EVEN IN
PARADISE

EVEN IN
PARADISE
CHELSEY PHILPOT

HARPER
An Imprint of HarperCollins*Publishers*

Library of Congress Cataloging-in-Publication Data
Philpot, Chelsey.
    Even in paradise / Chelsey Philpot. — First edition.
        pages   cm
    Summary: "Seventeen-year-old Charlotte 'Charlie' Ryder, a girl from a working class family whose talent for the arts has gained her entry into the exclusive St. Anne's school, is drawn into the circle of the larger-than-life Julia Buchanan, a former senator's daughter"— Provided by publisher.
    ISBN 978-0-06-229369-5 (hardcover)
    [1. Boarding schools—Fiction.   2. Schools—Fiction.
3. Friendship—Fiction.   4. Artists—Fiction.]   I. Title.
PZ7.P5496Ev 2014   2013047956
[Fic]—dc23   CIP
                                                                AC

Typography by Erin Fitzsimmons
14 15 16 17 18   LP/RRDH   10 9 8 7 6 5 4 3 2 1
❖
First Edition

With gratitude and love, this one's for my family:
My siblings, Natalie, Saeger, and Harris,
And my parents, William and Karen Philpot

"*Perhaps all our loves are merely hints and symbols;*

a hill of many invisible crests;

doors that open as in a dream to reveal

only a further stretch of carpet and another door."

—*Evelyn Waugh,*
BRIDESHEAD REVISITED

PROLOGUE

THE BUCHANANS' PULL WAS AS natural and strong as the moon on the tides, and when I was with them I was happy in the warmth of their reflected light.

If they had any sense of their collective charm, they never showed it. So self-assured were they all by nature that it never occurred to me to doubt that their perfection was predetermined by forces I did not understand. They were all royalty. They were all gods. They were all broken.

I could not tell you now, then, or really ever who I loved more—only that I did love her, and him, and them all with a fierceness that I didn't know was possible. They say there is nothing like your first love, but they have little to say about loving two people at the same time—or an entire family.

She was as fragile and full of life as a flute of champagne teetering on the edge of a table. He was strong enough to be the man he was born to be, but maybe not the one he would have chosen to become. As for the rest, they amaze me still.

Even knowing, as I do now, that grace, power, and, yes, love can hide the darkest elements of the human heart, I would do it all again. Beginning with the night I met her, then him, then the rest. I would do it all again just to know that for a moment I was one of the Great Buchanans.

THE BEGINNING

Et in Arcadia ego
(Even in Arcadia I exist)

ONE

I WAS JUST DRIFTING OFF to sleep when I heard someone throwing up in the bushes outside my dorm room. Before that unmistakable sound—a combination of heaving and throat clearing—the only noises coming through my open window had been the occasional barking dog and the rare sound of footsteps slapping on the concrete path that cut across the St. Anne's quad.

I glanced over at Rosalie, but she lay in her bed snoring softly, oblivious. In our three years of rooming together, she had trained herself to sleep through nearly anything. I shut my eyes tighter and willed the sound to be a dream.

"Julia, you okay? Hey Jules, what are you doing?" A girl's voice I didn't recognize seemed to be coming from right under the windowsill.

I heard another gut-clenching heave that made my throat hurt just to listen to it, followed by a low groan. I threw the covers off, waiting, hoping, to hear the sounds of the two girls shoving through the bushes. Instead, I heard a third girl join the other two.

"Jules, you've got to get up. We can't stay here." She spoke like someone was pinching her nose between two fingers. "This isn't the place to be sick. Mulcaster could come out her door any moment."

The only response she got was another low groan, followed by the sound of someone clearing her throat and then spitting whatever she had hacked up into the soil. In the darkness of my bedroom I wrinkled my forehead and sat up, rubbing at my eyes and searching the ground near my bed for the new bottle of water I had bought that afternoon in the campus store.

"Come on," the pinched-nose girl hissed. "We have to get back before the night patrol lady comes around and sees the door propped."

I heard what sounded like a bag of laundry hitting the brick wall, followed by a muffled thud of something landing on the dirt.

"Hell, Piper. Lemme alone," said a new voice, this one raspy and almost sultry. A voice I recognized but could not quite place. "Give a girl five minutes to enjoy her gin all over again." She snorted, and then giggled, before groaning. The retching began once more.

"Jules—" The second girl stopped speaking as the headmistress's voice trilled out from her front porch, just around the corner from my dorm.

"Hooper, come here, boy. Hooper."

"Shit. Jules, we need go," the first girl said, her British accent a little more pronounced than earlier. I gave up on finding the water and focused on fumbling for my slippers on the floor of my closet.

"Jules, come on."

I heard hands scraping against the wall.

"Lemme alone," the girl said, right before something tumbled through the bushes, cracking branches before landing in the dirt.

I threw my slippers on the floor and pulled a pair of jeans from the top of my hamper before slipping them on.

"We can't just leave her, Piper," the girl with the accent hissed.

"It's Jules; she can take care of herself or she'll talk her way out of it. I'm not getting work duty again because of her. Besides, there's no sense in all three of us getting caught," Piper said. I should have recognized her. I had heard her speak so many times in Geometry sophomore year.

Piper's friend must have agreed with her, because the next sound I heard was the scuttle of feet on the gravel of the dorm driveway.

"*Merde!*" The voice came from right under my window this time.

I paused with my hand on my doorknob, waiting for the

sounds of the friends coming back.

But the only noise I heard was the click of metal dog tags slapping against one another as Dr. Mulcaster's French bulldog explored the drainage ditch by the side of the science building.

I breathed deeply out my nose and eased the door open just enough for me to slip through and down the hall.

The common room was partially lit by blue moonlight that drifted through the ceiling-high arched windows. No matter what time of day it was, the common room smelled like burned popcorn and old sofa. Grabbing a wrinkled fashion magazine from the nearest armchair, I propped open the door to the quad and then crept into the dark.

The air was a New England April combination of the end of winter and the beginning of spring: a mixture of barely defrosted dirt, freshly mowed playing fields, and a hint of salt from the ocean miles away in Hyannis.

I slid with my back against the brick, trying to avoid the sharp branches of the bushes and give myself some cover. The back of my right thigh scraped against the wall as I rounded the final corner, and I had to pause and bite my bottom lip to keep from crying out.

Just under my window, I could make out the outline of a small figure with her head against her knees and her arms clinging to the wall behind her as if it alone was keeping her from floating away.

"Hooper, come here *now.*" Dr. Mulcaster's voice sounded

closer, and I could picture her standing on her front porch, squinting into the night for the small black dog that was nearly impossible to see in the dark. Dropping to the ground, I inched forward, pushing my hands into the soft dirt for balance until I reached the doubled-over girl.

"Hey," I whispered. "Hey, are you okay?"

Her thick, dark hair hung like a curtain about her face. Taking a hand from the wall, she pushed some strands away from her cheek and peered at me from under one thin arm.

I was right. I had heard her many times before, but it was the first time I had seen her close up.

Her dark eyes were bloodshot at the edges, and her fading spring-break tan and her sharp cheekbones made them seem enormous. Her nose was a little too large for her other features, but it made her more than just pretty. It made her interesting.

After staring at me for several moments, studying me so intensely I wanted to duck into the shadows, she asked, "Do you know who I am?"

I nodded. Of course I did.

"*Magnifique*, because I don't mean to be rude, but right now I don't have a clue who you are. *Merde!* I don't think I'm done yet."

She rose unsteadily to her feet, braced one arm against the wall, and threw up the rest of her stomach on my slippers.

"Crickets," she said, still bent in half. "I hope those weren't expensive."

I took a shallow breath through my mouth, willing the microwave noodles I'd had during study hall to stay down. "It's fine. They're wicked old. Let's go before Dr. Mulcaster sees us."

As if to prove my point, the headmistress, yelling, "Dammit, Hooper!" was followed by the sound of sneaker-clad feet thumping down wooden stairs.

The girl nodded weakly as she straightened up. I knew she was short, but even at her full height she barely came to my shoulder, and I had to hunch down to put my arm under hers. With me half carrying her, we shuffled toward the dorm door, where I kicked off my slippers and dropped them in the trash bin under the exit sign. Once we were in my room, I sat her on my bed and turned my desk lamp on its lowest setting.

She barely moved as I coaxed her out of her dirty clothes, and she kept her arms above her head like a toddler waiting to be picked up while I pulled a T-shirt over her.

"You're so pretty. So tall," she said as she flopped back on my bed. "My sister was tall. The rest of them are all tall." She frowned at some thought as I nudged her back farther on the bed until she no longer looked like she would fall off and then changed out of my shirt and jeans.

"Just so you know before we snuggle," she mumbled, "I like girls. Like *like* girls."

"Shhhh." I put my finger up to my lips even though her eyes were already closed. "I know."

She fell asleep while I was in the bathroom scrubbing my

feet in the middle shower stall. I walked on the balls of my feet back down the hallway, stopping to open the door to the quad just enough to grab a perfect white stone from the walkway before shutting it with a click. I kept walking on my toes even once I reached my room and slid the stone into the old wooden toolbox beside the duffel bag in my closet.

I did not need a memory to help me remember that night, but I wanted one anyway.

I climbed over her and squeezed in on the side of the bed nearest the wall. Her small body barely took up a third of the twin mattress. Before shutting my eyes, I glanced over at Rosalie. She had pulled her Canadian-flag quilt up over her head. I would be waking up to a very cranky roommate.

I stayed up half the night, unable to sleep with the strange feeling of another person's body lying so close. When I woke up, only a dent on the pillow where Julia Buchanan's head had rested next to mine gave any indication that she had been there at all.

AN APOLOGY

I found the package and flowers at my door when I got back from third period the next morning.

The flowers weren't anything like the plastic-wrapped ones my dad picked up from the grocery store when he forgot an anniversary. They were a collection of hunter green, pale green, and olive green flowers and ferns. Their scent was strong enough to smell from the common room.

The package contained tissue-paper-wrapped slippers from a department store I had only been in once. They were sweater soft.

Julia's note was tucked into one of the toes.

> *Please accept my most very, very sincere apologies.*
>
> *I'd say that's the first time I've found myself in such a predicament—but that would be a blatant lie.*
>
> *Drop by my room tomorrow afternoon so I can apologize in person. I'm in 5D, Pembroke Hall, North Tower.*
>
> *If you don't come I'll be heartbroken, which might lead me to drink again . . . and we don't want that, now do we?* ☺
>
> *Yours in contrition,*
>
> *JB*

TWO

AT ST. ANNE'S, THERE WERE some girls who wore their scholarship status like badges, flaunting consignment shop blazers in atrocious patterns that technically adhered to dress code, but also openly mocked it. There were girls who looked like walking billboards for Italian and French designers with names they struggled to pronounce blazed across their chests and butts. There were girls who wore clothes of such deliberate taste and quality that they might as well have pasted hundred-dollar bills on themselves. And then there were girls who didn't have to care what they wore. With them, the shabbier they dressed, the more important and older their family was. They didn't care because they could afford not to.

Pembroke Hall was generally where such girls and legacies lived. Thick maroon carpeting dotted with the St. Anne's crest ran the length of the fifth-floor hall over shining hardwood floors. The air smelled like lemon cleaner, as if one of the custodians had just been through. Three clunky chandeliers provided a dim glow that could not have been lower if they were using candles instead of lightbulbs. The navy blue walls were lined in perfect symmetry with sepia-toned photographs of smiling residents from past years.

I padded slowly down the hall, not particularly anxious to arrive where I was curious to go. The photos gave me an excuse to pause. In one, a girl in a long flowing dress stood on her tiptoes with her arms around the neck of a horse. Her face was half hidden against the horse's sides, but her small smile revealed that she knew she was being photographed. Her light-colored hair was wavy and fell just below her chin. I lifted my right hand to my mouth and began to chew at a hangnail.

"Oh, she's my favorite," a voice purred over my left shoulder.

I jumped. When the small of my back hit the molding on the wall behind me, my left hand swung out until I felt it connect with skin.

"Oh, my god. I am so sorry," I stammered. Julia Buchanan now stood in front of me, her hands clutching her right cheek.

"You startled me. Oh, God. I am so sorry. Does it hurt?"

Julia raised her eyes from the floor, her mouth opened in a small O. And then she smiled and dropped her hands. "Well now, I suppose we're even. I lose pasta night and a half a bottle of gin over your slippers and you whomp me in return."

I didn't say anything, but I smoothed my hair back from my face.

"You're right. Not fair at all. I should probably let you stomp on my foot to make things even." She laughed, and the sound was like hundreds of glasses clicking together. "Oh, ease up. I'm only joking." She smiled even as the redness on her cheek grew darker. "If I really wanted to be even, I would have given you a go at both cheeks; after all, I'm pretty sure I not only ruined your slippers, but also made off with a T-shirt."

"Don't worry about it," I said. "It's from freshman year."

"You shouldn't bite your nails, you know." Julia took my right hand in her pale palms. She raised it to her face and studied my fingers. "You have a piano player's hands."

With her eyes on me, I became all too aware of my broken nails and raw red cuticles. "Thanks, but I don't play piano. They're in wicked sad shape."

Julia laughed her clinking-glass laugh but did not let go of my hand. *"Et pourquoi ça?"*

I shook my head. "I don't speak French."

"C'est dommage," she said. "Where are you from?"

"What makes you ask?"

"The 'wicked' as an adverb. It's a New England thing, but you also draw out your vowels like they're stuck on your tongue."

I had no idea if it was good or bad to have tongue-sticking vowels.

"New Hampshire. Way up north. Practically in Canada."

"Live free and die. State motto, right?"

"Live free *or* die," I said. "We give you an option."

Julia smiled, biting the corner of her lip as if to keep her mouth from opening any wider. "You're funny. We're going to get along fabulously. Well, I suppose you should come say hello to everyone."

Julia turned and I followed her at a distance as she glided down the hall to the last door in the corner tower.

She threw the door wide open, causing it to hit the back wall with a thump. "Ladies, I hope you're halfway decent."

"Hell, Jules, must you shout all the time? You're going to piss off the whole floor, never mind bring every security guard on campus running."

I recognized Piper's voice immediately this time. Catching the door as it drifted back, I eased it shut behind me and let my eyes adjust to the low lighting.

The round room was stuffed with furniture. It resembled a murky antique shop bursting with piles of forgotten treasures more than a dorm room. The St. Anne's–provided dresser was weighted down with knickknacks, picture frames, and a shrunken cactus in a clay pot that looked like it hadn't been watered since the beginning of the school year. A mirror with a heavy gilded frame hung against one wall opposite a cream-colored chaise longue piled with clothes. Two beanbag chairs sat in the center around a low coffee table that was covered with textbooks with their broken spines in the air, wrinkled papers, and ripped magazines. Discarded clothing seemed to hang on every surface, dripping like the clocks in Dalí's paintings. And against the wall nearest the door was the standard twin bed found in every room. It was unmade and piled with a sun-faded quilt, decorative pillows, and even more clothing.

"It's a mess, isn't it?" said Piper as she stood up from where she had been sitting next to a stack of books on the floor near the window. "Jules just can't abide throwing anything out. She says it makes her feel bad."

Her full name came to me suddenly. Piper Houghton. St. Anne's was small enough that I knew she and Julia were insepa-rable. Teachers and coaches strung their names together like they were one longer word: PiperandJulia, JuliaandPiper. Last night was one of the handful of times I had seen them apart.

"It's true," Julia said as she moved toward her closet. "I hate throwing things out. What'll your poison be? I'm afraid selec-tion is pretty limited because somebody . . ." She cut her eyes toward the chaise longue. "Well, because somebody decided that it being a Wednesday was good enough a reason to drink half a bottle of rum." Julia started reaching behind the rows of clothes, retrieving three plastic water bottles with their labels peeled off and standing them up on the floor beside her like soldiers lining up for inspection. The way she handled them gave away their contents.

"It's four in the afternoon. How do you have all that in your room? Does your proctor even—" I said before Piper interrupted me.

"Yes, poor Jules just can't stand the thought of any broken knickknack, old dress, or, say, ratty old stuffed moose, or whatever the hell that germ trap is, going in the trash." Piper raised her arms above her head and arched her back like a cat stretching. "In fact, I'd say our Jules is a great collector. Stray dogs, dejected horses . . . people." She glanced at me and smiled with her lips tightly pressed together. She walked over to Julia and slid her arms around her waist, hugging her until her chin rested on the shorter girl's left shoulder. "But that's why we love her. Isn't it?"

Julia shrugged and twisted out of Piper's embrace as she turned with two plastic tumblers in her hands. "Piper, *ne recommence pas.*" Her voice sounded like loose gravel scattering down a hill. "Besides, you know how I feel about you calling Aloysius ratty."

Piper dropped her arms. She watched Julia weave her way toward me the way someone might watch a person board a plane to a war zone.

She shivered and then straightened her back, raising her chin again. "Whatever, Jules. You're just being pissy because we left you last night. And that thing *is* a health hazard. You better hope the nurse never gets her hands on him, or he'll end up in the graduation bonfire." She flopped down in one of the beanbag chairs and picked up a clear plastic cup containing a watery, pink liquid from the floor beside her. Her eyes met mine over the rim. She raised the glass in front of her and nodded her head at me before tipping it back and swallowing what remained of her drink.

Julia barely glanced at Piper's salute. I hadn't noticed in the hall, but Julia's cashmere sweater wrap had holes in the sleeves that she had forced her thumbs through, and her dark halo of hair looked as if it hadn't been brushed that day. The hands that clutched the two tumblers were long, but the nails were short and her red polish was chipped like she had had a manicure months ago and couldn't be bothered to get another.

"*Pour toi.*" Julia handed me a tumbler with a slight curtsy. "A toast to my rescuer. *À votre santé!*" She tipped her cup back and took a gulp before flopping stomach first on her bed. With her free hand she reached out and pulled a pillow to her chest.

"*A votey santi,*" I repeated and took a small sip. The pale green drink was surprisingly sweet. It tasted almost like a sports drink that had been left in a hot car too long. I took a second sip. This time I felt a burn in the back of my throat like a hot liquid was being poured straight from a kettle into my stomach. I slammed the cup down and pulled my sweatshirt sleeve over my right hand and clutched it to my mouth.

"First night on the town, sailor?" Piper said.

"I don't . . . really . . . drink," I wheezed out in between coughs. My eyes were watering. I swiped at them with my left sleeve.

"A toast!" a delicate voiced piped up from the chaise in the corner, but I could see only a tan hand raised in the air above the piles of clothing. A girl struggled into a sitting position. When she turned to face us, her sleek black bob highlighted her high cheekbones, slightly flattened nose, and almond-shaped eyes.

"Oh, Eun Sun. So nice of you to join us. How was your nap, sleeping beauty?" Julia's sarcasm barely cloaked her annoyance.

Eun Sun snorted. "Guess I overdid it last night." She struggled to sit up, as jerky as a robot. "Jules, you should have stopped me. You know once my face becomes all blotchy to cut me off." She had the studied accent of someone who has learned English via Europe.

"I tried, but you kept stealing my cup whenever my back was turned," Julia said as she sat up and folded her legs, never letting go of her glass. She tucked her sweater around her knees, making her look like a very small tent. "After almost three years, the one thing you should have learned at St. Anne's is how to handle your booze. Come say hello to our visitor, Charlotte Ryder. She's a junior, too. She was the one who rescued me after you *bêtes* abandoned me."

"Hello, visitor," Eun Sun said, rubbing her eyes and opening her mouth in a yawn that split her face in two. Sitting more upright, she blinked and then stared at me. "You're the girl who did those thingies hanging in that place, aren't you?"

"What?"

"You know." She exhaled loudly. "The art center. We only have assembly there like every day."

"The sculptures?"

"Yes." Eun Sun settled against the chaise. "Yeah. The metal thingies. I recognize you from the little photo on the wall." She snorted. "You look so pissed in that photo. Otherwise, I don't think I've seen you once in my life."

I straightened my back and crossed my arms across my chest. "I'm in the art studios a lot." I took another small sip of the drink, mindful this time of the burn.

"Some say to-may-toe, some say toe-ma-toooo," Eun Sun said.

"So what's your story, Charlotte Ryder?" Piper said. "Take a seat. Stay a while. Tell the rest of the class a little about yourself, since you and Julia already seem to know each other *so well*." Piper drew the last two words out, filling them with meaning, but of what I wasn't sure.

"Piper, stop it," Julia said. She had swapped the pillow for a stuffed animal that she clutched against her chest. Her tumbler was empty on the bedside table. "You're being mean and it's *not* attractive. Charlotte is *my* guest and you're in *my* room, drinking *my* vodka, so you'll play nice."

"Jules, I *am* being nice. I just want to know about your new friend. That's all." Piper twirled her long necklace with the hand that wasn't clutching her empty cup and shifted in the beanbag so she faced me, her back to Julia. "See, I've known Jules practically my whole life. Our families have summer places near each other. We basically grew up together, so when someone new comes along, I'm always just a little bit curious."

"There's really not much to tell," I said, holding my cup close to my chest and wrapping my fingers around it to hide how little I'd been able to drink. "I'm here. Next year, I'm going to apply to a bunch of art schools." I took another sip. "I'm going to be an artist."

Piper set her cup down on the floor and tried to adjust the beanbag chair so she could sit up straighter. "You either *are* an artist or you're *not*. It's not something you become," she said, giving up and flopping back down.

"Piper, stop it," Julia commanded from the bed.

"What? You don't think the soup can guy knew in high school that he was going to paint soup cans? Of course he did."

"Well, then, I guess I *am* an artist." I shifted from one foot to the other.

"Okay, as an artist, what do you think of this room?" Piper made a circle over her head. "Other than the mess, of course." She laughed. "How about those pictures over there?"

I set my drink down on the coffee table and walked over to the set of drawers with all the picture frames on top. A thin layer of dust coated the dresser surface and the tops of the frames. One picture was of a large gray house with a golf-course-green lawn rolling in front of it. Another was of a small red sailboat bobbing on dark water. But the one that held my attention was of a girl that could have been Julia's twin. Her face was fuller and her eyes gray instead of brown, but she had the same nose and the same dark, thick hair. She was squinting as if the picture taker had caught her by surprise. She shaded her eyes with one hand, and the other was slung around the mast of what looked like the little red sailboat from the other picture. She had on shorts and a red T-shirt and a smile that stretched as far as her face would allow.

"She looks like she's planning something funny. A joke or something." I picked up the frame carefully, tracing my finger lightly over the girl's face. "Either that or she's wicked in love with the picture taker. Your sister?" I asked as I turned toward Julia. "The tall one you were talking about the other night?"

She did not answer immediately, but she hopped off the bed and came to stand beside me. Once she was close enough for me to smell the vodka and juice that lingered on her lips, she reached out and took the frame from me. "Yeah. At Arcadia, our summer place. Her boyfriend, David, took the picture." She set the picture down at the same angle in the dust-free spot on the dresser and walked back toward the bed. "Her name was Gus."

"Was?" I said, still standing by the pictures.

Eun Sun shook her head at me from the chaise, and Piper pressed her lips together as she twirled her necklace. There had been a test, and somehow I had failed.

When I took my next sip, I could feel my throat working to swallow. The chapel bell started ringing, and for the first time ever I was grateful for formal dinner.

"I've got to go change, Julia. You can just keep the T-shirt," I said. If she said anything back as I shut the door to her room behind me, I didn't hear it.

THE MEMORY BOX

The box was just an old wooden toolbox of my dad's. It was rough-sided. The hinges squeaked, and it still smelled a little like sawdust and oil. It took up way too much space in my closet at St. Anne's.

But it held everything.

Postcards from Grandma Eve, letters, trinkets I'd won at arcade games, ribbons from elementary school, my mom's old locket. It protected my shells from summer vacations at Hampton Beach, buttons from old coats, and those colorful umbrellas they put in your drinks when you go somewhere warm.

It was heavy with ticket stubs, museum pamphlets, and so many of my memories.

I added Julia's note and closed the lid.

THREE

"**I HEARD SHE HAD, LIKE,** a mental breakdown and they kicked her out of Mansfield Academy," Amy said. She crunched down on a baby carrot as if to punctuate her point.

"Amy, you're full of it. Her family is the closest Massachusetts has to royalty. There's no way she would have gotten booted out of some tier-two boarding school," Rosalie said. Her Canadian accent became as thick as maple syrup when she was annoyed.

I poked at the pile of salad on my plate and let my eyes wander. The St. Anne's dining hall reminded me of a fancy ski lodge. Exposed wood beams ran across the high ceiling, partially blocking the enormous skylights. Floor-to-ceiling windows ran the length of the side that faced the quad. During free periods, when I didn't have my job manning the reception desk at the art gallery, I liked to sneak into the empty building and just watch the world happening outside those windows.

"Didn't she date Indira in the beginning of the year?" Amy had stopped chewing and her mouth hung slightly opened.

"Amy." I coughed. "Uh." I tapped the underside of my chin. She quickly shut her mouth, swallowed, and wiped her face with a napkin.

"Don't tell my mother I did that."

"Indira isn't gay. You're thinking of Ina," Jacqueline said from the opposite side of the round table, not bothering to raise her eyes from the textbook in front of her. "And when would we ever tell your mom that you eat like a little kid?" She pushed her glasses up her nose with one hand and continued flipping pages with the other. "Plus, your mom scares me."

Amy shuddered. "She scares me, too." She picked up a carrot, looked at it, and set it down before speaking. "You could totally say something parents' weekend. It's the last week in May, less than four weeks."

Jacqueline raised an eyebrow and looked up from her book. Rosalie laughed so hard she snorted.

"What?" Amy squeaked. She pouted, then picked up another carrot and pointed at me with it. "When are you going to let me fix your hair?"

"Uh, random," I said, reaching up to touch where I knew the blond ended and my brown roots began. "Does it look that bad?"

"If my mother were here, she would say, 'Charlotte, are you trying to look unattractive?'"

Amy's impression of her mom's high voice was so bad I nearly choked on a crouton. I was still coughing as I replied, "You know my stepmom, Melissa . . . promised . . . she'd fix . . . if I let someone else . . . too scarred . . . to finish beauty school."

Amy patted me on the back. "I wasn't trying to make you choke. Personally, I couldn't handle it, but . . . well, remember I offered."

My eyes still watering, I nodded. The conversation drifted to other topics after that. I was content to half listen, half watch the rest of the room.

Lunch at St. Anne's was loud, but never in an obnoxious way. Different groups had their established tables, but they were often an odd mix of girls and never firmly set. Academic overachievers were on the basketball team, drama girls on the student council, artsy girls in the debate club. That didn't mean that people forgot for a moment who everyone was and where they came from, but it meant I knew of a dozen tables where I was welcome if no one was at mine.

Maybe it was because to some of these girls I was still a curiosity, with my accent that caught on certain words like a long shirt on thorns, or maybe it was because I listened more than I talked, but I got along with most girls at St. Anne's. I was friendly with many, close to few.

Jacqueline and I had become friends after I stumbled on her crying in the Bio wing bathroom. She had just gotten a D on an exam and was so upset she ran from the classroom to throw up. I gave her my cardigan to cover up her shirt. I got to know Amy after she wandered into my studio, looking for someone to tell her whether or not her butt looked big in her *Guys and Dolls* costume. She ended up staying for half an hour and telling me about the diet tips her mother sent her and how she missed her cat back home in Connecticut. As for Rosalie, I had just been lucky. We were stuck in a room together freshman year. We bonded over both being from towns so small they didn't have traffic lights, and we had lived with each other since.

"Anyway." Rosalie shoved her tray out of the way, knocking my own so she could cross her arms on the table. "Charlotte actually got to go to her room the other day 'cause Julia felt bad about barfing all over her. So she would probably know more about the Buchanans than any of us, eh?"

Three sets of eyes turned toward me. "Why are we back to talking about Julia Buchanan?" I said as I dropped my fork on my plate, giving up on the salad. I wasn't hungry anyway. "I don't know any more than you guys."

"Come on, Charlotte." Jacqueline shut her book with a thunk. "You gotta be curious. It's weird. The girl starts here as a junior. Who does that?"

I glanced over my shoulder at the table in the far right corner. She was there today. When Julia came to lunch, I never saw her actually eating. Her chair was the farthest one from the entrance and when she wasn't there, it was left empty just in case. I doubt this was something her group ever did by conscious decision.

They just did it. She never sat facing forward with her feet on the floor. She perched and sprawled and once even stood on her chair until Dr. Blanche came to the table and suggested she get down. Today she had one knee up and the other leg resting on Piper's lap. She was gesturing wildly, and from time to time her entire table erupted with laughter.

"Earth to Charlotte." Rosalie waved a hand in front of my face.

"Huh? Sorry."

"I bet she got kicked out of all the other places for drugs so she *had* to transfer. Those kinds of girls." Rosalie nodded her head in the direction of the back table. "They're always into heavy stuff. I bet that was it."

Amy drummed her polished fingernails on the table. "That's ridiculous. Her dad was a governor."

"Senator," Rosalie said. "Her dad was a Massachusetts state senator. He dropped out of the race for governor when the press found out about all his affairs."

"You don't—" I started.

"No." Amy leaned forward and then, as if hearing her mother's voice in her head, took her elbows off the table. "He stopped running after her older sister crashed her car and died. Don't you remember? It happened like three summers ago. It was really bad. A boy died, too. It was all over the news for all of August."

"Guys, come on—"

"I remember that. The sister went here, right?" Rosalie shoved back her chair and stood up. "It was after a boat race or polo game or something. Her sister was wasted, but the guy was supposedly the one driving. Didn't his family sue?"

Amy shrugged and stood, too, sweeping her blond hair over her shoulders. "Don't know." She looked down at her plate, still full of baby carrots and celery. "I'm going to go get a cookie." She started toward the kitchen area and then stopped and turned to look at us. "Don't tell my mother."

I got up, grabbing my backpack from underneath the table and slinging it over one shoulder. "You coming?" I asked Jacqueline, who had opened her textbook again.

"Nah, I have free period." She glanced up at me. "You're not the least bit curious about this girl?"

I shrugged my shoulders, rattling my glass against the china plate as my tray jiggled. "Julia's nice and she has a really messy room. That's all I know about her."

"Charlotte, you're too much." Jacqueline propped her legs up on the chair next to her and settled her textbook on her knees.

I followed the path in the hardwood floor that had been scuffed to dullness by years and years of St. Anne's girls rushing in and out and shoved my tray on the dish room conveyor belt, remembering with a shudder when my campus job had been working in the kitchen instead of the art gallery.

Julia caught up to me when I was halfway across the quad.

"Where's the fire, Charlie?"

"Who?" I asked as I stopped and faced her.

"Charlie; do you mind if I call you Charlie? It suits you more than Charlotte," Julia said. She had her hands on her hips and a faint line of sweat at her hairline. "You walk really fast, you know?"

"Sure, I guess—"

Julia interrupted me. "Look, I'm sorry about Piper the other day. Her parents put liquid evil in her bottle or something. She'll behave next time. I promise."

"Next time?" I said. "I thought I . . . it's been three days. I thought you were mad at me—"

"Actually," Julia said, "Aloysius was wondering if you wanted to come hang out." She turned her back toward me so I could see the stuffed moose hanging half out of her black canvas bag. "In fact, he would like it very much. He was telling me." Strands of hair escaped from her lopsided bun and stuck to her face. She swiped at them absentmindedly.

I laughed. "I can't believe you carry him around. Please explain to Aloysius that I have a Latin test."

Julia wrinkled her forehead. "Why would anyone learn a dead language?"

I shrugged. "It's beautiful."

She scrutinized me as if trying to gauge whether I was joking or not. She must have decided I wasn't, because she nodded solemnly. "And that is why we are going to get along fabulously."

"How about after club period this afternoon?"

She exhaled through the side of her mouth. "Meet me in the chapel." She wrapped her arms around her ribs and turned to walk in the opposite direction, looking like she was heading into a cold wind instead of a warm spring day.

BOSTONGLOBE.COM

POLITICAL FAMILY LOSES BELOVED DAUGHTER

Augustine Rose Buchanan, the daughter of Massachusetts State Senator Joseph Buchanan and his wife, philanthropist Teresa Buchanan, died early Sunday morning in car crash on Nantucket Island. She was 18 years old.

"Gus," as family and friends knew her, was a champion sailor. She was recently named a "Top 10 under 30" by Yacht Magazine. On the night of the crash, she had been celebrating her victory at a party following the Nantucket Regatta.

"Gus was everything you want in an athlete," said Tucker Carroll, Ms. Buchanan's coach and family friend. "She was determined, smart, and generous. Losing her is a tremendous blow to the sport, but it's devastating to those of us who knew her and loved her."

David Cross, 19, Ms. Buchanan's boyfriend and the son of Cara and Jon Cross of Cross Farm on Cape Cod, and her sister Julia Buchanan, 14, were also in the car. Island police pronounced both Mr. Cross and Ms. Augustine Buchanan dead at the scene. Ms. Julia Buchanan was found miles from the accident site. A family member took her to Memorial Hospital, where she was kept overnight for a broken wrist, lacerations, and a concussion.

A police investigation into the exact cause of the crash is ongoing. Alcohol and speed have not been ruled out.

Senator Buchanan, who interrupted his gubernatorial

campaign to join his family at their home on Nantucket Island, announced Ms. Augustine Buchanan's death. Reading from a prepared statement, he said, "Gus was always the first to laugh at a joke, the first to think of a foolproof prank, and the first to be ready for adventure. She was talented, smart, and a devoted sister and daughter. During this difficult time, my wife, children, and I ask for your respect for our privacy even as we express our gratitude for the outpouring of support."

Ms. Augustine Buchanan leaves behind her parents; her sisters, Cordelia and Julia; and two brothers, Bradley and Sebastian. But she also leaves a promising life that was cut short far too soon.

I printed out the article, folded it into an origami rose, and added it to my memory box.

FOUR

I LIKED THE CHAPEL BEST when it was empty.
The ceiling went up and up and reminded me of the pictures
Grandma Eve used to send from Europe of the Italian cathe-
drals. The rows of dark pews shone in the places where gripping
hands had created half-moon indentations along the tops. The
stained glass windows glowed. The dust in the air caught the
soft afternoon sunlight in such a way that it looked like glitter
as it drifted down. The damp air was infused with an earthy
smell, as if the floor were made of dirt instead of scuffed marble.

No matter how softly I tried to put down my sneakers to
preserve the silence, I still created an echo as I made my way to
the altar, which stood before a massive pipe organ that looked as
if one note would be powerful enough to bring down the walls.

"Julia," I said, glancing in each row before arriving at the
front. She wasn't there.

"Pssst." Though Julia might have meant it to be a whisper,

the sound vibrated through the massive space. "Over here."

I let out a breath I hadn't realized I was holding. She was here.

"Julia?" I turned and walked toward the end of the first row of pews, bending down to run my fingers along the polished seat out of habit. The wood felt like the surface of a mirror under my fingertips.

"Warmer," she called. "Warmer. Hotter. Red hot."

At the massive pillar at the end of the row, I turned right and started moving toward the basement stairs.

"Getting colder. Colder. Icy cold."

I backtracked to the front row. "You know," I said, "this would go a whole lot faster if you just told me where you were."

Her giggle echoed off the walls, leading me to the pillar I had just passed. I wove around it. There in an alcove that could not have been more than four feet deep and four feet high, Julia sat on the floor with her knees pulled to her chest and Aloysius's stuffed legs dangling out from her lap.

"Extra, extra hot! Come on in," she said, patting the floor as she scooted deeper into the little cave.

I crouched down and crawled in beside her. The only way both of us could fit was if I pulled my legs tight enough to rest my chin on my knees and sat with my side completely touching hers. I was close enough to smell the fruit gum she was chewing and to see the loose threads along the hems of her jeans and shirt cuffs.

"Cool, huh? Bet you didn't know this was here."

"How did you—"

"Shhhh." Julia took Aloysius and pressed him against my lips. "Someone's coming." She dropped her hands and hugged him again.

I rubbed my mouth against my arm trying to get bits of fake fur off my tongue. The sound of hesitant footsteps and the creak of wood as someone settled on a pew reached us.

I stopped picking at the little fibers long enough to glance at Julia. She raised one eyebrow in response and put a finger to her lips. We sat in silence for nearly a minute before the visitor spoke.

"God, I know you're mighty busy. But if you could maybe . . ." The girl's intake of breath was as audible as her prayer. "If you could just help me pass this one test, just get me through it. If you do that then I'll go to church, I swear, every Sunday this summer. Swear. Amen."

Julia pressed her small, slightly sticky hand around my arm as soon as the girl stopped speaking and kept it there after the thud of the massive front doors shutting boomed.

"Awesome, right? The acoustics of this place are so amazing that even if someone is whispering in the middle it carries to this corner."

"How often do you sit here and listen to people pray?" I felt like I had just read pages from someone's diary or taken a glance at a letter not addressed to me.

Julia shrugged. "Sometimes you need to hide for a while. This is my hiding spot. Now it can be yours, too." She released her grip on my arm and hugged her knees closer to her chest. Her dark hair was coming loose from the messy bun piled on top of her head, and I could feel strands of it drifting against my cheek. Though they tickled, I did not brush them away. "I thought you'd like it."

"I do." I wiped at my mouth one more time, trying to catch the last threads of Aloysius's fur. "I guess . . . I'm not sure why you would share it with me. I'm just a girl who gave you a T-shirt."

"Are you always so modest?"

"Not when it's true." I tried to glance at her, but when I turned my head, my nose bumped her cheek, so I settled my chin back on my knees and waited. I was good at waiting.

"The other day in my room you saw things in my sister's picture . . . like that she was in love with David—"

"I'm so sorry I said that stuff about your sister. I didn't know that much about the accident and—"

"I just mean that you noticed things that no one else would have. You're *wicked* observant."

She pronounced "wicked" with a click, so I knew she was teasing me. I smiled to myself and waited for her to go on.

"See, even right now, you're just checking stuff out, watching, listening. You're pretty much the opposite of most girls here." I felt Julia's hand gripping my right arm again. "That's why I thought you'd like this place. You get *it*, Charlie."

I didn't know what *it* was, but a sense of warmth that began where Julia held my arm spread through me.

Julia let go and shifted, putting a sliver of space between us. "You know she went here, right? My sister, Gus, the one in the photo."

It suddenly felt like there was not enough air in our little cave. "Yeah. I heard that."

"When she went away to St. Anne's, I was just a little kid. I cried for a week. That's how badly I missed her."

"It must have been—"

"But," Julia continued as if she hadn't heard me, "what made it worse was that once she went away she became a stranger. Even during the summer, she was so wrapped up in sailing and David, I barely got to see her." Julia pressed one palm against the stone floor. "I like being here. Being where she went to school. It's like I get a chance to know her better. Does that make sense?"

"Yeah. It does."

"You probably think I'm—"

This time it was me who shushed her. The sound of rubber-soled shoes scuffing across marble made me reach out and put a hand across her mouth. I could feel her swallow her bubblegum and her warm breath against my palm.

This time a man's voice traveled to our cave. "Uh, Lord. I mean God." He sounded much older than the girl. I pictured a gray-haired man sitting in the front pew, his head bowed and his hands clasped together on his lap.

"I think you know this is a tough time for me." His voice quivered. "I just miss her so damn much." He was silent for long enough to make me wonder if he would speak again. "Just help me get through it, Lord. Just help me keep going. That's all I'm praying for. Amen."

I waited until we heard the thud of the chapel door before I removed my hand. The man's abrupt departure left as heavy a feeling in my stomach as his prayer. Julia moved even closer to me, settling Aloysius so he draped across our laps. It could have been two minutes or it could have been half an hour that we sat silently pressed together.

It took the chapel bells chiming five times for me to wake from my thoughts. "We should probably get going. Formal dinner's in an hour." I braced a hand against the cool stone wall and started to stand, ignoring the pins and needles in my legs.

"Wait," Julia said as she pulled me back down to my crouching position. "Let's just listen to a couple more. *S'il vous plaît!*"

So we did. We sat in the cave that Julia had made mine as well as hers and listened to voices we recognized and some we did not make their prayers. We listened until the warmth of our bodies had fused the skin on our pressed arms together and the multicolored sunlight that reached through the windows like fingers from an outstretched hand turned to the dark streaks of dusk.

HONORS ENGLISH WITH DR. BLANCHE

"Before we wrap up for the day, can anyone tell me where Huxley got his title *Brave New World*? Anyone? Ladies, I know it's spring and you are almost out of here for the year, but humor me for ten more minutes by at least pretending to be engaged."

"From Shakespeare?"

"Say it with conviction, Miss Piper Houghton."

"From Shakespeare."

"Yes, from the bard himself. Now, can anyone tell me what play? My good opinion is the prize."

"*A Midsummer Night's Dream?*"

"What do the judges think? Incorrect, Miss Eun Sun Lee, but thank you for playing. Miss Charlotte Ryder, you've been awfully quiet today. What do you think?"

"*The Tempest?*"

"Is that a question or an answer?"

"*The Tempest.*"

"Miss Ryder, you are . . . correct. 'O brave new world, that has such people in it!' says Miranda. Now, Miss Ryder, I will let you leave five minutes early if you can explain the meaning of the quotation to the rest of us."

I tapped my pencil against my desk. "Miranda says it near the end."

"Go on."

"Huxley might have been using her words ironically, because the world he creates is terrible, but when she says them she's being sincere. She's been sheltered from everything her whole life, but then people come to her island. She has adventures . . . falls in love. She's expressing awe that the world is so amazing and that she gets to be part of it."

"Charlotte, that was lovely. You may leave. Piper and Eun Sun, because of your efforts, you can join her. Go out and enjoy the day. *Experientia docet*. Experience teaches, as they say."

FIVE

AFTER THOSE FIRST FEW INVITATIONS, it was so easy to fall into Julia's world. So easy, I didn't even notice it happening at first.

I stopped seeing Julia with Piper. Did they have a fight? Did Julia leave her, or was it the other way around? I didn't pry and tried to ignore the gossip, but being the focus of so much curiosity felt as natural and comfortable as shoes that were two sizes too tight. I was stumbling all the time and always just a step away from falling on my face.

Despite Piper giving me ugly looks in English, and despite my own questions, I became Charlie, as in "JuliaandCharlie," and by mid-May, the rest of my friends had sort of drifted away.

I gave up moving from group to group during lunch and just got used to the looks that followed us as Julia and I walked across the quad or whispered together in the library, perplexed glances that seemed to say, "Why you?" I hated those looks for many reasons, but mostly because I was wondering the same thing.

She came to the studio and was surprisingly good about watching me work, unafraid of the torches, the banging, and never questioning why I could stare at a pile of clothes hangers, cans, or discarded lamps for hours before I knew where to begin. She'd bring her phone and play games, or a book she would usually only glance at. From time to time when I'd look up, I'd catch her watching me work. No one had ever found me interesting before. I was surprised by how much I liked it.

I went to watch her ride at the stables sometimes after club period or track practice. And during study halls, I'd settle into one of her beanbag chairs in her messy room and try to get work done. I never accomplished much.

Julia was always preparing to study, but never actually getting to it. She was forever searching for lost books or a pen that didn't leak. And even when she had an open notebook in front of her on her unmade bed, she was usually staring into space instead of at the pages.

It took a couple of calculus tests choked with red ink before I realized that if I was going to make the GPA requirement for my scholarship, I needed to retreat to the library instead.

Julia barely had to do anything to get her A's and B's, and she was honestly confused by my confusion when I didn't understand a physics problem or remember automatically the year that India won independence from Britain. But she was so generous with her offers of help and so matter-of-fact about the ease with which most things came to her that her intelligence didn't make me jealous—just amazed.

With St. Anne's being the fish bowl that it was, it did not take long for the rumors to begin.

Charlotte is totally a lesbian now. She's obviously in love with Julia.

Piper was crying in the dance studio because Julia's completely dumped her for Charlotte.

The Buchanans are paying her tuition. That's why she follows Julia around like a puppy.

But I was learning to not care what other people thought, and I found the less I cared, the more free I felt to spend time with Julia.

I learned to ignore Rosalie's sighing each time I left the room and to avoid Amy's hurt expression whenever I rushed out of Physics to meet Julia before lunch. As for Jacqueline, she was from New York City and tougher than the rest. She gave up on me before Rosalie and Amy did.

I knew what I was doing. I was becoming *that* girl, the one who drops all her old friends when a new, exciting one comes around. I knew what I was doing and I couldn't help myself. I didn't want to.

SIX

SPRING PARENTS' WEEKEND WAS LIKE a carnival—minus the animal tents and fried dough. Evergreen and ivory balloons with the St. Anne's crest were anchored to wrought iron benches and lampposts across campus. Sandwich-board signs stood outside all of the academic buildings, describing with the flair of travel brochures what happened inside. Teachers wore their college scarves over button-ups and blazers. There was even a bouncy castle set up outside the gym for the staff kids and visiting siblings.

I hated parents' weekends. Not because my dad, Melissa, and my younger stepbrothers, Sam and AJ, could never make it, but because it felt like a three-day invasion, like I was a native in my habitat and all these tourists had dropped in to observe me. There were parents in classes: gray-haired and balding dads who struggled to fit in the polished wooden chairs, and pearl-wearing moms who perched on their edges. Younger brothers and sisters ran around the dining hall, hopped up on sugar and the freedom of not being the immediate focus of their parents' attention. Grandparents were in the library, dorm common rooms, stable, gym, and greenhouse. The only place to escape to was the art studio.

The Saturday afternoon of that parents' weekend, I had to weave around the groups of families that crowded the path to the art center. Everyone was moving too slowly, taking too many pictures, talking too loudly. I kept my eyes down, knowing I wouldn't hear anyone call me. The past two years, I had received at least half a dozen invitations for lunch or dinner on parents' weekends. Most were from friends who treated getting off campus like leaving for San Francisco, Seattle, or some other huge and glamorous city instead of just downtown Hyannis. But some of them were desperate pleas, as if the girls inviting me could not stand being alone with their parents for the time it took to choke down salads and sandwiches. But I had given up those friends.

That afternoon, for the first time since becoming part of Julia's world, it felt strange to walk alone. Ignoring the path and walking across the grass so I could move quicker did little to ease the loneliness that hit me like a stomach pain that leaves you doubled over.

There was one invitation I dared to expect, but it was not delivered.

I saw Julia's family arrive on campus that morning on my

way to breakfast. And I swear even Dr. Mulcaster had stopped mid-conversation to watch as they slid out of a black town car.

Waiting for them on the sidewalk in front of Pembroke, Julia lunged for the door handle even before the car came to a full stop. A petite woman in a dark navy suit, her blond hair in a tight chignon at the nape of her neck and huge sunglasses covering half her face, jumped out of the driver's side and ran around the car to hug her. A tall guy with curly hair held the door as a little girl hopped out of the backseat and attached herself to Julia's side. The final person to emerge was a heavy-set woman with silver hair and high heels that would have been impossible for a woman half her age to walk in. Yet she moved from the car to the brick walk with the practiced balance of a beauty pageant contestant.

When Julia caught me watching she waved and mimicked throwing a noose over her head and pulling it tight. But she did not gesture me over. So I kept moving and tried to swallow my disappointment—but it was a tight fit down my throat.

I did not know the rules of our friendship yet. I only knew the boundaries.

The art center was the most hideous building on campus, an eyesore that had been designed, built, and paid for by a celebrity architect alumna. The roof was flat and constructed of reflective tin, and one side was covered with straw-like sticks of metal forming a faux barrier over the chipping brick. But inside the ceilings were high, and though the electric circuits were always blowing and the old radiators always put out too much heat in the winter, the art studio, a cluttered space with paint-splattered walls and a chipped cement floor, was a haven. A space as familiar to me as my childhood bedroom.

I kept the stereo playing whatever pop station the person who was there before me had left on and stretched dark goggles over my eyes to protect them from the heat of the small torch I planned to use with some stubborn metal. Out of the corner of my eye, I saw that Marsha, a sophomore, was working in the far corner. I waved at her before pulling on a pair of thick leather gloves.

I turned on the torch, felt that rush of heat against my cheeks, and some of the loneliness of walking by myself melted away.

I had been at work for only fifteen minutes when someone tapped me on the shoulder. Annoyed at the interruption, I pushed my goggles off so forcefully that they fell off the back of my head and hit the floor with a clunk.

"Oh Jesus. Sorry. Sorry. Didn't mean to startle you. I was just looking for the bathroom." A boy about my height, maybe a little taller, stood just a foot away from me, his hand still reaching out from touching me. A pair of aviator sunglasses hid his eyes and his curly brown hair stuck out at all angles from his head like he had just taken off a winter hat.

"All girls' school," he said. "I haven't been able to find a guy's room yet."

I tore my eyes away from his face. "Never surprise someone

with a flame in her hand." I shut off the torch, took off my gloves, and bent down to grab my goggles, hurriedly wiping the sweat off my face with my sleeve before I stood up.

"Yeah. Not the smartest thing I've done today. But might not be the dumbest either." I could tell by the way he delivered the line that it was something he'd said before.

I hadn't talked to a guy my age in weeks. I felt like I had to translate words before I could speak them. "There's a bathroom . . . other side of the building. It says 'faculty' on it . . . you can just ignore that though. They won't care on parents' weekend."

The boy moved toward my workbench. "Are these birds?" he asked, picking up one of the metal rods I had melted into a delicate v-like shape and taking his sunglasses off his face with his free hand. His eyes were mahogany dark.

"Do they look like birds to you?" I said, feeling a little less flushed now that we were talking art.

"They're seagulls, aren't they?"

"If you see seagulls, then they're seagulls. If you think they're pigeons or crabs or contortionists, then they can be those, too. That's the beauty of it all, really." I pushed the bandanna I had covering my hair back until it slid off the top of my head, remembering too late that the awful shade of blond and my brown roots were now exposed.

He looked up at me and grinned. His bottom teeth were slightly crooked, as if he'd had braces but couldn't be bothered to wear them for long and so the teeth had shifted back. "Well I think they look like the seagulls my dad tries to get rid of every summer. They're pretty, though."

I grabbed one and studied it to stop myself from staring at him. "I don't know what I'm going to do with them yet."

"Hey, Charlotte," Marsha called from the other side of the studio. She had moved from the corner and was perched on a radiator and looking out the large window that faced the library lawn. "Did you see the boat parked in front of Pembroke? You know whose car that is?"

Marsha had a Virginia accent as soft as warm honey and an interest in all things mechanical that could rival a NASCAR fan's. Because we didn't have an auto shop, she used the studio to weld parts together for a car she kept off campus.

I put down the metal and let my eyes drift once again to the boy's face. He had the thickest lashes I had ever seen on a guy. A scar cut a thin triangle into his left eyebrow, making it look like it was slightly raised and he was just about ready to wink.

"Yeah. It's Julia's," I called over my shoulder.

"Julia?" the guy said.

"Julia Buchanan," I said. "She's another junior girl. New this year."

He stuck his hands in his pockets and rocked back on his heels.

Marsha's pudgy tan hands were pressed against the glass like a puppy's paws in a pet store window. She whistled, then turned away from the window to look at us. "I hear the whole family's tied up in the Irish Mafia and that's where they got all their money."

"Really—" I started to say, but was interrupted.

"Actually, they're all secretly working for the CIA or FBI," the guy said as he winked at me. "I think I read it somewhere."

"Really?" Marsha's eyebrows couldn't go any higher. Her drawl made "really" sound as stretched out as a bubblegum balloon. "Reaaaaallllly?"

"Sure." He shrugged. "How else would they get a car like that?"

Marsha didn't reply, but she twisted to look out the window again, her mouth slightly open.

"Not nice," I hissed at him, trying to resist the smile tugging at my lips. Marsha was sweet, but way too gullible. The year before, someone had her convinced that Mrs. Kahn was a political refugee from North Korea. Marsha attempted to speak to her in Korean for months until Mrs. Kahn let her know she was born in Maine.

He looked down, then up at me. Still smiling. "You have lines all over your face from the thingies." He reached as if to touch my face. "Right here."

"Yeah. Thanks. Occupational hazard." I stumbled back, pushing aside my torch and gloves to set the goggles on my workbench. "So you must be somebody's brother? Cousin? Complete stranger sneaking on campus? Enjoying the carnival?"

I got snarky when I was nervous.

He tapped his feet against the side of a paint cabinet before answering. "It beats Spring Fling day at my college. At least you guys get a bouncy castle. We get a popcorn machine and bad local bands playing on the commons." He took a step closer to me. "Want to go check it out?"

"Bad local bands?"

"No, the bouncy castle."

"Uh, I'm pretty sure it's just for kids."

"Yeah, but I bet you it doesn't say that big kids are forbidden."

"I thought you had to go to the bathroom."

"Right. But as soon as I get back——" He was interrupted by a girl in a dress dashing through the studio door and attaching herself to his legs. She mumbled something incomprehensible into the back of his thighs.

The guy sighed and reached down to try to loosen her tentacle-like grip. "Oops, I can't understand you when you mumble. How about coming out for air."

The little girl muttered more into his legs, and he bent down to listen. "Fine."

"My sister is a little shy and would like to know your name before——" Metal hitting cement stopped him short as his elbow knocked a pile of hollow rods to the ground. They clanked against the floor one by one by one.

He jumped back far enough that the little girl was forced to look up from his legs.

"Sebastian, what'd you do?" she asked.

"Wait, you're Julia's sister." With her face free, I could see that she was the same little girl who had leaped out of the back of the town car. "Then you're . . ." The nose. The brown eyes. Of course he was Julia's brother.

"Sorry," he said as he began collecting the rods from the floor. Even as he knelt to reach under the tool cabinet, Julia's sister did not let go of his leg.

"You're Julia's brother," I said.

"Yeah." He stood up, setting a handful of rods on top of the counter. "Should have introduced myself. I'm Sebastian, and this monster is Cordelia, a.k.a. Oops."

Cordelia buried her face again in his side, but I think she said, "Nice to meet you."

"So do you actually know Julia?" he asked as he pushed the pile of rods back and then grabbed the final one from the floor, adding it to the pile with a wave. "Done."

"I do. Why didn't you say anything . . . about the car?" I wondered how much Julia had told them about me, if anything.

He tapped an uneven beat against his legs with his flat hands. "Wanted to see how far the joke would go. I always wanted to be in the mob."

"I—"

"Okay. Detach." He lifted Cordelia off his legs and onto his back. "Time to introduce." He looked at me, pausing before asking, "What's your name?"

"Charlotte," I said. "But Julia calls me Charlie."

He worked a phone I knew cost at least half as much as my laptop out of his back pocket and glanced down at it, his fingers skimming over the screen. "Well, Charlie, we are being summoned. Ready to meet the mobsters?"

I drew back from Sebastian's side to follow at a slower pace as he approached Julia and the silver-haired woman in heels. They were standing under a giant oak tree that was out of view from the art center windows. I was just close enough to hear Sebastian call out, "Julia, Oops and I stumbled on one of your friends."

Julia took her hands out of the older woman's. When her eyes reached my own, I was surprised at what I saw there. She was angry.

Her expression and the way she wrapped her arms around her rib cage let me know that in following her brother, I had messed up. I should have stayed behind.

Sebastian, oblivious, jumped Cordelia higher up on his back and stood on the other side of the older woman. Four pairs of eyes now looked at me as I walked toward the oak tree.

"Mon petit canard, présente-moi à tes amies." The silver-haired woman's voice was as smooth and sweet as cake batter being poured into a pan.

Of course she was French.

"Désolée," Julia said in response. "Nanny, this is my friend,

Charlie. Charlie, this is Nanny. I mean, Sophie Girard."

I shoved my hands in my shorts pockets, wishing I had thought to wash the streaks of soot off. When I reached the small group, Julia pivoted toward her brother.

"Mummy had one of her headaches and she wanted to talk to Dr. Mulcaster before the trustees' meeting, so it's just me and Nanny now. Maybe you and Oops should go check on her." Julia's suggestion was more of a command. She kicked at a root, not needing to look at him to know he would do what she asked.

"No worries. I'm still on a quest for a bathroom anyway." Sebastian saluted with one hand before hopping Cordelia higher up on his back again. "Charlie, nice to meet you. Oops," he said as he bounced. "Say good-bye to Julia's friend."

In reply she mumbled something into his back and turned her head the other way. He raised his arms out as if to say, "What can you do?" and then started toward the headmistress's house.

I watched him, smiling a little when he caught a foot on a divot and had to brace himself against a tree before starting out again.

Hands as soft as old leather on my cheeks brought my attention back to Julia and Sophie. The older woman held my face between her two hands, forcing me to bend so she would not have to reach so high and my eyes could meet her startling blue ones. *"Tu es très belle. Et tu as été une très bonne amie pour Julia."*

I squirmed, but not enough to loosen her gentle hold. "Uh, Julia, can you explain to your grandmother that I don't speak French? Well, I know a little. But that's French-Canadian I pick up from my roommate and most of it is swear words."

Julia snorted, and I saw her uncross her arms out of the corner of my eye. "Nanny's not our grandmother. She was our nanny growing up. Now she's Mummy's secretary. She speaks perfect English, but prefers not to. *Le français est plus élégant.*"

"My apologies, sweet child. I just said that you were very beautiful." She shook her head. "I am so used to speaking French with the family." She dropped her hands from my face. "It makes me happy to know that you are here watching out for *mon petit canard.*"

"Well," I said, "we watch out for each other." My neck hurt from bending down.

Julia leaned against the tree trunk. Her long skirt was coated at the bottom with grass. When she looked at me her expression was a clear slate, indifferent. Our staring contest ended when a bunch of freshman girls and their families passed by talking loudly.

Sophie smiled at the group. Once they were some distance away, she patted my arm and stepped backward until she was shoulder to shoulder with Julia. "You must come visit us on Nantucket, at Arcadia this summer. I'll make clafouti."

"Thanks." I could still feel the press of her long fingers on my face. "That sounds really great."

Julia softly but firmly grabbed Sophie's elbow. "Well, we'd better go find Mummy. See you, Charlie."

"Okay," I said, but if Julia heard me she gave no indication. As she and Sophie walked away, I took Julia's place against the trunk of the tree, watching them until they disappeared into the headmistress's house.

CONTRA MUNDUM

"You're pouting."

"No I'm not."

"Then why do you have that line between your eyebrows?"

"I'm trying to concentrate on the canvas and you're distracting me."

"Look. I'm sorry I didn't want to introduce you to my family yet. I just . . . I wanted to keep you to myself a little while longer. That's all. *Je te voulais pour moi.* You get it, right?"

I pretended to focus on mixing the right shade of blue.

"Right?"

I sighed. "I get it."

"How do you say 'just you and me' in Latin?"

"Uh, the translation would be pretty bad, but there's a phrase, *contra mundum.*"

"*Contra mundum.* What does it mean?"

"Roughly? 'Against the world.' Together against the world."

"*Contra mundum?*"

"*Contra mundum.*"

SEVEN

WE ONLY HAD TWO WEEKS left in our junior year the night Julia and I got in trouble. I was still wide awake when she came to my window.

I had taken to creating sculptures in my head—ridiculous things built more out of air and hope than anything that would actually stay together—to help pass the time between waking and dreaming, but that night I wasn't having any luck. My mind kept wandering back to the clumsy boy who also happened to be Julia's brother.

Her tapping was soft at first, like the branches of a tree scraping against glass, but when I didn't answer right away, she started pounding.

I jumped out of my bed and yanked the old warped window open. Her nose barely came to the sill, but her voice rang into the room. "Come on!"

I let go of the frame, glanced at Rosalie, who shifted beneath her covers. I caught the window just as it began squeaking down again.

"Charlie." Julia was standing on her tiptoes in the soft soil. Behind her the leaves of the bushes glowed and dimmed in turn as clouds passed in front of the nearly full May moon.

"Time. To. Have. An. Adventure?" Julia spoke like a drunk person pretending to be sober, enunciating her words as though it was the first time she had said any of them.

I leaned out the window. "Adventure? Where?"

She didn't say anything but released her grip on the sill, curling her fingers at me in a "come here" gesture as she backed out of the bushes.

"Jesus." I sighed and bowed my head, pushing my fingers against my temples before sliding on a pair of pants from my floor and my sneakers. When I left the dorm, I was careful to stick a *Vogue* from the recycling bin against the lock.

With a quick glance to the left and the right, I dashed around to the side of the dorm. It took my eyes adjusting to the bright moonlight for me to spot Julia leaning against the trunk of a large maple, twirling a leaf beneath her nose, one hand wrapped around what were once Aloysius's antlers but were now just stubs. She was tapping a foot against the ground as if I had kept her waiting for hours.

"*Dépêchons-nous.* We have to hurry. The night watch lady is on the other side of campus, so we're in the clear," she said. She started walking even before I reached her.

"Julia." I caught up to her in three strides. "Where are we going? I have my last Latin class tomorrow, and—"

"*La gloire se donne seulement à ceux qui l'ont toujours rêvée.*"

"I don't know what that means, Julia." She couldn't see me run my fingers through my hair, but she had to hear my annoyance.

"It means—" Julia stopped suddenly.

"It means what?"

"We're going to go check out some stuff about Gus. The year's almost done and . . ." She took a deep breath, pulling Aloysius toward her until his head rested under her nose. She whispered into his fur, "Please help, Charlie." Her voice quivered on "help," and that was all it took.

"Okay."

"Okay?"

"Okay."

So I turned off the smart part of me—the part of me that wanted to go back to my room, crawl into bed, and dream of a boy who was in college, and rich, and funny, and out of my league in so many, many ways. I followed her around the sides of buildings, trying to keep to the shadows as much as possible and running when we were out in the open.

The admissions and alumnae building was a small cottage on the far side of campus. It reminded me of a gingerbread house, with its candy-pink paint and swoops of white window boxes that looked like vanilla frosting. The back door wasn't locked—buildings on campus seldom were—but the door at the end of the entry hall wouldn't budge.

I was ready to turn around—to sneak back down the hall over the thick oriental carpets, out the door, and back across campus—but Julia was determined.

"Charlie," she whispered. "Boost me." She pointed up at the slit of a ventilation window just above the door. It could not have been open more than a crack.

I shook my head.

"Why not?"

"You'll break yourself getting down on the other side."

"Charlie, please."

Even in what little light we had from the exit signs and the lampposts that lined the paths outside the buildings, I could see that tears had pooled in the corners of her eyes, threatening to overflow onto her cheeks. I sighed and bent on one knee. She wiped her face and then clamored onto my shoulders, and after her small hands were grasped around the top of the door I stood up, bracing myself against the wall, until she was able to swing one leg over, then the other, and drop as smoothly as a shadow to the other side. The door clicked open a moment later, revealing Julia with her arms held above her head in a V, her face a glowing red from the exit lights.

"Ta-da!"

"Shhhh," I said, holding a finger to my lips.

Julia mirrored my gesture, but did it with a smile, so I'd know she was making fun of me. She went into the office before she could see me scowling.

The admissions office was cheerful and cozy. Wooden chairs in the St. Anne's colors lined the walls of a small waiting area, where brochures and old yearbooks were displayed on a large wooden coffee table. When I had visited for my interview, my dad had sat bouncing his knee and tapping his cap against his leg while I folded brochures into origami swans. By the time I was called to the back room for my meeting with the head of admissions, he was pacing in the entry hall and I had created an entire glossy flock of birds.

I grabbed a brochure and started folding it. Just one. "What are we doing here?" I asked after I tore the paper to make a square.

"*I'm* going to look for Gus's record," Julia said. "It looks like *you*, however, are having arts and crafts time."

"Sorry." I set down the swan in progress and joined Julia at the reception desk. "Old habit."

"You are so wonderfully strange," Julia said as she began opening drawers. "Where do you think they keep the alumnae files?"

I watched her riffle through the office supplies in the center drawer, which she left dangling open when she moved to the file cabinets behind it.

"Well? Are you going to help?" She wrapped her fingers

around a file cabinet handle. She had to jerk it several times to get the drawer to open.

I stepped up to the desk and wiggled the drawer she had left open shut. "Julia, what exactly do you think you're going to find out?"

"*Rien. Quelque chose. Tout.*" She shuffled the files, glancing at the labels before shoving the drawer closed.

"Meaning?"

She didn't look at me as she opened a new drawer, this one full of stationery with the St. Anne's crest at the top and on the envelopes. "It doesn't matter what I *think* we're going to find. It matters *what* we find."

I wished I could make out her expression. I picked a handful of paper clips off the desk and started hooking them together.

For a minute, the only sounds were the buzz of the exit signs and the scratch of paper against paper as Julia knelt to the carpet and riffled through a file box on the floor.

I waited.

"I got to walk away and they didn't. After the accident, Gus and David didn't get to walk away."

"Julia, is that why—"

"I cannot begin to explain how unfair that is." Her back was to me and she was bent over the box, as if she was trying to protect it and make herself as small as possible at the same time.

"Okay . . . let's see what we find . . . I'll go look in the back offices," I said. I went down the hall that led to the office where

I had had my interview. I wanted to give Julia her space.

As I peeked in the various doors, I could hear Julia opening and closing drawers in the front.

The room at the end of the hall was wall-to-wall file cabinets. It took me two minutes to find the drawers marked "B" and a matter of seconds to find Gus's record. I shook the dust off the folder as I made my way back to the reception area.

"Look," I said, holding the file above my head.

"Where was it?" Julia leaned forward across the reception desk, climbing half on top of it to snatch the manila folder from my hands.

"There's a room of cabinets in the back. I think it's where they put all the records for students who . . ." I swallowed. "For all the alumnae. It's another alumnae file room."

Julia flipped quickly through the slim folder. "There's only three sheets of paper in here."

"That's it? Didn't she go here for four years?"

Julia slapped the folder shut. "Yes, since she was a freshman. She was an honors student and the best one on the sailing team. She was more than three sheets of paper." She sounded like she was on the verge of tears again.

"I bet . . . I bet they gave everything to your parents. After . . . after it happened."

Silence.

"Look," I said, gently taking the folder from her and opening it across the desk. "There's plenty of info in here. The dorm she lived in. Her advisor. Her senior project. Sports stuff. This is really good."

"*Ce n'est pas grand chose.*"

I didn't bother her for a translation. The hunch of her shoulders told me all I needed to know. "Let's go."

Julia shut the folder, tapped it against the desk, and nodded. We left all the doors open on our way out, which ended up being a good thing, because we had just let the outside door click shut behind us when Julia stopped so suddenly I ran into her.

"I forgot Aloysius. Here." She thrust the folder at me. "Hold this. I'll be right back."

Not two seconds after Julia slid back into the building, I heard heavy footsteps slapping across asphalt.

"Shoot!" I said, louder than I meant to.

"Found him," Julia said, flinging open the door hard enough to make it smack the side of the pink building.

"Shhhh," I hissed. But it was too late. The figure in the parking lot by the campus store turned and jogged our way.

The door clicked shut, and at the same time a bright light blinded us. We stood there, each with one arm raised to shield our eyes and blinking like we had just stumbled into daylight. The moment the flashlight pointed to the ground, Julia grabbed the file from my arms, lifted up my sweatshirt, and shoved the folder down the back of my pants.

"Julia—"

"Ladies, I think you better come with me," the night guard

said. She patted her flashlight against her palm before standing with her hands on her well-padded hips.

I couldn't help it. The file scratching my back and making my underwear slide down, the lack of sleep, the guard's ridiculous TV-cop stance, and even Julia's ratty Aloysius were all of a sudden the funniest things in the world. And once I started giggling, I could feel Julia shaking beside me. I didn't need to look at her to know she had lost it, too.

"I'm glad you find this funny, ladies," the guard said. "I'm sure your parents and Dr. Mulcaster won't be so amused." She began walking, knowing we had no choice but to follow.

We both looked at the ground so we wouldn't glance at each other and erupt again.

I started after the guard first. When Julia caught up to me—Aloysius tucked under one arm—she slid her hand into mine and squeezed twice. *Contra mundum.* I squeezed back. *Contra mundum.*

I lost weekend privileges for the rest of the year, was thrown back in supervised study hall and given two weeks of kitchen duty, and had to call home to explain what I'd done. My dad mumbled something about not telling Melissa.

Julia got it worse. Dr. Mulcaster wanted to prove something with her. She got hit with everything they could throw at her—work detail, study hall, community service—but she didn't get suspended, which is what mattered most.

GUS'S FILE

I had been too optimistic. The three sheets of paper in Gus's folder didn't tell us much at all.

The first listed her advisor (Dr. Blanche all four years), senior classes (AP Calculus, AP English, Honors Spanish Four, Honors Environmental Science, and AP Art History), activities (Debate and Sailing Team), and dorm (Pembroke, which didn't surprise me).

The second described her senior project (poetry writing with Dr. Blanche).

The third was a chart of colleges with thick checkmarks next to most of them—except for Harvard. The box next to Harvard was blacked out, and a huge red question mark was drawn off to the side.

Harvard, question mark.

EIGHT

THERE WERE FEW PLACES I could be found on campus in June. If I wasn't in class, I was fulfilling my work hours with the kitchen staff. If I wasn't in the kitchen, I was in study hall. And if I wasn't in study hall, I was trying to squeeze in time with Julia, who had her own punishment obligations. If I wasn't in any of those places, then I was in my room, which was not a particularly great place to be.

By the second day of finals, I was no longer able to ignore the fact that Rosalie was avoiding me. Since I'd snuck out with Julia, she'd only come into the room to swap her books between classes or to change before she went to crew practice. She stayed out until check-in, and then when she came in, she changed into PJs, opened a textbook, and read silently on her bed until lights out.

The night before my physics exam, I reached my breaking

point. It was 10:33, and I couldn't get comfortable at my desk. My chair seat felt lumpy and one of the wheels kept squeaking. I couldn't remember the equation for Coulomb's law, and electric circuits were never going to make sense without Julia explaining them to me. I crossed my arms and put my head down on the open book on my desk. "You don't like Julia Buchanan, do you?" I said into the pages.

I heard Rosalie toss a book on the floor from where she was sitting on her bed. "I'm indifferent."

"No, you're not. I can hear it in your voice you're not." I raised my head from my desk and slouched down in my chair, daring her to argue with me.

"Fine." She opened another book. "I don't like the fact that you two are obsessed with each other. You'd never been in trouble before she got here, and now you're on lockdown until the end of the year."

"I'm not obsessed." I swung my chair from side to side.

"If you're not with her, you're texting her, and when you're not texting her, you stare at your phone like you hate it for not buzzing."

"I'm not—"

"Whatever, Charlotte. You can spend your time with whoever you want. It's none of my business." She flipped through the pages of her book like they had offended her. "You were the one who asked me what I thought. Don't get mad just because you don't like the answer."

"Fine," I said, opening up my laptop.

"Fine," Rosalie echoed.

Later that night, when we were both pretending to be asleep, I whispered, "I'm still your friend."

Rosalie took a sharp breath in and then let it out in a low whistle. "You haven't been acting like it."

"I know. I'm sorry. I wish you would give Julia a chance, though. She's really nice and funny and smart. She's not like most of those girls she hangs out with. She's not snotty at all, and she's been through a lot. You know her older sister?"

"The one who died?" Rosalie sounded like she was talking with her quilt over her mouth.

I glanced across the room. She was facing the wall, her quilt pulled up to her ears.

"She was here, at St. Anne's. Julia's curious about what she was like when she was in high school. That's why we snuck out. We went to the alumnae house to see if we could find her file."

"The dead sister's file?" Rosalie said as she turned over so she was facing me.

"Yeah. I don't know if I'm supposed to tell anyone that that's what we were doing." Suddenly my covers felt too warm. I kicked them off and pushed them over the bottom of the bed with my feet. "You can't tell anyone."

"It sounds like you're wrestling with a bear. What'd that blanket ever do to you?"

"I got hot. Seriously, you can't say anything."

"I'm not going to." Rosalie propped herself up on her elbows. "Sounds like a classic case of survivor's guilt."

"What?"

"Well, Julia was in the car crash, too. Right?"

"Yeah."

"But she lived and her sister and the boyfriend died and now she's trying to feel better about that by asking you to break into buildings and run around campus. Eh?"

"Eh?"

Rosalie sighed. "Don't make fun of the 'eh.' Anyway, like I said, classic case of survivor's guilt."

This time I sighed.

"What? I'm taking psychology with Mr. Campion."

"Yeah, because you think he's sexy."

Rosalie giggled. "True. But I can't help it if I learn something while I'm picturing him naked and naming our imaginary children."

"Gross." I leaned over the edge of my bed, grabbed one of the slippers Julia had given me, and threw it across the room.

"You bitch," said Rosalie. "That hit me in the elbow."

"What happened to being a tough Canadian, eh?"

Rosalie answered by chucking the slipper at my leg.

"Ow!" I threw it back at her; then she tossed one of her pillows at me.

When I didn't have anything left to throw, I crossed the

room to pick up my pillow. "Fine, I give up. But only because I'm a bigger person than you."

Rosalie tossed one of my slippers at my butt when I turned around to go back to my bed. "Now we're done."

"That was totally against the rules of combat," I said, but I was smiling when I finally fell asleep.

AN UNNECESSARY GIFT

Dear Charlotte,

Mr. Buchanan and I feel terrible about the trouble Julia got you into. (Don't worry. She told us sneaking out was her idea and that you went with her because you're a good friend.)

Please accept this token as an apology. We really do feel horrible.

I'm sorry I didn't get to meet you over parents' weekend, but Sophie said she invited you to Arcadia this summer. The whole family would love to have you!

Until then . . .

Sincerely yours,

Teresa Buchanan

The small box was wrapped in purple paper. The silver watch inside had a delicate oval face, Roman numerals, and a rich brown leather band.

I had never owned a watch before, and I didn't know if I could keep this one.

LOCKDOWN

J: Hope u like the watch! Lockdown is terrible!

C: It's amazing

C: Watch. Not Lockdown! Can't keep watch. Way 2 much!

J: U have to. Mum didn't keep receipt

J: that might be lie. But could be true. ☺

C: Meet me after 1st exam tomorrow? Studio?

J: Ugh. Have community service at 12

C: After Second exam?

J: Come to my room instead. Will make "refreshments." ;)

C: K. Gotta go study. TTFN

J: CM?

C: CM

NINE

THE SCHOOL YEAR ENDED AS it always did, with a frenzy of finding boxes, packing, and hugs good-bye to graduates, who I knew from experience would forget their promises to keep in touch almost as soon as their taillights passed through the St. Anne's gates. Why we bothered with the rituals of email and phone number exchanges was a mystery.

Not that it really mattered much to me that spring. I had few people to say good-bye to. My world had become Julia's world, and I knew I would miss it when I went home.

We began the summer talking or texting every day. But by mid-July she had stopped replying, and I stopped trying. I could imagine the life she had returned to, and I had mine: waitressing at the resort, helping my dad in the garage, watching Sam and AJ, while Melissa went to her classes, and working on my sculptures.

I tried not to think about Julia—but the more I tried, the more I failed to think of anything else.

Home was a dirt driveway three miles after the turnoff for the old ski lodge. It was the smell of pines and deep snow in winter and burned dirt and shady woods in summer. Home was a small house that had grown in a haphazard way—a new deck here, a mudroom off the kitchen, an enclosed back porch—until the original cabin seemed as lost in the sprawl as a tree in a shopping mall parking lot. It was forest and the sound of trucks passing on the highway on their way to Canada. It was too many people in too small a space.

Between Sam and AJ being four and five and Melissa being from New Jersey and my dad's garage being a hundred yards from the house, most of the time I could barely hear my own voice over the noise, never mind really think.

I had been back a little over a month when the din drove me outside again. The thin walls were no match for the shouting of two mud-covered boys home from the first afternoon of day camp.

I pulled on Melissa's barn coat, more for protection against mosquitoes than for warmth. My paperback copy of *The Great Gatsby* fit perfectly in one of the large front pockets, even though the sleeves barely came to my wrists. I closed the screen door gently behind me before I jogged across the backyard to the giant trampoline near the edge of the woods.

When the trampoline was new, before Dad had even met Melissa and before they got married and she moved in with Sam and AJ, I had entertained myself for hours on it. I did back flips, jumped off tree limbs into the center, and pretty much did everything the safety manual told you not to, and never broke a bone. But then I went away and we forgot to take it down in winter. Eventually the middle started to sag, the springs started to creak, and rust covered the poles.

It was lousy for bouncing, but great for hiding. I tossed the book first, then hefted myself up and did an ungraceful roll, landing on top of *Gatsby*. For two precious minutes I did nothing but stare up at the tissue paper ceiling of green leaves.

"What you got there?" My dad's voice was low and rough like sandpaper against a freshly sawed board. When I sat up on my elbows the trampoline springs protested with sharp squeaks. I shielded my eyes with one hand to look up at him. The early evening sun silhouetted him, and his Red Sox cap was slightly askew. After my eyes adjusted, I could see that he was grasping a crate between his hands; his expression was easy, his posture relaxed. It had been a good day in the garage.

"Summer reading. *Great Gatsby*. I have to finish before tomorrow and get it back to the library," I said.

My dad scratched his nose on his shoulder. "You should meet up with some kids your age."

I flopped on my back. "Who am I going to hang out with around here? I don't know anyone anymore." A bird flew below the tree line, and I paused to admire how its shadow crept across the leaves: a streak of black paint over a background of green.

"Besides, you know if I go out that means Melissa will make dinner. My stomach might never recover from last week's macaroni surprise. I wouldn't wish that on anyone."

My dad chuckled and set the crate down at his feet. "Nah. I wouldn't either." He ran his hand across the five o'clock shadow that covered his jaw. "Charlotte, your mom called again this morning. You gotta call her back. She's your mom. She deserves a phone call. She's lonely out there now that your grandma's gone."

"Does *she* know she's my mom?"

"Don't be a smart-ass." He put both hands on the springs and pushed them down, bouncing me in small waves. "And lay off teasing Melissa about her cooking. Her mind is half on the boys and half on hair dye and shampoo these days."

I struggled into a sitting position, wrapping Melissa's coat tighter around me as I crossed my legs. "I'm not trying to start anything. Look at what I let her do to my hair." I pointed at my brown roots. "And she *still* hasn't fixed it."

"Yeah." My dad gave the springs enough of a push to make me fall backward. "I would maybe wait until she actually graduates from beauty school before you let her test anything else out on you." He swiped his cap off his head and wiped his forehead against his T-shirt sleeve. "Just cut her some slack. Get what I'm saying?"

"Yup," I said, lurching back up. I ducked my head down, picked up my book, and started to read.

"Hey, Charlotte!"

I turned and saw Sam half in and half out of the front screen door.

"Mom says to tell you to come answer your bleep bleep phone before she backs over it with the truck. It's been buzzing all afternoon," he shouted.

"What's my 'bleep bleep' phone?" I called back.

"She won't let me say the bad words." He spun around, the door slamming behind him.

"I better go. With all those chemicals on her brain, she *would* run it over." I bounced to the side of the trampoline and dropped to the ground, *Gatsby* clutched in one hand.

"Yup." My father shook the springs one more time. "This thing's a death trap. We gotta take it down."

"You say that every summer."

"Yeah, and I mean it every summer. Hey, before you go in, I found some good stuff at the dump this morning for you to use." He rustled in the crate and then stood up. He held an uneven circle of glass in his palm. It had probably once been the bottom of a beer bottle, but now, with its edges worn down by time, it looked like a precious stone. "There's lots more in the box in the bed of the truck when you need it."

"Thanks." I took the glass and held it up to the sky. "You told Henry I want to use the tools in the garage Sunday, right?"

"I'll tell him tomorrow. Shouldn't be a problem."

"You going to meet the guys before dinner?" I asked.

He straightened up and tapped the brim of his cap like he was tipping a top hat. "Two beers. Scout's honor."

"You were never a Boy Scout." I smiled.

"It's a good thing, too. I'm terrible at starting campfires." He looked down at the crate, kicking it gently with his boots. "You better get up there and check your phone before it goes out the window."

I slid the piece of glass into one of the large coat pockets and then knocked my dad's cap so it fell off his head. I caught his choice words just as I reached the porch.

THE INVITATION

J: hope u are smashing!! miss u much. so dull here

J: If I see 1 more guy in pleated khakis . . . .girls too. Ugh. Not cute!

J: When are u coming to visit?

J: Are u mad? Sorry, am rotten @ email

J: am rotten @ text too

J: I feel like death! Might have cold or bubonic plague

J: Have never felt so bad in my life. might never get out of bed again

J: Nanny says could be fu!

J: Meant flu. Could u come to ACK real soon?

J: Are u not answering because ur mad!?!

C: Just got texts. K will try

J: am buying u a bus ticket from NH to Hyannis JIC. Will email tix. ☺

J: ???!!!???!!!???!!!???

C: Can leave Sat or Sun, need to get sub for work. Bus to Hyannis then ferry to ACK. What should I bring?

J: Just u! ☺ get here yesterday!!!!!

TEN

THE BUS TO HYANNIS HAD been stuffy, loud, and crowded. When we reached the final stop, I unfolded myself from my seat, feeling like the smells of the cheesy popcorn the woman next to me had been eating and whatever terrible chemical they put in the closet-size bathroom would never come out of my skin. I saw Sebastian while I was reaching for my bag in the overhead bin. He was pacing in the travel center parking lot in front of a billboard advertising deep-sea fishing and whale-watching tours. His cell phone was pressed to his ear. He had just started kicking at a dandelion tuft that had broken through the pavement when a man behind me in the aisle coughed.

"Oh. Sorry." I shuffled the rest of the way off the bus, my duffel bag smacking against my leg the whole time.

I stood near the travel center entrance, wishing my phone hadn't died on the ride down so I could at least pretend to check emails or text while I waited for him to see me. I saw him put his phone in his pocket out of the corner of my eye, so I started inspecting the box of chocolates Melissa had insisted I bring for Julia's parents. The bow was crumpled and one side had a footprint from when I had set it on the floor.

"Hello again."

He was just as cute as I remembered. His collared shirt was missing a button at the bottom and hung loosely over expensive-looking dark blue jeans. His eyes were hidden behind the same aviator sunglasses he had been wearing parents' weekend. I saw my distorted face in them as he stepped in front of me. He stretched one hand out and reached the other up to remove the sunglasses—a move that would have been smooth if he hadn't sent them clattering to the pavement.

"Shit," Sebastian said as he scrambled on the ground, kicking the glasses twice before grabbing them. He straightened with a jerk. "Sorry." He stretched a hand out once more. "Sebastian. Nice to meet you again, Charlie."

I shook his hand, feeling every inch where it covered my own. Remembering the cheesy popcorn and bathroom chemicals, I dropped it and stepped backward, shifting my duffel on my shoulder. "Where's Julia?"

"Pip doesn't drive . . . I mean, she knows how . . . she just doesn't do it," he said, slipping his sunglasses back on.

"Okay. Does that mean she's not here?"

"Nope. Plus, she's on her deathbed and all," he said.

"She's that sick?"

He shook his head. "Nah, just that dramatic." He looked down and kicked at a stone. "Let me guess. She didn't tell you I'd be picking you up."

"Ah, negative."

"Typical." His brow wrinkled and he shoved both his hands into his jeans pockets. "That's Pip. She's not one for details. She's more of a big, huge picture kind of person." He scooped my bag from my shoulder. "I'm parked around the corner at the coffee shop."

Once his back was turned, I pressed my T-shirt to my nose. No bathroom sanitizer or processed cheese. Thank God. I tried to smooth my flyaway strands back into a ponytail. After cursing Julia for not warning me, Melissa for ruining my hair, myself for wearing my oldest jeans, and anyone else I could think to blame in that moment for the marbles in my stomach, I followed him.

He led me out of the parking lot to a red car with a fabric roof and curved lines from another era. It was rusty near the fenders, and I could see through the driver's-side window that the dash was scratched and the leather seats had stuffing poking through. There was no backseat. It was a car held together with glue, duct tape, and hope.

"Is that a seventies Vantage?"

He tilted his head to the side, letting the handle of my duffel slip off his shoulder to the crook of his elbow. "I wish. It's an '87 fixer-upper. But it's my baby. How'd you know it was an Aston Martin?"

I tugged at the passenger door. "You own an Aston Martin, my dad works on them." The fifth time the door finally lurched open. I climbed in, and after his own battle with the driver's-side door, Sebastian did, too.

The short drive from the bus station to the ferry was punctuated by squealing brakes (ours) and honking horns (other cars'). Sebastian drove the speed limit exactly and at each stop sign gripped the wheel so tightly I wondered if his knuckles hurt.

When we arrived at the docks, the man shepherding cars onto the ferry, a mass of metal that floated at the end of a long pier like a huge dog tied to a tree, waved Sebastian on with a flourish.

"Thanks, Mike," Sebastian shouted with a wave as we inched by. He drove up the ramp into the ferry like he was going through a series of stoplights. Stop. Go. Stop. Go. Stop. Go. We parked in the last row of cars, right behind a produce truck.

I pulled myself out of the car as soon as we stopped. My wrists were sore from bracing against the dashboard.

Sebastian turned off the keys and looked up at the truck in front of him. He froze. "Shit."

"Is everything okay?" I ducked my head down and peered at him through the passenger door. He looked confused, like he had just woken up in a bed that wasn't his own.

I followed his gaze to the truck. "Cross Family Farm" was all it said across the back. A cartoon cow and bushel of fire-red apples were painted below.

"Sebastian, you okay?" I said, leaning half in the car. When he didn't respond, I started to slide back into my seat.

I was just about to swing my legs in when he ripped the keys out of the ignition and jumped out of the car. "Yeah. Great. Never better." The sound of his door slamming shut hit the walls of the ferry and bounced back at us. "After you." He gestured toward a flight of metal stairs at the far end of the parking level.

I wove around the other cars and led the way up the stairs. When I stopped at the top, Sebastian was only halfway up and staring at the truck.

"Being parked behind a truck always makes me nervous about the car. Is it okay if we go to the upper deck? It's the best view."

"Sure." I stood to the side to let him pass. His arm grazed my shoulder when he stepped by me up the second set of stairs, and that moment of touch and the citrus smell of his shampoo were enough to make me choose to stop wondering why he was acting so strange.

Sebastian found us a bench in a hidden corner of the upper deck, where we were shielded from the wind and the railing and lifeboats didn't cast shadows. From time to time he would glance up, frowning slightly, as if he was looking for someone. But then he would catch me watching him, and his smile would return and he would go back to pointing out landmarks. And when the shore disappeared and a field of water was the only view, I went to the snack bar and bought us hot chocolate made from powder and dehydrated mini marshmallows.

Sebastian tried to pay for them, and even though I refused to take his money he seemed grateful that I had been the one to go below to the second deck.

It was a perfectly ordinary trip—sun, wind, and water—but it seemed like a journey to me. Like I wasn't just taking a ferry to somewhere, but taking it toward *some place* and that everything would be different when I got there. I already felt like in a way I did not yet understand, my life had changed.

By the time our hot chocolates were just crumpled cups lying at our feet, Nantucket Island had begun to rise on the horizon like a blue-green promise. Gray houses with white trim and shutters stood on the perimeter, undulating like the waves that surrounded them. The dark windows were eyes looking out at the boats passing by.

A faded fishing boat roared to the side of the ferry, dipping left and right. But the men on board, baked and hardened by lifetimes of working outdoors, did not pause from their pulling and hauling—not even when their boat leaned low enough to one side that waves washed up on the deck.

The island interior was a landscape of rooftops, and in their center, a white church steeple rose into the sky like a hand reaching for the sun.

Sebastian leaned across me pointing to a peninsula that was just coming into view. "See that lighthouse there?"

"I see a tower that could be a lighthouse."

"Okay, well take my word for it. On that point, there's a lighthouse, and every time you pass you throw a penny and make a wish. I've never missed it. Not since I was little."

"What do you wish for?"

"You can't tell. It won't come true if you do."

"Well, I wouldn't use a penny. Pennies are probably bad for the fish. I would throw something else."

"Do you have anything else right now?"

I pretended to pat my pockets. "Gosh. No."

"Well then a penny for your thoughts." He slid a coin that was warm from being in his pocket into my palm. I didn't want to throw it because it had been his.

"One. Two. Three."

We tossed them simultaneously, both pennies falling yards and yards short of the peninsula.

Once we got back in the car, Sebastian went from the guy who could laugh and make wishes to a guy who grasped the wheel like it was a rope and he was hanging over a canyon.

We were the first ones off the ferry. He insisted. He slunk

low in his seat and rolled down the ramp to the shore, glancing only once in his rearview mirror at the still truck as if it might give chase even without a driver.

He had to slow to a creep once we reached the cobblestone streets of downtown. We bumped by red brick shops with bright T-shirts and gourmet foods on display in the windows, overflowing flower pots, and cars that I had only seen on the calendars my dad liked to order for the garage.

People milled about with sweaters knotted around their necks, wearing polo shirts in Easter-egg blues, greens, and pinks. Shirt collars were popped against tanned necks, and flip-flops were as common as loafers. An older couple, the man with leather-brown skin and a straw fedora set at a rakish angle on his head and the woman in sunglasses and a bright patterned dress, held the hands of a boy and a girl who couldn't have been older than AJ. The children were dressed like their outfits had been planned for adults and then shrunk in the wash to make them kid-size. When Sebastian stopped to let them cross the street, the little boy waved to me, and as I waved back I was happy to see his hands were covered with what looked like chocolate ice cream.

Once the cobblestones ended and the pavement began again, Sebastian finally spoke: "Mind if I put the top down?" His shoulders, which had been raised near his ears since we had driven off the ferry, were now dropped, but his arms were stiff in front of him. He was pressing against the wheel as much as he was turning it.

I relaxed my grip on the door handle. "I've never ridden in a convertible."

"Really?"

I glanced at him to see if he was making fun of me, but he looked genuinely surprised.

"That is something I'm going to have to rectify." He slowed the car to a stop, pulled a switch near his door, and hopped out. "Ow. Shit. That hurt."

"Can I help?"

"No, I got it." He wrestled the top down and then climbed back into the driver's seat. There was a fresh cut across the back of his hand.

"You're really accident prone, aren't you?" I asked as he jerked the car back onto the road. His eyes were so intensely focused on the pavement, I couldn't help adding, "Do you want me to drive? I'm a really good driver . . . I've been doing it since I was thirteen."

His lips became a straight line, and he started drumming his fingers on the steering wheel. He finally replied, "We grew up driving, too . . . thanks though." He seemed to be talking more to himself than to me.

"K," I whispered. I rolled down my window and pretended to be watching the bikers and joggers on the path next to the road. I was really more interested in stealing glances at him out of the corner of my eye.

In profile, I could see that his nose had a slight bump in the middle, as if he had broken it once and then broken it again with little time in between to let it heal.

I let the wind fill my ears, and tried to figure out what to do with my hands. Gripping the door meant his driving was bad. Crossed arms might make him think I was angry. I had settled on holding them in my lap when Sebastian leaned over me and reached toward my feet, taking the steering wheel and the car with him.

"Sorry." He sat back up, steering the car to the left. "I had a drink down there. Do you see it?"

I bent down and ran my hand across the floor, grateful for the distraction from how close his face had just been to mine. I closed my fingers around a glass bottle under the seat and pulled it out. "This?"

"Yeah. Thanks." He took it from me, opening the top and handing me the cap without ever taking his eyes off the road.

"What's the fact of the day?"

"Fact?"

"What's it say on the inside of the cap? These guys that make them, they're from the island and they put these great factoids inside the caps." He took a gulp so large I could see his throat working.

I flipped it over and read aloud, "Love produces the same physiological reactions as fear: pupil dilation, sweaty palms, and increased heart rate." I clicked the center of the cap back and forth between my fingers. Fear and love. Love and fear. One and the same.

"Huh. Pupil dilation, really? Want a sip?" He held the bottle toward me.

And even though I hadn't had lemonade since I was a kid when my dad would make giant pitchers of it with tap water and a powder mix, I took the bottle from him and sipped from where his lips had been. It was too sweet, too warm, and the bottle was too moist and dirty from rolling around on the car floor. It was delicious. I handed it back just to touch his fingers one more time, but I kept the cap, shoving it into my pocket.

"What are you studying?" I liked that I had to shout to be heard and then lean in to get his answer.

"What else? Government and economics. I'm being groomed to take over the family business." He had a wrinkle between his eyebrows that hadn't been there before.

"Politics?"

He fiddled with a knob near his window. "I didn't even have to worry about finding a freshman advisor this year. My guy's been coming to my parents' parties since I was in diapers—a fact that he unfortunately made clear at a meeting first semester." He hummed and drummed his fingertips against the wheel. "What about you? Julia says you're the greatest artist since Picasso."

"Hardly. Julia needs to get to a lot more galleries and museums, if that's what she thinks." I pressed a hand against the cap

in my pocket. "It's more that art's the only thing I can picture myself doing all the time. I've tried. Teacher? Nope. Chef?
Disaster."

"Actor in a haunted house?"

"Not scary enough."

"Interpreter for the United Nations?"

"I take Latin."

"Phone psychic?"

"I can't even predict what I'll have for breakfast tomorrow."

Sebastian laughed. "Guess you better stick with art then.
That's great . . . that you know what you want to do."

I shrugged, forgetting that he couldn't see me because he
was looking at the road. "Most of the time I feel like I'm mud-
dling my way through." I wove my right hand through the
wind, catching and falling, spreading my fingers to feel every
bit of it. "I mean I might know, but that doesn't mean I'm certain. Does that make sense?"

"Yeah," Sebastian said, his hands still grasping the wheel like
he was afraid it would try to escape from him. "That actually
makes a ton of sense."

"You're lucky, too. That you know what you want to do,"
I replied.

"Maybe . . ." He glanced at me, then quickly put his eyes
back on the road. "I had it handed to me. You figured it out all
on your own, though. That's pretty cool."

I kept weaving my hand through the wind. "Until I fall

on my face and become another starving artist with a useless degree and live out the rest of my existence as a cliché."

Sebastian rewarded my sarcasm with a smile. "You're different from anyone else Julia has invited to Arcadia. That's a good thing, Charlie."

I let his words soak in like sunscreen through my skin. "Different" never sounded so good.

Sebastian slowed the car to a crawl before we turned through a wrought iron gate that was surrounded on both sides by dense hedges.

The main house was a sprawling, white, colonial-style fortress. Three porticoes held up the face, and green shutters at every window seemed placed more to break up the ethereal whiteness of it all than to actually shut out the sun. A large porch stretched around half of the front and disappeared into the back. A green lawn rolled out from the porch steps, stretching down and down and down, right to the edge of a thin beach. A small red sailboat bobbed next to a dark dock and boathouse that leaned in the back, like a dog settling on its haunches.

The sign above the front door could have been ripped from the back of a boat: "Arcadia." It was crooked.

Sebastian pushed open his door and reached for the bag at my feet. He walked behind the car, opening and shutting the trunk, fumbling for a bit, and then continuing around to my side. I was still staring at the house when he started pulling on my door. He got it open before I even had a chance to undo my seat belt. I grabbed the battered box of chocolates from the floor and stretched out of the car with all the grace of a corpse coming to life. As I stumbled up, I came nose to nose with Sebastian. I forgot to exhale.

"Full confession." Sebastian took one step away from me and looked down as he kicked at some broken shells in the driveway. "The way I drove took twice as long as the one I should have taken." He glanced at me through those thick lashes. "Don't tell Pip. She'll tar and feather me."

I made a zipper motion across my lips. I felt a rush as unsettling and sweet as sugary coffee on an empty stomach.

"Here you go." He handed me my bag, my fingers meeting his for longer than necessary.

"Thanks," I mumbled, shifting the straps onto one shoulder.

"Well." He clapped his hands together and then rubbed them as if trying to keep them warm. He looked down at his feet again, then up at me, then down. "I have to go. People to see. Things to do and whatnot."

"You're leaving?" I hoped that I didn't sound as disappointed to him as I did to my own ears.

"Summer classes. Little too much time at Grendel's Pub and a little too little time showing up to English class to actually discuss *Beowulf*." He laughed. "Plus, Boom wants the car back on the mainland. I kind of volunteered to chauffeur when I heard you were coming to rescue Pip."

"Throw a penny for me on the way back then."

"I'll do that," he said, tilting his head and shielding his eyes with one hand. "I'll throw two." He climbed into the Aston Martin over the driver's-side door instead of bothering with trying to open it and backed slowly out of the drive, honking three times once he reached the road. The gravel was still settling when Julia called to me from the porch.

"You survived being in a car with Sebastian. He drives like an old man with a stick up his *arrière-train*." She slid down the banister and landed with a thump on two feet.

"I thought you were on your deathbed," I shouted.

"I got better. What are those? It looks like the box survived a trip from Fiji."

"Chocolates. I brought them for your parents."

"Well they're not here yet, so we'll just have to eat them ourselves. Come on. I've been waiting forever for you to get here. We'll share them with Nanny. She loves chocolates."

I held up the battered box: the ribbon was nearly shredded on one side, it was dented, and the top corner had a footprint on it—mine. Julia started up the porch stairs. I tucked the box under one arm and moved across the lawn to join her.

She paused when she got to the top step. "He has a girlfriend, you know."

I was grateful her back was to me, so she couldn't see the heat creeping across my face. "Who?" I asked lamely.

"My brother who could charm the underwear off a nun."

She turned around at the door, one hand on the knob. "Come to think of it, he probably has charmed the granny panties off a nun. He did go to a Catholic high school. Come on." She disappeared inside.

I reached in my pocket and wrapped one hand around the bottle cap. I did not trust myself to say anything in response.

A HANDFUL OF WISHES

I found the pennies when I was alone and unpacking in my guest room that first night. There were sixty-four of them; I counted.

A pile of copper underneath my jeans and pajama bottoms.

He must have thrown them in when he went around the back of the car.

I took one for my memory box. The rest I put in a clear glass and set on my bedside table, so I could look at them before I fell asleep.

ELEVEN

"**WHY DO THEY CALL IT** a widow's walk?"

"Because a sailor's wife would come up here and pace and look for her husband's ship to come in," Julia called over her shoulder as she continued up the ladder to the roof. "If it never did, she was a widow, watching for a someone who wouldn't ever be coming home. Here, take this." She lowered the bottle of champagne she had been holding down to me on the floor and began pounding at the ceiling with her two fists.

"What are you doing?"

"The only way to get up is through the trapdoor, but no one goes up here, so it's stuck," she huffed.

As Julia pounded, I looked around the attic. Like the rest of the house, it was elegant but shabby, like a wedding dress slowly turning yellow in a storage box. Downstairs, the carpets had worn patches, the sofas sagged in the middle, and the antique vases all looked like they could use a polish.

Upstairs, the attic looked like a playroom that time had forgotten. The floor was scuffed in places so badly it appeared as though someone had run across it wearing ice skates. Drooping dolls hung out of a red toy box. Plastic truck parts and board game pieces were scattered around the room like confetti. The only thing that seemed to be intact was a child-size wooden sailboat with a sun-faded blue sail. I did not have to ask Julia whose toy that had been or guess why time had held it together so well.

"Enfin!" A square of light suddenly flooded down from above Julia's head as the door swung back on its hinges, landing on the roof with a crack. "Come on then," she called over her shoulder. "Bring the champagne." She disappeared through the hatch.

I followed her, holding the bottle and cups under one arm and clinging to the ladder with the other. When my head was above the opening, I stopped. The sky was so densely blue it looked like you could push against it. On one side I could see the outline of the roofs of downtown, including the spire of the church that I'd noticed when driving with Sebastian. On the other sides, I saw miles and miles of scrubby trees broken up by squares of lawn and gray houses, some of them even larger than Arcadia. "Holy *merde!*" I whispered.

"See, you do speak French. Now get off the ladder so we can close the door."

"Julia, this is amazing," I said as I finished climbing.

Julia shut the hatch and took the bottle from my arms. "I thought you'd like it. *Un. Deux. Trois.*" She popped the bottle, sending a shower of champagne into the wind. "Welcome to the home of the Great Buchanans!"

"Thanks." I wiped at the spray on my face with my sleeve. "The Great Buchanans? You make your family sound like a bunch of circus performers."

Julia put the cups on the railing and started pouring, letting foam run over the sides and drip down the roof. "Oh, if nothing else, the Great Buchanans are performers. Don't you know? We're all acrobats and lion tamers. We make caramel popcorn good enough to tempt dentists, and our trapeze act has brought royalty to their knees with awe." She took a deep drink of the cup she had poured herself. "Oh, not bad." She filled the second and handed it to me. "Yes, Mummy is the master of ceremonies, Boom is the businessman counting the cash in some poorly lit tent, my oldest brother, Bradley, is the lion tamer, Cordelia is the elephant trainer, and Sebastian is the juggler. God forbid he drop a ball or else the world might stop spinning."

She threw back her head and drained her cup. "These things are stupid," she said. "All the froth goes everywhere. *Au revoir!*" She flung her cup off the roof, giggling when some champagne drops flew back and hit her. "Just the bottle for us."

I settled into a sitting position with my feet planted flat against the roof so I could shoot up and grab Julia at the first hint of her swaying. "And what about you? What do you do in the circus?"

Julia looked at me, her head tilted to her left shoulder. She tapped a finger against her lips. "*Moi?* I'm the resident clown. I can ride a unicycle, or I'm sure I could if I wanted to. I can stuff myself in a car, take a pie in the face, and disappear and reappear when you least expect me—or maybe that makes me the resident magician? I'd never pull a rabbit out of my hat, though. Too cruel. I'm more of a saw-women-in-half kind of girl." Julia raised the bottle, splashing champagne near her feet. The bubbles sizzled and then disappeared. "What would your family's act look like?"

"It wouldn't look like an act at all."

"Oh?" Julia said, raising an eyebrow. "Do tell."

"There's not much to tell. My real mom is in New Mexico. Santa Fe. She moved out there after the divorce to be with my grandma Eve. Grandma Eve was great. She used to take me to museums, these crazy modern dance shows, and weird hole-in-the-wall galleries every time she came to Boston. My mom stayed out there even after she died."

"Do you miss her?"

"Grandma Eve? All the time."

"No, your mother."

"This January, I threw her week-late Christmas card in a bonfire at the skating pond. It was, as Dr. Blanche would say in

English, a cathartic ritual."

"You really *don't* miss her then?"

I shrugged. "If anything, I miss the idea of her, but maybe not *her* her."

Julia sat down across from me and gestured for me to continue, a hand pressed against her forehead to shade her eyes from the sun.

"I have a stepmom. She's great. Two Animal Planet–obsessed stepbrothers. My dad. I love them, but it's wicked crowded when I'm home. I don't even have a bedroom anymore." I laughed, thinking how ridiculous I must sound to someone who had two houses. "I sleep on a futon in the den over breaks. It's all really boring. Not like here." I took the champagne from her and gulped, letting the bubbles trip along my tongue. "Your turn." I pointed the bottle at her.

"Fine," Julia said, swiping the bottle back. She sipped, handed it to me, and then spoke. "I can't come here on my own anymore, even if Nanny's here, too. There always needs to be two other people besides me. Nanny's cousin stayed three extra days until you could get here." She turned her head to look at me, one cheek resting on her knees. "There was an incident, and after that Mummy won't let me be alone." She reached for the bottle again, gulped, and held on to it this time. "Part of the deal with me being allowed to go to St. Anne's was that I had to find a friend who could come with me to Arcadia."

Now I hugged my knees to my chest and looked out at the

ocean. Not wanting to watch her watching me. "So that's why you texted me? Why didn't you just ask Piper or Eun Sun or one of those girls you used to eat lunch with?"

"Oh no, I didn't mean it like that. That came out all wrong. Don't be upset with me. I want you here because you're Charlie and you get *it*. I would rather be with you than any of those *filles aussi stupides que leurs pieds* at school. You're so, so, so much more interesting." Julia scooted closer to me and put her head on my shoulder. "And you're fantastic on the eyes and that's always a plus," she said, winking.

I felt my cheeks get prickly. "Flattery will get you nowhere." I took the bottle from her, grateful for the distraction of the bubbles exploding in my mouth.

Julia stood up. "I've hurt your feelings? I know how to make it up to you. I will perform part of the Great Buchanans acrobatic act, a breath-catching, show-stopping, world-famous defiance of gravity!" Julia put both her hands on her hips and started kicking her legs in front of her like a can-can dancer.

I tried really hard not to smile.

"What? Madame is not impressed." Julia stopped kicking, her chest heaving in and out. "I can tell ze Madame is a lady of *exigeants* taste. Perhaps zee ballet dancing is more to her liking, *oui*?"

I nodded.

"Well I shall perform zee Swan Lake for zee discerning Madame." Julia raised her arms and bounced on the balls of her sneaker-clad feet with small, barely discernable fluttering motions.

"You're really good for a pick-up ballerina."

"Thank you, Madame," she huffed. "Mummy insisted on zee ballet lessons since zis ballerina could barely walk. Too bad I have the height of a munchkin instead of a dancer. And *maintenant pour le grand final!*" Julia moved closer and closer to the edge of the widow's walk until she was less than a foot from where it ended and the sky began. She stopped and drew her arms into a circle in front of her. She looked at me, winked, and then began raising her left foot until it formed a triangle against her right knee. She slowly moved it behind her, lowering her chest toward the railing as her leg climbed higher and higher behind her.

"Julia." I dropped the empty champagne bottle and had to clamor for it as it rolled toward the edge. I grabbed the neck and stood up. "Julia, stop. I'm impressed, okay. Now move away from the railing, please."

Julia didn't break her slow graceful motion except to raise her head to look at me. "Say you forgive me."

"I forgive you."

"You forgive me for what?" She kept stretching her back leg even higher, and I could see her standing leg start to wobble.

I moved toward her, and this time when I dropped the bottle I let it roll off the roof. It hit the gutter with a thud and then sailed over the edge, crashing in the bushes three floors below.

"I . . . I forgive you for saying you invited me because you always need people with you when you come to Arcadia."

"I'm not sure I believe you." Small sweat beads gathered near her hairline.

"I do. It's true."

"Good." She lowered her leg. "Because I am hopelessly out of shape. Let's go down to the edge. The view's better there."

She had one leg over the railing before I had begun to exhale normally again and was lifting the other when her sneaker got caught in the corner. Without thinking, I reached and grabbed her wrist. She stumbled, but she didn't slip any further. For a moment I just held her, feeling her heart pounding, feeling the adrenaline pump through my veins. Still holding her arm, I guided her back over the railing, until she was inside the widow's walk once again with me.

Clinging to me, she raised her face up toward mine. First, her breath on my face: sweet, fruity, and warm. Then her lips on mine: soft, gentle, and curious. Then she was kissing me. She tasted like champagne and salt, so I didn't think. I just kissed her back.

We stopped kissing when a seagull's caw pierced the barrier of our little world. I ducked my face away from hers and reached to push back my loose hair. I felt her gaze on my face and that my skin was flushed with champagne, and heat, and I don't know what else. I looked up.

"You're blushing," she said, leaning against the railing. "It's

cute. Right now I can totally picture five-year-old Charlie getting caught stealing a cookie or trying on your mom's jewelry.
Tu as l'air d'une enfant coupable."

"Julia, it's just that . . . I don't know. It's just that I can count
on one hand the number of people I've kissed in my whole life
and . . . I don't know."

"Oh, Charlie. You saved my life, so I kissed you because I
felt like kissing you. We're not lezzing it up for a bunch of boys
behind the gym at a dance. *"Profite un peu de la vie!"* she whispered, her voice smoky.

"What does that mean?"

"It means you should drop Latin and take French. Come on,
let's go inside and see what Nanny left us in the kitchen. Practically dying has made me hungry."

I followed her through the hatch and down the ladder,
stumbling at the bottom over a plastic dump truck. If I hadn't
bumped into Julia on the attic stairs, I wouldn't have noticed
the room at all.

"*Oomph.* Sorry. Julia?"

Julia was staring down the hall. I followed her gaze to the
green door at the end. It was slightly ajar and dust drifted in
the slant of afternoon light coming from within the room. The
metal plate near the top was so dull that I couldn't make out
the writing.

"That room should not be open." As Julia strode to the end
of the hall I jumped the rest of the way down the steps. She

slammed the green door with a bang loud enough to make me reach to cover my ears.

"Jesus, Julia!"

"Nanny knows I don't like to have the door open." She spun and started down the stairs to the first floor. "It's Gus's room." Her voice was a filled sink in danger of overflowing.

I took one more glance at the closed door before padding after her, the cork from the champagne bottle safe in my pocket.

Julia was quiet the rest of the day. Nothing Sophie or I said or did could bring her back. After dinner, she went to bed early, so I did, too.

I had learned to accept her laughter as my reward for never pushing her too far and her silences as answers.

TWELVE

I WENT INTO THE ROOM while Julia was riding at the farm across the road. I went in because I was not supposed to, and because I was curious and bored and because I wanted to know the unknowable girl who haunted Julia and Arcadia itself.

Just turning the doorknob made my heart clatter like a box of nails dropping onto the floor of my dad's garage. I found myself walking on the balls of my bare feet and preparing excuses in case I got caught:

Oh, that's Gus's room? I got confused.

I got lost.

I'm sorry. I thought you were joking when you said no one went in here.

They were all lame. None of them would work.

The room was black as the bottom of a sealed box, and the hot dusty air made me feel like I was trying to breathe inside a balloon. When I couldn't find a light switch, I tiptoed across the floor with my arms straight in front of me until I bumped against the far wall and the edge of a curtain.

"Ow!" I pushed the dense fabric aside with one arm while trying to grip my stubbed toe in my free hand. The rectangle of morning coming through the window cut across the space like a flashlight, illuminating the objects directly in its path and throwing the rest into shadow.

The room was spare and lonely. There was no carpet on the scuffed floor. The whitewashed bureau was tired and leaned on the uneven floorboards like one side of it had melted. A navy and ivory comforter and throw pillows with cartoonish nautical designs—anchors, fish, and mermaids—topped the twin bed. It was a bed for a little girl or a girl who couldn't be bothered to get a grown-up one.

Trophies of various sizes, many with plastic sailboats on the top, lined the bookshelves to the left of the bed, interspersed among knickknacks, half-used candles, and photos without frames, their edges curled in. I stepped toward them, picking up the first object that my fingers could reach: a miniature stuffed moose, a smaller version of Julia's Aloysius. I set the creature down as carefully as I had lifted him, adding a pat on his head for good measure. Someone must have loved him for his antlers to be so worn.

I reached for the photo nearest to me. Its edges were uneven with age and faded, but the center was still vibrant. In it, Gus looked about the same age as in the photo in Julia's room. Her smile was wide and strands of her dark hair blew in her face. She was perched on a railing, her head resting on the shoulder of a guy with red hair and freckles across his burned nose. He wasn't looking at the picture taker. He was looking at Gus. He was a lottery winner who couldn't believe his luck. A guy holding a statue made of crystal and gold that he was terrified of dropping. They looked happy. They looked in love.

I was about to set the photo in front of a dried corsage when I heard soft footsteps behind me.

"Chérie?" a delicate voice said over my right shoulder, barely above a whisper.

I tried to put the photo back, but in my panic I dropped it and knocked my elbow against one of the metal latches of an upright trunk behind me.

"Ow! Oh, my God. I am so sorry. I . . . I was just—" Gripping my elbow, I looked up at Sophie. Her perfect posture reminded me of a post stuck in the earth. Her expression betrayed nothing. "I was just looking."

"Une porte fermée est toujours une tentation." She leaned in toward me. "Truth be told, I like to come in here, too. Sometimes it's nice to look at her things." She reached down and picked up the photo. "She was such a pack rat, this one." She pointed to the center, her finger pressed right below the face of the dead girl with the beautiful smile and eyes full of love. "She saved everything. Passed the habit on to Julia, too. That child

has had that *élan* since Augustine put it in her crib."

Her sharing made me momentarily forget I had gone into a room that I had no business going into. "She looks like Julia . . . or Julia looks like her. She and her boyfriend, they're . . . they were . . ." I searched for a word. The right one wouldn't come to me. "Vibrant?"

Sophie sighed and set the photo back on the shelf. "That's her David. They were very in love. *C'était beau à voir.*"

I let go of my elbow and shifted so I stood next to her, both of us looking at the shelves that now seemed more like a shrine than a girl's collection. "He was in the car, too? The driver, right?" I knew the answer, but I asked anyway.

Sophie clicked her tongue. She studied the space in front of her for so long, I thought she didn't hear me.

"Was he—"

"There was only one David in Augustine's life. She met him and that was it." She reached forward and swiped at some dust on one of the shelves, leaving a wide streak where her fingers had touched. "I need to convince Julia to let me clean in here. *C'est très sale.*"

"Nanny, I mean Sophie," I said. "Why did she get in a car with him if he was drunk? Why would she let Julia? Gus loved him. Wouldn't she want to protect him?"

"Is that what Julia told you? That David was drunk?"

I let my fingers trail across the top of the trophies, avoiding Sophie's gaze. "Julia talks about Gus a lot, but I heard that from . . . well that's what the papers imply, and then some of the girls at school—"

"Tu ne devrais pas croire tout ce que tu entends." Placing a hand on my back, she guided me away from the shelves. *"Ma douce, l'amour peut faire des choses folles."* She lapsed into French as gracefully as she moved me toward the door. When we reached it she turned and held my face, her piercing eyes fixed on my own. *"Tu comprends?"*

I didn't understand at all, but I nodded anyway.

"If not now, someday you will. Come, let's go see what's in the kitchen for lunch."

I followed her out of the room, and only after she had shut the door with a click did I find my voice again. "Is it okay if we don't tell Julia about this?"

"I already have a lifetime of secrets, *chérie*. I think I can keep one more."

STAY/SCULPTURE I

"I have to go home eventually."

"Why?"

"For starters, because I have a job, and I'm probably already going to get fired."

"Quit."

"I need the money, Julia."

"Stop being so damn responsible. I'll talk to Mummy about it. We'll figure it out. Plus, I must, must, must take you to get your hair fixed."

"It's really that bad?"

"Oui."

"I also need to check on the boys. Melissa is the worst cook in the world. She could ruin instant rice. And my dad hasn't been allowed to make anything since he put aluminum foil in the microwave."

"What do they do when you're at school?"

"They get by. Eat a lot of pizza, Chinese takeout, frozen lasagna."

"What are they doing right now?"

"Probably the same. Getting by."

"Exactly."

"Exactly?"

* * *

So I stayed. And I started sketching an idea for a sculpture.

I wanted it to be something sturdy that would last through snow, rain, and time, but was also as delicate as a memory.

A structure of driftwood. Stained white like bleached sand. A thing with sea glass that reflected the sun during the day and caught the lights from the porch at night. A piece of art that would look so natural, it would seem as if it had always been there.

THIRTEEN

SKINNY-DIPPING WAS, OF COURSE, Julia's idea.

"What do you mean you've never been?" she shrieked. We were lounging in the Adirondack chairs on the lawn. She had grown bored with her game of solitaire and had switched to mindlessly shuffling cards. I was sketching the line of kayaks leaning against the side of the boathouse, trying to capture the strange shadows they made in the midday sun.

"When would I have gone skinny-dipping? Family vacations?" I raised my sketchbook, hoping Julia would drop it and start another game.

She didn't.

"Swimming naked is delicious. The water feels like silk and goes places you never would imagine you'd be able to feel it go."

"You're just trying to make me turn red and it's not going

to work this time." I was bluffing. My face felt like I had just opened an oven door. "Stop distracting me."

"Charlie." Julia put a hand down on the top of my sketchbook and lowered it until I was forced to look up at her.

"Yes?" I kept my pencil raised so she'd know I wasn't going to stop drawing.

"What kind of artist are you if you're so embarrassed by the human body, so, dare I say, represssssed?" She drew out the "s" sound like a snake hiss. "So uptight that you've never even *enlevé tes sous-vêtements* and taken a little dip."

"I'm *not* repressed. And I'm not ashamed of nudity. I've been to tons of life drawing classes. I've probably seen more naked people than any other girl in our year," I replied, snapping my sketchbook shut. "I just don't feel like swimming now, that's all. Plus, I really don't feel like Sophie needs to see my *derrière* hanging in the breeze."

"Nanny went to town ages ago and she takes forever at the grocery *and*—" Julia smacked the arms of her chair for emphasis. "If you're *really* an artist, you have to experience everything once and that includes skinny-dipping!"

Julia was off across the lawn before I even had a chance to argue again. As she got closer to the boathouse, I saw her kick off her flip-flops, then wiggle her shirt over her head. She was shaking her baggy pink shorts off before she even passed the shoreline.

I tapped my sketchbook against my forehead, sighed, and

then set it down on the seat of my chair. I dropped my shirt on the lawn and my shorts at the start of the beach. My bathing suit bottom was the last thing to go as I charged off the end of the dock.

Julia and I were shouting so loudly and so focused on spitting water at each other and diving into the waves that neither one of us heard the sound of a car pulling up the gravel drive.

"Oh, *mon Dieu!*" Julia stopped splashing me and ducked into the water so that just her nose and mouth were above the surface.

"What?" I smoothed my now-short hair back from my forehead and rubbed some of the salt water from the corners of my eyes. When I spun around, I was much less eloquent than Julia. "Shit!"

Sebastian stood at the end of the dock with my shirt in one hand. His other hand covered his eyes. He laughed. "Well, I've been called worse things, I guess." He gave a little wave with my shirt. "Nice to see you again, Charlie. Don't worry, I've seen nothing. Promise."

"What the hell are you doing here? You're—" Julia shouted, but a wave caught her by surprise, filling her mouth with sea water. Coughing, she tried to keep going. "You're not . . . until . . . second week . . . August."

"It *is* the second week in August," Sebastian called down from the dock, one hand still clamped over his eyes.

"Well, Nanny didn't warn me you were coming," Julia said,

as if that would make him disappear from the dock and every-thing right again.

"She didn't know. Mum didn't tell her."

"Mummy's here?" Julia's voice lost its anger. And she suddenly sounded weary from treading water for so long.

"We're all here. Mum, Cordelia, Bradley, Boom. Don't tell me you don't remember what Saturday is?"

"I remember," Julia shouted half into the water. "I just chose to forget for a bit, that's all."

I had slowly been moving out deeper, where I knew the water was dark. Following Julia's lead, I ducked beneath the waves until just my nose was above the surface. Sebastian had on a navy T-shirt from some college I had never heard of, and his cheeks and the bridge of his nose were slightly burned. Even though he continued to hold one hand over his eyes, I tried to tread water and cover my chest with my hands, just in case. I ended up sputtering and spitting. Julia swam over and tried to pound me on the back, but she just splashed more water in my mouth.

"Look, why don't you be a gentleman and give us our clothes and then go up and distract Mummy, Boom, and the lot so we can go change," Julia shouted after she gave up trying to help me. "Don't they teach you manners at Harvard?"

Sebastian tried to lean against one of the dock posts while covering his eyes. He ended up stumbling and nearly falling off the edge of the dock. After he righted himself he replied, "Most days I don't think they teach me much at all."

"*Well.*" Julia dipped her voice in the way that meant a biting remark was coming. "If you weren't so busy playing around, maybe you'd at least learn the basics. Red means stop, green go. Dogs chase cats. Too much boozing equals skipping class—"

Sebastian laughed. "*Touché.* Tree pose?"

"Fine," Julia shouted, lifting her mouth above the water. "Tree pose."

"Tree pose?" I shivered, making small ripples around me. "I need my clothes for yoga, Julia."

"No." Julia started swimming for the dock. "It's shorthand for truce," she shouted over her shoulder. I stayed out in the dark water.

"She speaks!" Sebastian turned his head in my direction and I swear his fingers were spread just slightly, like a little kid peeking during the scary part of a movie. I ducked back into the water so that up to my mouth was covered again.

"Of course she speaks. Now, will you grab our clothes and go get Cordelia started on reciting the European capitals or anything else to distract her? Keep Mummy and Bradley out of the kitchen and Boom in his office. We'll go in through the side door and they'll just think we've been in town."

Sebastian, his eyes firmly covered once again, gave a little bow in Julia's general direction. Only after he turned around did he drop both hands by his sides. As he walked back to the shore he stopped to pick up our bathing suit tops and bottoms.

He pivoted about, gathering all the clothing into a pile at the end of the dock. When he was done he waved at us, then jogged up to the house.

As soon as his back was turned, Julia climbed up the dock ladder. I floundered after her, missing the bottom step twice before I got the footing. I tried to pull on my shorts at the same time as I was yanking my shirt over my head. It didn't work. I had to stop with my shorts around my knees to get it right. Neither Julia nor I bothered with our bathing suits. Holding them to our chests, we dashed to the kitchen door, and only when I tried to turn the knob with my wet hands did I realize how hard I was laughing.

By the time we managed to get the door open, I was hic-cupping and Julia had to cross her legs as she shuffled across the kitchen because she swore she was going to wet her already soaking shorts.

When I got to my room, I felt something in my shorts pocket. I pulled out a bottle cap. It was one for peach juice this time.

It is physically impossible for you to lick your elbow.

I tried. It was true.

"Fascinating," I whispered and put the cap in the side pocket of my duffel bag with the other.

I had just stepped out of my room, wearing jeans, sneakers, and a long-sleeved shirt—even though it was midafternoon

in August, I was set on covering as much skin as possible—
when Cordelia, in shorts that matched the pink in her floral
top, appeared from around the corner.

"Oh, there you are. Nanny said that Julia had a friend here.
Do you speak French? *Parlez-vous français?* I'm practically flu-
ent, but I'm taking Chinese because Boom thinks China is the
future. Do you go to school with Julia? I'm not going there.
Mummy says that I'll probably get into one of the Phillips
because my grades are so good. I skipped second grade, that's
why I'm the shortest one in my class. What's your name again?"

"Charlotte," I coughed. "Charlotte Ryder. But your sister
calls me Charlie. We met at my school. Remember? You were
hiding behind your brother." I paused. "I thought you were
shy."

"I'm only shy when I'm not here," she said slowly as if she
were explaining directions to a foreign tourist. "It's good you
already have a nickname." A little bit of her belly stuck out over
the top of her shorts and her cheeks had a roundness to them
that made her look like a well-fed doll. Her hair was dark like
Julia's, but a mess of curls instead of pin straight, and the bridge
of her nose was covered with freckles and peeling from a recent
sunburn.

"What's yours? Your nickname, I mean," I said.

"Well, Bradley calls me Pest, Nanny calls me her *petit canard*,
and Mummy used to call me cheeky monkey. But Sebastian and
Julia call me Oops because they say Mummy and Boom weren't

expecting to have another baby, but here I am."

"Yes." I bit the inside of my cheek to keep from laughing. "Here you are."

"Come on." She grabbed my hand and pulled me toward the stairs. "Julia is having one of her college talks with Mummy and those can go on forever. Come meet Casanova."

"Is that a pet?" I asked, letting her lead me down the curving front staircase.

Cordelia sighed so dramatically that her bangs flew up on one side. "My brother, Bradley. That's what Julia and I call him. He dropped out of law school, but it's okay because now Sebastian is the one who's going to be a senator like Boom, and Mummy thinks Bradley's a genius and that he's going to sell his techy company for millions. But he's never serious. Julia says he can't go to Rome 'cause he'd try to flirt with all the naked lady statues."

"What?"

Cordelia, her hair swinging back and forth across her shoulders, tugged me into the library. The light streaked across the floor, filling the space and making the gold threads in the carpet glisten. A guy about a foot or so taller than me was standing by the far window, looking at his phone and smiling as if he were reading a secret. His fingers danced across the screen.

"Hey," Cordelia called as we entered, but he barely shifted in our direction. "Come meet Julia's friend. Her name's Charlotte, but we're calling her Charlie. Charlie," Cordelia said formally, "this is Bradley. Bradley, this is Julia's artsy friend Charlie who Nanny told us about."

Bradley met us in the center of the room. His face was square-shaped just like Sebastian's. But that was about where the resemblance ended. He was classically handsome in the way that catalogue models and actors in commercials are: perfectly proportioned nose, even-set eyes, side-parted hair. When he smiled at me, I saw two rows of white, straight teeth.

I stretched out my hand. "Nice to meet you, Brad."

"It's Bradley," he replied, shaking my hand firmly. "I go by Bradley."

"Bradley." I clenched and unclenched my hand once he let go, trying to get some circulation back into it. "I'll remember that."

"Just kidding. You, Charlie, can call me whatever you want." He winked. His posture was relaxed, yet full of energy, as if he could walk out of the room and be ready to play a round of golf or talk to a room full of investors without changing his stance either way.

I would have kept staring at his blue eyes, but the sound of Julia's voice made me spin toward the door.

"Hands to yourself, Bradley." Julia plodded across the carpet and slipped her arm through mine.

"Oh." Bradley lifted one eyebrow and both hands. "Pip, Oops didn't say this was a 'special friend.'" He made air quotes.

"We're not . . . I'm not . . . Julia and I aren't together . . .

not like *that*." I mimicked his air quote gesture and glanced at Cordelia, who had settled stomach down on the sofa and was staring up at us, her chin in her hands.

"Charlie's my *friend*, you moron," Julia said. "Besides, she's not my type."

"Why not?" I said.

Bradley clapped his hands. A little boy delighted at the trouble he'd caused.

"Julia, there you are!" A half-naked man stood in the door of the library. His arms opened wide as if he wanted to hug the whole room.

To be fair, he was wearing a bathrobe, but I still got a glimpse of his fleur-de-lis boxers when he flung his arms around Julia.

"Miss me, kiddo?" His voice was deep and thundering like a radio news announcer or the referees who call the beginning of boxing matches on TV. His round stomach pushed against the sash of his robe, and his bare legs were tan and thick with dark hair. His face was as ruddy as a construction worker's. He had deep wrinkles at the corners of his eyes that could only have come from a lifetime of loving the sun.

"*Mon Dieu*, Boom. Could you put some pants on? Or at least wear underwear that's not boring," Julia said, her face pressed against his chest.

He released her as suddenly as he had hugged her and turned toward me. "This must be the lovely and talented Miss Ryder."

"Her name is Charlie, Boom. We're calling her Charlie."
Cordelia jumped up from the couch and started tugging on his
sleeve.

He reached down and picked her up with one arm, extend-
ing his free hand to me. "Welcome to Arcadia, Charlie. I was
in such a rush to see my adoring daughter here"—he jerked his
head toward Julia—"that I forgot a few things."

Bradley chuckled. And out of the corner of my eye, I saw
that even Julia couldn't help smiling.

I shook his hand. "It happens, Mr. Buchanan."

"Call me Boom."

"Okay, Boom." I tested the word out. "Boom." It's so rare
that names, or even nicknames, capture exactly who we are. It's
a matter of luck really, what we end up answering to. Was I a
Charlotte? A Charlie? I wasn't sure, but he was unequivocally
a Boom.

Julia grabbed my arm. "Charlie and I are going riding at the
Homers' before Mummy comes down the stairs in her bra and
underwear or Nanny streaks across the lawn." She started tugging me toward the door. *"Ma famille est folle!"*

"Can I come?" Cordelia wiggled out of Boom's arms to
stand by my side.

"Are you going to be a pain?" Julia had to lean in front of me
to see Cordelia since she couldn't see over me.

"No!" Cordelia jumped. "I'll exhaust maturity. I'll even
ride the pony so you can have Little Miss Sunshine."

"Don't you mean 'exude,' Webster?" Bradley asked.

"That's what I said. Exude, to project or display abundantly. Exude. And I prefer the Oxford English Dictionary over Webster's." Cordelia put her hands on her hips.

"Oh, come on, Oops," Julia said. *"Les deux clowns, on vous verra au dîner."*

Boom made a motion with his hands as if he was trying to keep a bee away from a glass. He then clapped an arm across Bradley's shoulders and gestured toward the sofa. He was in no rush to go upstairs and put on pants.

"She called them both clowns," Cordelia whispered to me right before Julia yanked me through the front hall and out the door.

By the time Julia had saddled up Little Miss Sunshine and Cordelia had outfitted the aptly named Gumdrop at the farm across the road, the sun was beginning to set. The scrappy pine trees that dotted the edges of the riding ring cast shadows on the faces of animals and riders. Cordelia's eyes were as much on Julia's back as they were on her reins. Every time Julia sped up, Cordelia kicked her heels into poor Gumdrop's side, and he would trot a few feet and then resume his languid walk. Eventually she gave up and let him plod in a small circle in the center of the ring as Julia rose and fell with her horse's graceful canter on the outside. She was beautiful anyway, but on a horse she looked like she was meant to have wings.

"She's always been a magnificent rider," I heard a low, rich voice say behind me.

When I turned around I saw a petite, finely boned woman just slightly taller than Julia walking toward me. She had on navy slacks that grazed the freshly mowed grass and sandals that showed her red toenails. The white sweater looped loosely around her neck only made her look more delicate, emphasizing the narrowness of her shoulders and her perfect posture. Her blond hair was pulled back into a smooth bun. The closer she came, the more I was able to see Julia in the high, sharp line of her cheekbones.

I wiped my hands on my pants and stepped away from the railing.

When she was just feet away she uncrossed her arms and raised one hand to her mouth, using two fingers to make the kind of ear-splitting whistle I had only seen and heard women do to hail cabs in old movies. Almost instantly, three dogs charged from the direction of the back field: a fat black pug that I could hear snorting even when it was yards away, a silver greyhound that ran like a horse and was tall as my waist, and a golden retriever that loped on three legs and looked like it was smiling with its tongue hanging out of its mouth.

"Meet my other children." The woman began furiously petting the golden retriever, which was almost knocked off its three legs by her enthusiasm. Then she bent down and grabbed the pug, hugging the little dog to her chest as she stood. "This monster is Henry." His bug eyes looked ready to pop out of his head. She pointed to the retriever, which was watching Julia ride and shaking its tail so hard that its entire body was moving side to side. "That's David, but we sometimes call him *toui*." She reached down with one hand and stroked the silk ears of the greyhound. "And this dignified lady is Thoreau because she's the smartest of the bunch." She kissed the snorting pug on the nose.

"They're very . . . canine," I stammered as David loped over and put his nose under my left hand. I started petting him, shaking the fur that came off with each stroke onto the lawn.

"And I'm Teresa, Julia's mother." She kissed the pug one more time before pouring him onto the ground. When she stood up, her entire front was coated in fur. She reached out one hand. "It's not particularly original to say this, but I feel like I know you already, Charlotte."

"I . . . I think I saw you at parents' weekend at St. Anne's," I said, grabbing her hand. It felt as fragile as a tightly stretched canvas. "Thank you. For . . . for everything. For the tickets . . . for having me here. And the watch. I brought it with me. I can't . . . I can't keep it."

"It's a gift, dear. Please, you must." She crossed her arms, stepping closer to the railing. "Well, I'm glad you've been able to keep Julia company this summer. Been enjoying yourself?"

"It's been amazing." I moved to stand beside her. "I brought chocolates, but Julia and I ate them a while ago."

She smiled. "Normally I'm here all summer, but Cordelia had her camps, and then work at the office has been crazier than usual. I feel like my eyes are permanently squinted from reading grant proposals." She raised her manicured hands to her eyes and rubbed at them dramatically.

"What do you do?"

She dropped her hands and tilted her head. "Julia doesn't tell you much, does she?"

I started to shake my head, but then thought better of it, and shrugged.

"I work for my husband's foundation. We basically channel money to deserving organizations for, as Bradley calls them, our 'do-gooder' projects." She tapped her fingers against the railing. "If I'm not reading grant proposals, then I'm on the phone bugging one of Joe's former colleagues for money or a favor. I'm just happy someone was here to keep Julia out of trouble in my absence." She raised her eyebrows and looked at me as if asking a question. I didn't know what else to do, so I leaned on the fence and pretended to be fascinated with watching Julia turn Little Miss Sunshine one way, then the other, as if she were pivoting around poles.

"She's always been so good with animals. As a little girl, she was forever picking up creatures and trying to rehabilitate them. Frogs that were half dead from being squished in the road, baby birds with broken wings, a cat with an injured paw. God, she must have only been ten the time she dragged David home after he was hit by a car." Mrs. Buchanan propped herself against the railing, resting her small chin on her arms as she gazed across the ring.

"That doesn't surprise me," I said, mimicking her pose.

Mrs. Buchanan sighed. "She's something."

The mixture of pride and sadness in her voice was enough to make me turn my head to look at her. She had her fingertips pressed to her temples and her eyes squeezed shut.

"Are you all right?"

"Oh, dear, it's nothing. Just a headache. I'm going to go back to the house now to lie down." She dropped her hands and straightened up. "If you need anything at all just let Sophie know. And if you need anything ironed or steamed for the party tomorrow, give a shout, okay?" She patted my arm and gave a sharp finger whistle. The three dogs were immediately by her side, circling around her as she made her way across the road to the Arcadia gate.

"Party?" I said, more to myself than to her.

"Yes, we have one every August." She stopped and looked over her shoulder at me. "I'm surprised Julia hasn't told you all about it." She frowned and shook her head. "Or maybe I'm not." She began walking again.

While I was watching Mrs. Buchanan, Cordelia had dis-appeared into the barn with Gumdrop, but in the ring Julia hopped down from Little Miss Sunshine. Standing next to him she looked so small, so fragile that I wanted to swoop in and drag her away—anywhere where she'd be safe from the too large hooves and oversized teeth. Instead when she began to lead him out of the ring, I stood where I was, and waited for her to come to me.

THE PARTY

"So you met Mummy, then?"

"Yes. She's wicked nice. Not what I—"

"Let me guess. The dogs jumped all over you and then she charmed you and left."

"Well. She had a headache, but she was very nice."

"You already said that. What did you two talk about?"

"Something about a party tomorrow?"

"*Merde!* We don't have to go. We can go into town and sneak into Melville's. If we close the place out, the whole lot of them might be gone by the time we get back."

"A party here could be fun."

"It's going to be *un spectacle de merde.*"

"Translation?"

"A shit show. Buchanan parties always are."

"If it's terrible, we can hide in Sophie's house with junk food and watch old movies until our teeth rot or everyone leaves . . . plus your mom did kind of invite me. I'd feel bad just leaving."

"Oh, Charlie. The things I do for you."

FOURTEEN

I HAD HEARD THE TENT going up and a crew of men and women clicking, clacking, and shouting around the yard, setting up tables, bars, and a dance floor in front of where Cordelia told me the band would play. Through the open window of my room, I heard the musicians tuning their instruments, bottles popping, and the sound of tires on gravel as the first guests arrived.

But the sounds did not prepare me for the sights of my first Buchanan party.

The one dress I had thought to pack at the beginning of the summer was all wrong. I had found it one Saturday afternoon in the dollar-per-pound pile at the Garment District. I had loved the pale gray, the way the thin straps twisted and came together in the back, and how the soft cotton hit just above my knees. But the night of the annual party at Arcadia I couldn't stop tugging at the bottom as if I could stretch it to cover more of my legs and then yanking at the top to try to stop my chest from spilling out.

I was standing on the landing and was just about to go to Julia's room and beg her for a cardigan, even though anything of hers would cover me as much as a postage stamp covers an envelope, when Sebastian came down the hall, shoving his arms into a dark blazer. He stopped fumbling as soon as he saw me, dropping his arms, his blazer still half off.

"Wow. You look as good with clothes on as you do with them off." With his tie looped loosely around his neck, his slightly wrinkled shirt untucked, he looked like one of the freshman boys who stood gawking any time St. Anne's invited a boys' school for a dance.

I crossed my arms in front of my chest, but that only seemed to make the cleavage situation worse. "You *were* peeking," I said.

"Nah." Sebastian shook his head and slid his arms the rest of the way into the blazer, then began to tuck his shirt into his pants. "I was a gentleman. I swear."

I tried not to notice that I could see the top of his boxers as he finished getting dressed. "Do you often do that?" I asked as he straightened his tie and then attempted to smooth down his hair.

"Get dressed? I try to every day. Doesn't always work out, though." When he looked at me his smile came up slightly higher on one side and he rocked back and forth, toe to heel, his restless fingers drumming against his legs.

I rolled my eyes. "Say one thing then say the opposite?"

"Never . . . always. Come on. Julia's already outside with the others." He spun around and then slid down the polished banister, jumping off the end. He looked up at me and bowed. I patted the palm of my hand like how I imagined women clapped at the opera. He grinned and then disappeared through the front door. I took the stairs, but I took them two at a time.

Two hundred, maybe three hundred people swarmed across the lawn. It was hard to tell how many. The party was both so crowded and so spread out. Arcadia had been transformed over the course of the day. Small white lights covered the bushes that lined the porch and Sophie's cottage, and white candles in navy hurricane lamps decorated the tops of tall tables whose ivory tablecloths grazed the lawn like the trains of wedding dresses. Catering staff milled around with trays, and a small bar had been set up in the front corner of the porch, complete with a bartender who looked as animated as a piece of furniture.

Men in light suits and women in wispy dresses that swished with every movement were standing in groups, chatting over the music coming from a five-member band that had set up on a small dance floor under a cream canvas tent. Salt air mixed with the sweet-smelling white flowers that had been woven into greenery and wound around the porch railings, the rich musk of expensive perfume, and the sharp evergreen scent of gin.

Even the ocean seemed to have been warned that a Buchanan party was happening that evening. Instead of crashing against the dock and pounding on the shore, it lapped at the sand.

I saw Piper surrounded by Eun Sun and a bunch of other St. Anne's girls standing near the tent. Her blond hair was twisted into a complicated mess of curls on the top of her head, which she kept turning to search the crowd. I recognized some of the girls from Pembroke Hall. They all watched Piper with a mixture of fear and awe, following each sweeping motion of her hands. Piper saw me just as she was finishing her story, and it was like a bucket of ice water had been thrown on her. She dropped her arms and pressed her lips, and her eyes went cold. Her look was enough to make me shiver.

Eun Sun turned to see where Piper was staring, saw me, shook her head, and then forced Piper to move so her back was facing me.

She hated me. I didn't know why, and I couldn't do anything about it.

I could hear Boom somewhere in the middle of the crowd, his voice carrying like a foghorn over flat water. Sophie had on her unreasonably high heels. They were sinking into the grass like pegs for a tent as she talked with a handsome man in a dark suit. There was an actress I recognized, clinging to the arm of an attractive guy who looked young enough to be her son. I saw an older woman covered with so many gold necklaces either they had to be fakes or she had just robbed a jewelry store. A group of guys about my age suddenly appeared from behind Sophie's cottage, their ties already loosened and their pants sagging. When they walked by the unmistakable skunk smell of pot surrounded them.

A man with salt-and-pepper politician hair was unbuttoning his shirt on the dance floor, flapping his arms like a duck trying to take off from mud as the woman he was dancing with swished her skirt and pumped a fist in the air. The sound of glass breaking against glass came from a bar set up close to the driveway, but no one paused their conversations, and few even turned their heads.

The air was swollen with music, shouting, and something I could not quite place—a feeling of happiness, but happiness with an edge, a sense of joy that was all the more meaningful because it was so fleeting.

It was a scene that had to be painted from a distance, because up close the colors would begin to blur. It was wild and lovely. Shocking and elegant. It was, as Julia had promised it would be, *"un spectacle de merde."*

When I saw Julia cutting across the lawn toward me, I started down the steps to meet her, but then she held up her hand. "Bar first or I don't think I'll make it." Her hair was pulled back in a low ponytail and she had a huge white flower tucked behind one ear. Her strapless pale blue dress made her look like a bridesmaid, even though the top was crooked and she had one of those stupid loops that are meant to help the dress stay on hangers dangling out from under an arm.

I tucked it in when she joined me on the porch.

"Thanks," she muttered as we walked toward the bar. "Two gin and tonics. Doubles please." If the bartender even thought of hesitating to ask how old we were, his unfocused expression gave no hint of it.

"*Mon Dieu!* I hate these parades." Julia sighed before taking a deep drink from her glass. "Come on. Mummy wants you to meet some people. Let's down these. Chat and then come back for another. Mummy doesn't care about wine and champagne, but she pretends to have a problem with gin and whatnot."

I took a sip from my narrow glass and had to press my lips together to stop from coughing. The bartender either followed Julia's request a little too well or just didn't care enough to add more than a splash of tonic. Julia, however, finished hers in a few gulps and then grabbed two champagne flutes from a passing waitress. I tried for another sip, but this time I couldn't stop myself from sputtering.

"Oh, here." Julia thrust one of the flutes at me. "I'll finish it." Still coughing, I handed her my glass. She threw back her head and gulped until the lime inside knocked against her teeth before setting the glass behind some fancy-looking crackers on a nearby table. Shaking her head, she started walking down the porch stairs. "Come on, then. Let's face the firing squad."

She walked over to where Mrs. Buchanan was standing with Sebastian, a short older man, and a tall, thin woman in an orange dress that showed off her tan arms. I followed her, tugging at the top of my dress with one hand.

"There you are, girls," Mrs. Buchanan called when we reached the edge of their circle. "Tom, Claudia, you know my daughter Julia."

"Of course." The man bowed in our direction. "You've turned into quite the young lady." The woman in the orange dress smiled tightly, as though to move her lips any more would pain her.

"And this is her friend Charlotte Ryder." Mrs. Buchanan gestured toward me. "She's at St. Anne's with Julia." Turning to me she said, "Tom used to work on Joe's campaign, but now he's in the Boston district attorney's office."

"Great place, St. Anne's. I was at Choate myself. We used to come around for dances. Descend upon the girls like a bunch of sailors on leave," the man said as he chuckled and reached out his hand, shaking my own so vigorously that champagne splashed over the side of my glass. The woman only pressed my hand long enough for me to notice her oval pink nails.

"Nice to meet you," I said, trying to subtly wipe the champagne off on the back of my dress.

"Now, what year are you girls? Seniors?" He gulped his dark drink until the ice cubes clinked against the glass.

"Yes, this fall," I replied. Julia said nothing.

"Well I know this one," he said as he pounded Sebastian on the back with a thump that sent Sebastian lurching forward and some of the ice jumping out of his drink, "is a Harvard man. What about you girls? Where are you going?"

I caught Sebastian's eye as he stepped away from the group to shake whatever drink had once been in his glass off his arm. And just like Julia did at parents' weekend, he quickly made a gesture of tying a noose and slipping it over his head. He shook his arm one more time and then moved back near our circle, setting his drink down and leaning against one of the tall tables.

"Julia," Mrs. Buchanan said, leaning into the circle, "is still thinking. She might take a year off. Help me with Joe's foundation." She started smoothing Julia's hair down with her long fingers. "She might go some place nearby. Wellesley is my alma mater."

Julia still said nothing. She had her arms wrapped around her ribs, her muscles tense as if she was trying to collapse herself inward. Her eyes were fixed on some point in the navy night beyond Sebastian's shoulder. Her glass was empty.

"Good to stay close to home. What about you, Charlotte?" The man raised his cotton-ball eyebrows as he tipped his glass to his lips for another long pull. "Staying in Boston?"

"Oh. Well, no." I shook my head a little and dropped my hand. I hadn't even realized I was reaching toward Julia. "I'd like to apply to some art schools. I guess some are in Boston, but a lot aren't."

"She's very talented." Just as suddenly as she had disappeared into herself, Julia reappeared, grabbing another flute from a waiter and placing her empty glass on his tray as she spoke. "It's a shame about the police record, though."

"What?" The woman's voice reminded me of a door that needed its hinges oiled.

"Oh, yes." Sebastian moved away from the table back into the circle, his expression somber. "It's a shame arson stays with you so long, isn't it, Julia?"

"Yes. Terrible business, getting out of jail after something like that. But I will give you credit." Julia raised her glass as if to toast me. "When you burn something down, Charlie, you do a thorough job. That factory didn't know what it had coming."

"How about that historical home in Cambridge?" Sebastian asked, looking around the confused circle as if inviting them to comment. "That was some good work."

"Some of your finest." Julia raised her glass to me, her lips pressed together to keep from smiling.

"I didn't . . . I would never . . . I'm just . . ." I stammered, turning toward the couple, whose mouths were both hanging slightly open.

"Julia." Mrs. Buchanan clutched her wineglass tightly between her two hands. "Stop teasing Charlotte. Arson is not a joke."

Sebastian chimed in. "Of course it's not a joke. Charlie takes it quite seriously. She plans to move up to becoming a hit woman. She's ambitious, this friend of yours, Pip. Ambitious *and* beautiful." He winked at me. "It's a lethal combination."

"Oh, murder for hire is really only the beginning. It's what she does when she's feeling lazy. Her real pastime is plotting military coups. Poor North Korea." She made a sympathetic clicking sound with her tongue, shaking her head mournfully from side to side.

"I . . . I don't really set things on fire," I said, looking from the woman in orange's shocked expression to the man's amused one. "I make sculptures—"

"One woman's art is another woman's life of crime," Julia said, her words keeping the beat of the chorus of whatever song the band had just started playing.

"Julia, darling, lovely, perfect daughter. Can I see you in the house for a moment?" Mrs. Buchanan put a hand on the nape of Julia's neck and steered her toward the porch. "Will you excuse us?"

The man chuckled into his drink and nodded. "We've got to find the Gorensteins anyway." He raised his chin toward me. "Charlotte, I'm glad to meet someone else who can put up with the Buchanan sense of humor. Sebastian, I want to talk to you more about that internship before the night is over."

The woman fidgeted with the thin gold chain around her neck and whispered good-bye before she joined him across the grass.

I saw Mrs. Buchanan swat Julia on the back of the head as

they walked up the porch steps and into the brightly lit house. As soon as they were through the door, I slipped my wedges off my feet.

"Come on." Sebastian wrapped his fingers lightly around my wrist. "Before we get trapped again. I think I see Mrs. Hughes-Green heading our way. When I was ten—"

"As in Hughes-Green shampoos?" I asked as I followed him in the direction of the shore.

"That's the one. She kept me up until midnight at one of these parties rambling on about free trade agreements with South America. I remember clutching a fistful of candy and promising God I would give it up forever if only he would res- cue me. He didn't. But eventually Julia did by throwing a huge tantrum in the other room."

"She was passionate. That's not a bad thing." I felt like I could make out his individual fingerprints on my skin. Could you feel touch in your veins? As he held my wrist it seemed possible.

"Sure. Passionate to give Boom money for his campaign, so she would have an invitation to his election party."

Sebastian led me out to the end of the dock. When we stopped, he suddenly seemed aware that he was holding on to me and dropped his hand. He sat, leaning against the last post. I set my flute and shoes down and perched on the edge of the dock, letting the waves wash over my feet. The salt stung when it hit the cuts my shoe straps had made, but I kept my feet in the water. I could still feel where Sebastian's thumb had touched the inside of my wrist. I focused on that.

"You and Julia have quite the shtick going. You should take it on the road."

"Sorry. Did we embarrass you?" He bent forward over his knees.

"I survived half a semester at St. Anne's with a dye job so bad that the school counselor gave me a pamphlet about self-destructive habits. You and Julia have nothing on that." The few slugs of gin and the small amount of champagne I had drunk gurgled in my stomach, spreading warmth from my center to the edges of my fingers and toes like I was standing next to a bonfire.

The music drifted down the lawn and floated across the surface of the water as he spoke. "I meant to tell you I like your hair like that. It suits you. Shows off your ears and whatnot."

"My ears?"

"Yup. You have very show-offy ears."

"Thanks. I think."

"You don't judge people, do you, Charlie? You just kind of watch them." He changed topic without missing a beat. The lights from the party let me see enough of his face to know that he was looking at me, trying to read my expression.

"There's a lot to see." I gestured back toward the house, and then kicked at the water, watching the spray rise and ripple on the black surface.

"Not even the Buchanans can shock you?" He slouched a little lower against the post. "Pip will be disappointed. She lives to astound."

"People don't really shock me much in general. Julia surprises me . . . she likes to tease and embarrass me . . . but shock? That's different."

"How did a girl from the middle of nowhere get to be so worldly?" he asked, angling his head in that way that I knew meant he was really listening. His eyes met mine. "I'm . . . I'm not trying to be rude. Just curious?"

I shrugged, breaking his gaze before I lost myself completely. "Even in a town with more snowmobiles than people, everyone has a story. Everyone has something they're hiding, right?"

Sebastian shifted closer and I could feel the warmth radiating off his legs, or maybe I was imagining it. I closed my eyes and breathed in the salt, the music, and whatever liquor had been splashed on his sleeve. I breathed in the lights from the house reflecting off the water like someone had lit a thousand candles and let them float on the waves. I breathed it all in because then maybe, just maybe, it would never have to end.

When I opened my eyes, he was searching my face with a mixture of confusion and curiosity. I leaned. Then he leaned. Our faces got closer and closer until his was so near mine I could feel his breath on my cheek. I closed my eyes again as he whispered, "Everyone has something to hide."

His lips hovered. I waited.

"Helllllooooooo. Anyone home?" Julia's voice floated down from the lawn. "Charlie, come out, come out wherever you are!"

I opened my eyes again to find Sebastian staring at me. Without looking away he shouted, "Down here, Pip. We're on the dock."

Julia wobbled toward us. The way she held her arms out from her sides and the sharp angles of her dress lit from behind made her look like a walking paper doll. "I hope you two have been behaving yourselves." She came to a few feet from where we were sitting and crumpled to the dock in a swish of dress and air. "Tsk, tsk." She wagged a finger at Sebastian. "What would H.G. think?"

"Who's H.G.?" I asked.

Sebastian sighed and leaned back against the post. "H.G. is what Pip calls my girlfriend."

"Girlfriend?" I couldn't help myself.

"Horrible Gwyneth." Julia lurched like someone was pressing down on her shoulders as she stood up. "She really is a monster."

I didn't say anything, hopeful that my face was in shadow.

Julia flung her arms above her head. "Mummy had to say her piece. Blah. Blah. Blah. Then Boom tried to be strict. Then I had to talk to that terrible woman with the ugly shoes because she's a cousin three times removed or something. Blah. Blah. Blah." Julia opened and closed one of her hands like she had on a sock puppet. "Then that gorgeous waitress was looking at me, and so I followed her outside." Julia paused. "Well, *that* wasn't blah, blah, blah."

Sebastian stood up. "Pip, I really don't want to hear about your conquests."

"Fine. Then promise to never tell me anything about H.G., and I'll promise to keep you in the dark." She looked at me with her hands on her hips, still swaying a little, like a newly planted tree in a strong wind. "Poor Charlie. You must be very bored."

"No. I'm—"

"Come on. I'll entertain you." Julia tried to pull me up, but I had to grip her forearm to keep her from falling over. "Let's go get more champagne."

Sebastian waved his arm as if to say *after you*. I slipped my shoes back on and followed Julia. She was wrong. I wasn't bored. I was stupidly wistful. I wanted to go back to the moment before I heard Sebastian say he had a girlfriend. The moment when I thought he was going to kiss me. I wasn't bored. I was an idiot.

When Julia reached the edge of the party she jogged toward a waiter and grabbed three full flutes before turning and thrusting one at me and another at Sebastian. "Cheers. It's time for One Up." She took a deep drink.

Next to me Sebastian groaned. "Pip, not tonight. Mum will kill us."

"One up?" I asked. Sebastian clicked his tongue and shook his head at me.

"There are too many people at this party. She won't even see." Julia looked at Sebastian over the rim of her glass. "Fine. I'll start." She dropped her nearly empty flute on the grass and lifted up a side of her dress and tucked it into her underwear.

"Julia!" I said, coughing on the sip I had taken. "What are you doing?"

She smiled, shrugged, and walked toward a circle of two women in floral sundresses, a man wearing a bowtie, and another man who stood so straight he looked like he had a rod taped against his back. She touched the silver-haired woman's arm and pointed at the large rings on her fingers. Moments later, they were talking, both gesturing with their hands.

"So what now?" I whispered to Sebastian.

He groaned. "Now I have to one-up her."

When Julia waved good-bye and began to make her way toward another circle, the woman she had been chatting with raised a hand to her mouth and the two men sputtered into their drinks at the sight of Julia's dress tucked into faded yellow underwear. The other woman reached as if to touch Julia on the shoulder, but she was pulled into a new group and began talking with a man whose bald head looked as polished as his white teeth.

"Okay." Sebastian sighed.

"What are you going to do?"

"Well, I can't let her win." He took one more sip from his

glass before splashing what was left on the front of his pants.

"Sebastian?"

"Yes?" he asked as he straightened his tie.

"You know what that looks like, right?"

"Just be glad I didn't need the rest of your glass as well. Okay. Gotta go join Pip." He jogged over to Julia's side, introducing himself around the circle and then settling an arm over her shoulders. The man standing next to him tried to whisper something in his ear, but Sebastian waved him away and turned to the plump middle-aged black woman with wildly curly hair across the circle from him. Next to him, Julia clasped and unclasped her hands. She was the life of the circle. The center of the conversation. No one in the group would meet their eyes, except for an older man leaning on a cane who nodded his head agreeably with everything Julia said.

The moment Cordelia dashed off the porch to stand next to Sebastian with a four-foot trail of toilet paper stuck to the heel of her shoe, the laughter that started as bubbles in my stomach erupted into giggles. Sebastian slid his other arm around her and continued chatting to the blinking group.

I tried to wipe the tears from my eyes, but I had to clutch at my stomach with both hands to breathe. I couldn't see Sophie, Mrs. Buchanan, or Boom, but on the porch, I saw Bradley talking to a woman at the bar. He shook his head, but he was smiling.

If I had to pinpoint one moment, pick an exact second when it happened, I would say it was that night—when Julia, Sebastian, and Cordelia stood side by side daring, just daring anyone to say anything to any of them—that I fell in love with the Buchanans.

VOTE FOR BUCHANAN!

As a state senator, Joe Buchanan was the chair of the Joint Committee on Children, Families and Persons with Disabilities, vice chair of the Joint Committee on Health Care Financing, and a member of the Senate Committee on Global Warming and Climate Change. He proposed bills to strengthen gun control laws and provide universal kindergarten to all of Massachusetts's children.

As your governor, he'll continue to fight for education, affordable health care, and funding for renewable energy research.

A vote for Joe Buchanan is a vote for what's right!

I found the creased pamphlet in a copy of *Leaves of Grass* in the library. Boom's photo on the front showed him standing on the steps of the statehouse building in downtown Boston. His gaze was fixed beyond the picture taker, and the set of his mouth and sharp focus of his eyes suggested that he was looking into the future itself.

I took the pamphlet for my memory box. It was faded and forgotten, and I didn't think it'd be missed.

FIFTEEN

AFTER THE PARTY—AFTER THE little white
lights had been packed up, the tables dismantled, and the tent
taken down—Arcadia felt as empty as a small town once the
circus has left. That was fine by me. I was ready to have Julia—
to have them all—to myself again, before I had to go home.

The hours were long and filled with trips to town and the
lighthouse, lazy games of cards, and dinners on the porch where
ten conversations always seemed to be happening at once—
most of them going over my head. The Buchanans had their
own language: code words and nicknames for everything and
everyone. I didn't need to understand. I was happy to listen.

When I called home, I struggled to describe it all to my dad.
How to convey the ridiculousness of the way Boom sang while
making coffee in the morning but was often quiet at night, how
Bradley's flirting was unnerving and flattering, how impossible
it was to try to both avoid and be near Sebastian, and how the

afternoons lounging on the porch with Julia and not talking at all were some of the best conversations I'd ever had?

I could not capture it in words. So I tried to draw it on paper. Even then, the sketches I made for myself were never quite right.

The hours were long, but the days were short, and as much as I willed it to never come, the end of summer arrived anyway.

I woke up early on the Sunday I was finally going to go home. I had put it off too long and now only had days to get back, apologize to my boss for quitting so suddenly, and throw my life in boxes and then in my dad's truck for the trip to St. Anne's. I crept down the front stairs. The sun had barely reached the drapes in the front hall. When I was outside, I slipped my shoes on and grabbed one of the sun-bleached plastic pails from beneath the kitchen steps.

The wet grass soaked my sneakers on my way to the beach, but my wet feet didn't bother me. It was one more way to take Arcadia with me when I left.

The seagulls didn't care that I had nothing to give them. They swooped behind me as I bent to pick up a shell, a bit of sea glass, or an ocean-smoothed coin of driftwood, ever hopeful that I was dropping food as I made my way down the sand.

"You're up early."

I glanced up from the shell I had been studying. Boom stood where the lawn met the sand. His khakis were so wrinkled it looked like he had slept in them. The collar on his dark shirt was flipped up against his neck and a pair of sunglasses hung on a cord around his neck. Henry, David, and Thoreau weaved around him as he lumbered like a bear just waking up down the slope toward me.

"I wish you could influence the rest of the house. They'll all sleep through lunch if I let them." He laughed. "These guys," he said, reaching down and scratching Thoreau's head, "are the only ones who will seize the day with me." He bent to pat Henry's head, groaning a little as he stood up. "It's a toss-up these days what hurts more in the morning: the knees or the back." He pressed his hands against his lower back, his shirt pulled tight against his watermelon stomach. "Well, at least I have the mutts in the morning to sound the alarm when I fall in the sand and can't get up . . . and now you, it seems."

The morning suddenly felt a little bit warmer. The wind less chilling. "I wanted to take some shells before I leave. I hope you don't mind," I said.

He waved an arm. "Not at all; take whatever you like, kiddo. You know." He paused, shuffling his feet in the sand. I could see where Sebastian got his fidgeting from. "I wasn't going to disturb you, but I doubt Julia offered you a car if you're a churchgoer. Just because we're a family of sinners doesn't mean we need to drag our guests down."

"Oh." I looked up from my bucket. "I don't . . . my family isn't really . . . no. Thank you, though."

He kept kicking at the sand. "We used to go . . . to church, that is. I'm sure Julia complained to you. I made all five . . . all four of them go every week." He bent down to pick up a rock. As he stood, he squinted into the sun, which was creeping bit by bit across the sand to where we stood. "But then we kind of lost our religion, I guess." He paused. "Or maybe it lost us. Who knows?"

Since I had met him in the library, Boom had looked ready to give a speech at a second's notice—to shake hands and kiss babies and listen to the needs of strangers. But at that moment on the sand, he looked tired—or maybe pensive was the better word. He was a man watching a memory flit away as though it was a balloon disappearing into clouds.

"I never understood how you could 'lose' a religion . . . where does it go? It's not like a watch or a set of keys . . . something that can disappear in a purse," I said, stumbling over my words to fill the silence.

Boom shook his head, clearing his thoughts. "Charlie, you ask the strangest questions. I understand why you and Pip are joined at the hip." He chuckled at the rhyme.

He gestured down the beach, bowing a little as if asking me to dance. "Can I walk with you?"

"Yeah. Sure. I mean, yes." I reached up to tuck my hair behind my ears, forgetting it was short now, then bent to work a shell out of the sand at my feet.

"Pip used to be inseparable from this girl. Her parents have a place nearby," he said, vaguely pointing back toward the house. "Piper. But I haven't seen her since last spring. You kids are teenagers, I know, and I don't pretend to understand her relationships, but . . ." He sighed. "Well, I'm just glad you're around to watch out for her."

"She's my best friend." I fell into step beside him, letting the pail hang from my wrist and bump against my thigh so I could shove both my hands into my sweatshirt pockets.

"Just friends?"

"Just friends."

Boom stared straight ahead, but his squinted eyes didn't look like they were taking anything in. "After Augustine, I wasn't much help to her. I protected her, but I also lost touch with her for a while. Lost touch with reality for a while." He laughed, but there wasn't any joy in the sound. "I'm trying now, but it's hard to make up for vanished time. Most days I'm just happy if I put my shoes on the right feet." He coughed, both swallowing his words and clearing his throat.

I nodded, sensing I was not expected to say anything.

He exhaled loudly and bent to pick up a stone and toss it in my pail. "Sorry. Guess I'm a little melancholy this morning. Well, I'm not telling you anything those gossip-mongers at St. Anne's aren't spreading around anyway. I'm good friends with the headmistress and know more than Julia would like about what goes on at that place." He forced a smile. "My spies tell me you're quite the artist."

I shrugged.

"Have you thought about schools? Colleges?"

I ducked my head. "I'm going to apply to a lot of places. Anywhere that'll give me a scholarship would be great."

"You must have a dream school."

I looked at my feet. "I'd like to go to RISD most. I guess. But it's wicked competitive and expensive and—"

"Got to reach for the stars, kiddo. Let me make some phone calls. I know a couple of trustees on the board over in Providence." He laughed, a deep chuckle that sounded like it started in the very center of him. "One of the perks of being an ex-politician is knowing an awful lot of awful people in an awful lot of great places. For what it's worth, I could write you a letter of recommendation, too."

"Thank you. That's . . . really, wicked generous." I again reached up to tuck my nonexistent hair behind my ears.

"Not really," he said. "You see, my offer is purely selfish. I've got a favor to ask."

"Okay?" I picked a piece of sea glass out of my bucket and ran my fingers around its smooth edges. How could *I* possibly help Boom?

"I was wondering if you wouldn't mind rooming with Julia this year. She'd murder me if she knew I was asking." He cleared his throat again. "She was so stubborn about going to Gus's school . . . and your parents would probably tell you this, too, but half of being a parent seems to be second-guessing every decision you make, but . . ."

He put a hand on my shoulder and we stopped walking. He twisted me gently to make me look at him, leaning down so his eyes were level with my own. "You're good for her. I haven't seen her this happy since . . . since a long time." He dropped his hand, but the weight of it lingered on my shoulder.

"Mr. Buchanan, I—"

"Call me Boom. Just think about it. Okay? You don't have to let me know right this instant. Now." He clapped his hands and rubbed them together. "Let's find you some treasures."

I took the gray shell he handed me, and bent down to rinse the sand from it in the wave that drifted toward my feet. I didn't drop it in the bucket, but slid it in one of my pockets. I would keep it somewhere special. Somewhere just for me.

So we walked, turning back toward the house only when the sun was hot on our faces and the wind had picked up enough to whip the top of the waves into white froth.

Had I known the heights of the joy and the depth of the hurt to come, perhaps I would have been smart. Perhaps I would have left the beach that day and taken the ferry for the safe world I had always known: a world of art made in a garage, car parts on the kitchen table, and Latin tests. Perhaps I would have been rational and chosen to have no more to do with the Buchanans.

But I have no illusions. Even knowing everything, I would have chosen the same.

It's only in hindsight that we can point, as easily as finding a town on a map, to the moments that shaped us—the moments when choices between yeses and noes determined the people we became.

SCULPTURE II

It was the last thing I packed to take with me to St. Anne's.

I covered what little sculpture I had started at Arcadia in bubble wrap and an old fleece blanket and made room for it on the backseat instead of the bed of the truck with the rest of my things. I didn't care that I had to push my seat all the way forward for the long drive.

I would have held it on my lap, but I already had my memory box. Its weight against my legs anchored me as I stared out the window at a view I had seen countless times before that was now forever changed.

THE MIDDLE

Non est vivere sed valere vita est
(Life is more than just being alive)

SIXTEEN

THAT FALL WAS LIKE IT had been the spring before—except things with Rosalie went from a tentative truce to her outright avoiding me again.

After I told her that I was rooming with Julia, if she saw me walking in her direction, she turned and went the other way. If I was in the front row in Environmental, she sat in the back. If we were stuck at the same formal dinner table, she placed herself on the other side. The few times I tried to get close enough to explain, her eyes were so full of anger and hurt that it made my insides twist. Each time my practiced speech seemed stupid and superficial. Each time I lost my nerve.

Once again, Julia and I made our own little universe and found that this time the gossip had moved on to fresher faces and rumors with more grit to them. Julia gave up Pembroke Hall and her tower room with all its furniture to live with me in Campion, closer to the library. She was just as much a slob as when she had had her own room, but she was quick to apologize for a wet towel carelessly thrown on my bed or her river-drenched sweats left in a pile in the middle of the room after her morning crew practice.

We went to the dining hall when we had to for formal dinners, but by and large we survived on microwave noodles and the massive care packages Sophie sent each week.

Sebastian came to campus a handful of times to check in on Julia. We were awkward around each other. Or maybe I was just especially awkward around him.

The time Julia left us alone together in the school store while she ran outside to talk to her crew coach, I tipped a large coffee onto a pile of newspapers with my elbow and he knocked over a display of Halloween candy. He made me clumsy. He made me tongue-tied and sloppy and nervous and want what was not mine to have.

Even when it was all three of us, there were strange lapses in the conversation. Sebastian's teasing had stopped entirely, and the time he brought H.G. with him to campus—despite the fact that Julia begged me not to leave her alone with them—I hid in my studio until I was sure he was gone. I hated disappointing Julia, but I couldn't handle seeing the girl he was with. If she was even half as flawless as she was in my head, then she was still beautiful and brilliant.

I spent September bending and unbending coat hangers into useless shapes while my sculpture for Arcadia collected dust in the corner of the studio.

When Julia showed me a post from a Harvard gossip blog saying Sebastian and H.G. had broken up—a big scene at a French restaurant in Cambridge, apparently; she threw a glass at his head, or so I read—I tried to keep my face blank. I think I even said, "How sad," or "That's too bad." If Julia didn't buy my act, she kept it to herself.

That final fall, I was both detached from life at St. Anne's and hyper-aware of every corner and cranny on campus.

I couldn't help myself from pausing in the long photo-lined hall of Keble, the English and language building, each time I left Latin IV. I knew that searching for truths in the faces in old photographs was like looking for love in a painting—you might see its shadows there, but it's not the real thing. Yet I stopped and hoped for clues I didn't really expect to find. Gus's picture was near the end, by the faculty offices. In it she was laughing, and her smile was Julia's smile, and her eyes were Mrs. Buchanan's eyes, and the cocky angle of her head made me think of Sebastian with a twinge. Her arms were over the shoulders of two shorter girls whose faces had been cropped out of the picture.

That such a girl could be anything less than immortal was one of the universe's cruelest jokes I had encountered—to that point, at least.

AP ENGLISH WITH DR. BLANCHE

"To those of you who took my honors class last year, welcome back. To those who have never had a class with me, believe everything you hear. I am indeed a merciless tyrant with unreasonable expectations. So I am assuming that you ladies did your summer reading like the dedicated AP English students I know you all are." Dr. Blanche paused behind his desk and scanned the classroom.

Giggles.

"I take your silence as a yes. Well then, let's get right into it. On the surface, F. Scott Fitzgerald's *Great Gatsby* is the story of a man who desires to be something he's not. He wants to become part of an upper-class world he wasn't invited into. On another level, it's a cautionary tale about the futility of the American dream and the endless optimism of the human spirit. 'So we beat on, boats against the current, borne back ceaselessly into the past.'"

Dr. Blanche leaned forward over his chair. "Who liked the book? Who thought it was a waste of time? Who loved it? Who hated it? And please don't let the fact that I considered it *the* great American novel influence you."

More giggles.

"Did you lose your voices over the summer? Yes, Miss Amy Worthington. Your thoughts, please."

"I liked it. I liked Gatsby. I felt bad for him."

"Why?"

"Because he tries so hard to impress Daisy and then he just winds up dead."

"For those of you who didn't finish the novel, there's your ending."

"Oops. Sorry. Was I not supposed to tell?"

"Serves them right, Miss Worthington, for not doing their homework. Yes, Miss Charlotte Ryder in the back row. Thoughts?"

"It's kind of beautiful that he tries."

"Who tries what, Miss Ryder?"

"That Gatsby tries so hard for his dream. That he wants to be part of Daisy's world so badly that he'll do anything. He believes in her long after he shouldn't. His hope is beautiful. It's what ends up killing him, but it's still beautiful."

"*Dum spiro spero.* While I breathe, I hope. Remember that, ladies. Okay, let's read aloud some sections to get a sense of Fitzgerald's language. Miss Rosalie Bernard, why don't you start from the beginning?"

I kept my eyes forward, but I let my mind wander. I didn't raise my hand again for the rest of class.

SEVENTEEN

EVEN IF JULIA HADN'T BEEN the coxswain, I would have gone to the fall regatta out of habit. Rosalie was the senior captain, and when we were roommates and friends, I had watched every one of her home races. Though weeks had passed and we were more than halfway through October, she still wasn't speaking to me. Nonetheless, I pathetically hoped that seeing me on the sidelines as she rowed would soften her a little.

Plus, I loved the river.

The fall regatta was the sort of event that ended up in all the photos in the St. Anne's admission catalogues. The air was popcorn and blueberry muffins mixed with leaves and the brackish scent of the river itself. Groups of parents and teachers stood over picnic tables or piles of discarded backpacks and jackets. The hum of conversation mixed with the hum of the water, their harmony occasionally broken by a coach shouting something to his or her team over by the trailers that covered the boathouse parking lot. It was exactly what Grandma Eve described when she was convincing me to apply to St. Anne's. It was a bit of paradise.

Julia looked more put together than usual for the occasion, dressed in matching wind pants and jacket in the St. Anne's evergreen and ivory. Her uniform was only a little too big for her, and her hair was back in a tight braid that someone else must have done. As she approached me, her face was red with the effort of carrying a burlap sandbag in her arms.

"What are you doing?" I said. "Watching you hold that is painful."

"How do you think I feel? I have to carry it. It's pathetic. I should have put stones in my pockets or drunk a gallon of water before weigh-in."

"Julia, you sure you got that?"

"Oh, don't worry. I gave Cordelia the other one to carry."

I looked over Julia's shoulder, and there was Cordelia behind her, dragging a sandbag across the ground, leaving a path of plowed grass in her wake. I could hear her grunting and see how hard she was pulling in the tension in her back.

"You are a heartless and twisted individual," I said, looking square at Julia.

"What? She wanted to carry it. Fine, Bradley," she yelled over to where Bradley was leaning against a boat rack, talking closely with Coach Hassle. It looked more like they were standing in a dark bar than by a river on a bright fall afternoon.

"Bradley!" Julia shouted again. "Are you telling Coach Hassle about the time you got so scared during the Fourth of July fireworks that you peed—"

"Coming, darling sister," Bradley said, smiling his game-show host smile at Coach Hassle before jogging up the hill toward us. "Wow," he said, slightly out of breath at the top. "You sure know how to kill a guy's game."

Julia snorted. "Game? That's what you call game?"

"Well, I got her number," he said, holding up a piece of torn notebook paper between his two hands.

"Bradley, you're disgusting. That's my coach."

"Yeah, and she's hot," he said as he folded the paper up neatly and put it back in his pocket.

Julia hefted her bag up higher in her arms. "Casanova, go help Cordelia bring my sandbag down to the dock. She's going to pass out if she keeps trying to pull it."

Bradley gave her a sharp salute and mussed both our hair before striding to Cordelia.

"It's amazing," Julia said, watching him. "He's six years older than me and is trusted with running a company, and yet most of the time he acts like he's thirteen." She grunted and tried to shift the sandbag more to her left arm. "Okay, I've got a boat full of girls to yell at and a regatta to win. See you after?"

"I'll be here," I said, pointing at the ground.

"Kiss for good luck?" Julia puckered her lips.

"Get out of here." I shoved her toward the dock.

"Right," Julia said as she made an exaggerated sigh. "Not on my team. Okay. Well, your loss." She turned and lurched down the hill, stopping from time to time to bounce the sandbag higher on her hip.

I wandered behind her, stopping at the water's edge to breathe in the river. It didn't smell as good as the ocean at Arcadia, but it had its own fantastic scent: a combination of dirt and decay that to most people would have been disgusting. But I loved it. I loved the way it turned black in the middle and there was nothing on the other bank but a wall of trees with electric red, orange, and yellow leaves. Groups of parents and students dotted the bank beside me, talking loudly, as coxswains, many of them Julia's size or even smaller, led the eight girls carrying their sleek racing shells in wide circles around the spectators.

I watched Julia work her way up and down the dock as the rowers in her shell screwed their oars in place and settled into their seats. I was grateful to see that Rosalie gave her a nod when Julia leaned in and said something to her. She might be mad at me, but at least she wasn't going to take it out on Julia and the team. As soon as everyone was in the boat, Julia climbed into the stern, half-disappearing in the tight space. She adjusted her mike, and then they shot away from the dock, slowly rowing, their oars creating synchronized arches over the water as they made their way toward the old railroad bridge and the start of the race.

"Charlie!" Boom's shout caused half the people on the top of the hill and me to turn around. "There you are. Come up and say hello." He gestured with one hand, and with the other he plucked an unlit cigar from his mouth.

When I was within arm's length, he reached out, keeping the cigar clenched between his teeth, and pulled me into a bear hug. "Aren't you a sight for old eyes?" he said, squeezing me one more time before releasing. My bones felt slightly crushed.

"Joe, give me that," Mrs. Buchanan said, walking over from the coffee table and grabbing the cigar from his mouth. "You can't smoke on campus, and you know what your doctor told you. Sometimes I think you have a death wish!" She stuck the cigar in her purse and smacked him lightly on the back of the head with the hand that wasn't wrapped around a paper coffee cup.

"What if they win?" Boom said, rubbing his head like Mrs. Buchanan's tiny swat had actually hurt him. "It'd be rude not to celebrate."

Mrs. Buchanan rolled her eyes as she sipped her coffee. "If they win, darling, then you may smoke half of it when we get home tonight and I'll only tell your doctor if you keep trying my patience." She gave him one more playful swat.

"Hello dear," she said, leaning in and hugging me with one arm, kissing both my cheeks. Her musky perfume was the perfect mixture of flower and vanilla. "My husband might be a child sometimes, but he's right," she said, squeezing my arm. "You look lovely."

"Well kiddo, why aren't you on the—"

"Sebastian, doesn't Charlie look lovely?" Mrs. Buchanan said, cutting Boom off and turning toward Sebastian, who had appeared with his own paper cup of coffee. He was wearing his aviator sunglasses, slouchy jeans, and a faded long-sleeved T-shirt.

"Hello," he said, his fingers opening and closing around his cup.

"Hi," I replied. My hands felt tingly, like the blood was rushing back into them after they had fallen asleep. I was grateful for the October air across my cheeks.

"Why don't we go over to where Dr. Mulcaster is standing, Joe? I want to ask her about the new science facilities," Mrs. Buchanan said, raising her cup to point to where the headmistress was holding court near the docks.

"Lead the way, beautiful," Boom said, winking, then ruffling Sebastian's hair before shambling after Mrs. Buchanan.

"Hello," Sebastian said, once it was just the two of us. He pushed his sunglasses onto the top of his head.

"You already said that." I waited until his eyes were on his coffee cup to touch my cheeks. They were still way too warm.

"Yeah, it's the next part that's always the trickiest." He took a sip of his coffee and grimaced as he swallowed. "This stuff's disgusting. I don't know why I keep drinking it."

"How about 'how are you'?" I said. "That's usually step two."

"Okay, how are you?"

"Good. How are you?" I watched him take another drink of coffee. Even with his mouth twisted with disgust, he was so cute it hurt.

"Good," he said before draining the rest of his coffee and crumpling the cup. "There was no reason for me to drink that. It was like chewing mud." He tried tossing the cup in a nearby trash can, but missed. "Shoot. There goes my NBA career," he said, picking it up and dropping it in the can very deliberately. "Well, 'how are you' didn't give us much to go with."

"Nope."

"Want to go watch the race?"

"Yup."

"Where's the best spot?" Sebastian stood on his tiptoes, trying to see over the rows of people that had already started to line the shore in anticipation.

"Follow me," I said as I started toward the boathouse. I led him around the side to a door that blended in so well with the rest of the building that it was easy to miss. It took a couple of hard pulls, but eventually it swung out, and I gestured for Sebastian to slip inside before I followed him.

"Awesome," he said when our eyes had adjusted to the low light.

Rows and rows of shining racing shells, small sailboats, piles of gigantic oars and lifejackets, and a dilapidated and useless lifeboat crowded the floor. The rough floorboards creaked under our feet as I led him to the stairs in the back of the barn-like space.

"They always lock the front door, but my roommate—ex-roommate—told me about the side one freshman year," I said. We climbed the stairs, and I was painfully aware of how closely he followed me. With every step I forced myself to think, *He's Julia's brother. He's Julia's brother.* But the mantra did nothing to calm my dancing heart.

The loft was dotted with extra boat parts, life jackets whose stuffing was beginning to come out, and a pile of trophies loosely covered with a sheet that must have been white once upon a time. The roof came down steeply at the sides, but the center was tall enough to require a ladder to reach the top. Sky-lights lined the ceiling, creating yellow rectangles on the wood floor. The smell of plastic tarps and motor oil hung in the air.

I led the way across the long space, grateful that I could put some space between Sebastian and me by weaving through the piles of boxes and forgotten tools, and flung open the small door at the end, stepping back to let Sebastian look. "Ta-da."

"Once again, awesome." He glanced out, then quickly stepped back in, his face a little paler than before. "Prob-ably should have mentioned that I kind of have a thing about heights."

I leaned out the door, glancing at the ground, which sloped toward the docks and was feet and feet below. I heard the crack of the gun signaling the start of the race and bent a little farther out, gripping the side of the door for balance, to find Julia's boat. His hand at my hip startled me enough for me to shiver. He pulled on my sweater, bringing me back into the boathouse.

"Sorry," he said, dropping his hand. His face was no longer just pale; it was ashen, and he was biting his bottom lip so hard it was a wonder it didn't start to bleed. I had to resist the urge to reach up and hold his face between my two hands.

He's Julia's brother. He's Julia's brother. He's Julia's brother.

I coughed and straightened my sweater. "Wow, you're really afraid of heights, aren't you?"

He shrugged, shook his head, then nodded, looking up from under his lashes. "You were making me nervous."

"I make you nervous?" I leaned against the doorframe, but not outside of it this time. I started skimming my fingers over the wall beside me so I would stop staring at him. For a moment, we were both silent, watching the boats glide in slow motion across the river. I kept running one hand up and down the wall, forcing myself to concentrate on the race and not the fact that his body was so close to mine. Just as the first boat was crossing in front of the boathouse, my fingers snagged on an indent in the wood. I took my eyes off the water and glanced at the carving in the wall.

"Hey, feel this." I grabbed Sebastian's hand and traced it over the wood. "Someone's initials. It feels like a D, a C, and then down here," I said, lowering his hand, "an A, another A, O, N, and a B. They're really deep. God, the second person had a ton of names. That must have stunk when he had to fill out the bubbles on the SATs."

"Yeah," Sebastian said. He switched our hold so his hand now covered mine. I could feel his touch in the small bones of my fingers as he pressed my hand down over the second set of initials. "It could have been a she, though."

"What makes you think that?"

"They could be Gus's."

I glanced at him. "Really?"

"Yeah, D.C. for her boyfriend, David, and then her full name was Augustine Rose Buchanan. But we called her Augustine 'Any Other Name' Buchanan because of the part in *Romeo and Juliet* where Juliet says something about a rose by any other name still smelling sweet. As a joke, she went by A.A.O.N.B."

"Oh, my God. Julia's going to hit the roof," I said, still running my fingers over the initials and taking his hand with me.

Sebastian released his grip and I dropped my hand against my side. It was still warm from where my skin had been touching his. He shifted until he was staring out the door again and I couldn't see his expression. "They're going around the final bend. I think Julia's boat is second," he said.

"Where?" I replied, standing on my tiptoes so I could see from his height.

On the water, three boats fought for the lead, their bows cutting through the river like snowplows through powder, leaving only ripples behind them from where the oars had dug into the water.

"There," Sebastian said, bending down so his eyes were at my level. "Her boat's the farthest from us. You can't even see her she's so tiny."

Maybe it was because his face was so close to mine, or maybe it was because I was so happy to be able to show Julia the initials, or maybe it was because he smelled like coffee and laundry detergent, but whatever the reason, I turned at the same time he turned and we kissed.

I don't know if I kissed him first or he kissed me. I just know that suddenly his mouth was on mine and his body was pressing against my own. His hand at the nape of my neck. My hands on his arms. Drifting down his sides. Clutching where his pants met his hips. My nose bumped against his and I giggled. He tried to hold me closer but stumbled, losing his balance and pulling me with him until his back was against the wall. I laughed some more, but kept kissing him. Below us, the crowd erupted into a loud cheer. Somebody had won. Somebody had lost. But we kept kissing.

When at last we broke, we stood staring at each other. His lips were still slightly parted, and my own felt bruised. For a moment, we did nothing. Just stared.

"Sebastian . . . I'm so, so sorry—"

"Shit. Sorry. I wasn't—"

"No, it's my fault. I kissed you—"

"No, you're totally right. So stupid," he said as he ran a hand through his hair, then leaned against the wall, well away from the open loft door.

What I did next was impulsive and so unlike me. I reached behind his neck and pulled him to me again. My lips hurt in the best way possible. His lips were warm and sweet with coffee and sugar. I had no room in my head to worry about betraying Julia or that he had just broken up with his girlfriend or that he was a Buchanan and I was just Charlie. I could only think about how amazing it felt to kiss him and how I never wanted to stop. It took the crowd below us exploding into a second and louder roar for me to realize what I was doing. I pushed him away.

"I'm so sorry," I said. "I'm . . . I'm going to go." I stepped back, tugging my sweater down from where it had ridden up and gotten caught in the clasp of my bra. Once my stomach was covered, I turned and ran down the stairs, leaving him standing at the loft door, lit from behind by the hazy October sun, a bewildered expression on his face.

WHY NOT?

"Tell me again why you won't come to Arcadia for Thanksgiving?"

"Because I have to go home."

"Will you look away from the canvas for one moment? What is up with you lately? *Très, très fou.*"

"Nothing," I mumbled as I dropped a paintbrush with more force than I meant to into a jar of murky water, splashing my pants. "Shit."

Julia raised an eyebrow. "Well if you won't tell me, you should at least tell Aloysius. He's very concerned that you're acting like such a *folle personne.*" She held out the stuffed moose from her perch on the studio radiator like I might actually start talking to him.

I smiled despite myself. There's no way I could tell her. I stirred the paintbrush in the jar vigorously and dumped the water in the studio sink, wiping at my eyes at the same time. They stung from the paint fumes.

"Hey, Charlie, catch!"

I turned just fast enough so Aloysius thudded against my face before crumpling to the paint-splattered cement floor.

"*Mon Dieu.* You're just as coordinated as Sebastian."

At his name my chest hurt. I bent over to pick up Aloysius, lingering so I could hide my expression. "I just wasn't prepared for a stuffed moose to be flying at my head, that's all."

"Hey, cranky pants, let me tell you a story."

"Oh, it's story hour now?"

"Yup. So when Gus was a sophomore, she was so tired from staying out all night after winning the Atlantic Coast Championship Regatta that when she went to practice the next morning she stepped in goose *caca* and slid right off the dock into the river."

"Who told you that?"

"Coach Kellogg."

"So, I guess Gus was clumsy, too."

"*Oui.* Now will you tell me the true reason you won't come for Thanksgiving?"

"I really do need to go home, I swear. Thanksgiving, unfortunately, is Melissa's favorite holiday. She's nuts about it."

"Okay," Julia said, jumping off the radiator. "If you swear, but you're still being weird."

"I know."

"*Merde!* It's going to be so dull out there without you." She slapped the wall for emphasis.

I smiled. "I'm sure you guys will find a way to entertain yourselves."

"Still won't be the same. Mummy and Boom are going to be disappointed, too. They consider you an extra Oops, another daughter they didn't expect, but kind of wanted."

I just shook my head, afraid that if I opened my mouth I would let her know how much I wanted to go. I hated the thought of not seeing her for a week and of missing them all. But I hated the thought of seeing him more . . . almost as much as I hated not seeing him.

"Fine, you're off the hook for now. These paint fumes are obviously messing with your brain, but you're coming out for New Year's, and I won't accept any excuses."

"None? What if I lose a leg in a tragic dining hall salad bar accident?" I said. "What if I'm sick in the hospital with food poisoning, or I come down with some rare tropical disease that's never been seen before?"

"Nope. Not even if you lose all your limbs in a car—" Julia's face fell just as quickly as her smile had risen.

I closed the space between us in a few steps. Her eyes were stretched at the corners and tears were threatening to spill over her lower lids.

"Hey, here," I said, thrusting Aloysius at her. "It's okay. I was just kidding. I'll get out there over winter break even if I have pinkeye, mono, and some incurable and highly contagious STD."

"That's disgusting," she said, but she was smiling through her sniffling. "Now I'm not sure if I want you to come after all."

"Too late. You're stuck with me."

"Promise?"

"Promise."

To: cryder@stannes.edu
From: tbuchanan@buchananfoundation.org

Date: November 29

Subject: Checking In

Dear Charlotte,

We missed you for Thanksgiving! However, Julia has
promised me that you'll be joining us over St. Anne's
Christmas break. I bought you a ferry ticket just in case.
I'm sending it back with Julia along with some goodies
Sophie baked for you. She says to tell you, *"Tu nous as
manqué, ma chérie!"*

With much affection,
Teresa

To: cryder@stannes.edu
From: littleduck24@yahoo.com
Date: November 29
Subject: This is Cordelia NOT SPAM

Charlie,

Why didn't you come see us? Julia promised you would.
Is it because Nantucket is too cold in November? My
friends think we're all crazy for coming out here all year
round.

The Homers got another horse, so next time you come to Arcadia, you, Julia, and I can all go riding at the same time. You know how to ride, right?

Write me back. I check my email every day!!
OXOXO
Cordelia (You can call me Oops if you want)

To: cryder@stannes.edu
From: bradley.buchanan@investtech.com
Date: November 30
Subject: Phone

Hey Charlie,

Why'd you bail on Thanksgiving? You missed meeting crazy grandma Gertrude . . . and trying one of Sophie's pies. The latter's more significant and more digestible. Ha ha.

I'm sending Julia back with a phone to give to you. (She told me yours is pathetic.) I just got it, but before I even opened the box they came out with a new model. Don't let her lose it! If you need help setting it up, you know where to find me.

--B

P.S. Julia's been moping all week. You can't do this to us again. She's a terror without you.

P.P.S. Seriously don't lose this phone. It's awesome. It does everything but the dishes.

To: cryder@stannes.edu
From: jbuchanan@buchananfoundation.org
Date: November 30
Subject: New Years Eve Party

Happy belated Thanksgiving! Julia tells me you're coming out for New Year's. We'll get an extra ticket for the party at the White Elephant just in case.

Let Sophie know if you need anything.

Cheers,
Boom

To: cryder@stannes.edu
From: sebuchanan@harvard.edu
Date: December 1
Subject: So . . .

Charlie,

Hey. So I got your email address from Julia. I hope that's okay. And I hope that the reason you didn't come out this week wasn't because of me. Julia would kill me if that was why.

I'm sorry for screwing up. But I'm also not sorry. Does that make sense?

Sebastian

> To: sebuchanan@harvard.edu
> From: cryder@stannes.edu
> Date: December 1
> Subject: Re: So . . .

It makes more sense than you know. You didn't mess up. I did.

I wish I could explain better.

I don't want to hurt Julia. I hope that makes sense, too.

Charlie

EIGHTEEN

WE HAD BEEN AT THE New Year's Eve party at the White Elephant Resort for a little over an hour before Julia insisted we leave.

It was my first New Year's on Nantucket, and I wanted to stay. I could have stood by the Buchanans' table near the dance floor and done nothing but watch people until midnight and it still would have been one of the most amazing nights of my life. The men were in black tuxedos and the women wore the kinds of dresses I'd only seen in Melissa's gossip magazines. The waiters and waitresses had on white gloves and the ballroom was dotted with candlelight and saturated with classical music. It was like being dropped into a Renoir painting.

But Julia was bored. Julia wanted to go. So I moved to the door and waited, smoothing the black cocktail dress I hadn't worn since the last and final time Grandma Eve had taken me to the ballet. I saw Julia grab Sebastian's arm and whisper something in Boom's ear. He shook his head, listened, and then shook it again. After a long pause and a deep drink from the dark liquid in his glass, he nodded and pointed first at Sebastian and then at me. Julia jumped up and kissed him on the cheek. She pulled Sebastian so he walked beside her. The straps of her red dress kept slipping off her shoulders as she crossed the dance floor. When she reached me, I slid them back up.

"Allons-y!"

I hadn't been so close to Sebastian all night. It was as if we both knew that our email exchange had actually been an agreement to avoid each other. I tried to keep my eyes on the couples on the dance floor, but I couldn't help glancing at him. His tie was loose and his tuxedo jacket too big, like it was borrowed from Boom or Bradley. His feet tapped and his eyes rested everywhere and anywhere but on me.

I forced myself to look at Julia. "What'd you tell Boom?"

"The truth," said Julia. "That we were leaving."

"And he's okay with that?"

Julia tugged on my arm. "Not really. Usually we're all together at midnight, but he'll be fine. Let's go. I want to do something different this year, and this place is as exciting as watching water freeze."

"What about Bradley?"

"Oh, he disappeared half an hour ago with an ex-ex-ex-girlfriend. He knows where to find us. Besides." She pointed in Sebastian's direction. "Boom's making Sebastian come with us, so we already have a babysitter for the evening."

"And where will Bradley find us?"

"The Chicken Box, of course." Julia hugged me, dropping
her purse on the ground in her excitement. *"Il est temps de faire
la fête, Charlie!"* She ran out the ballroom door while my arms
were still raised from being around her waist.

I picked up her purse and followed her. I couldn't believe
that I was leaving a place called the White Elephant for one
named after a barnyard bird.

As we passed through the lobby door into the December
dark, I saw Boom watching us from near the check-in desk.
His forehead was wrinkled and he had one foot in front of the
other, as if he might spring after us. When our eyes met he
raised his glass and smiled that wide Buchanan smile, mouth-
ing something to me that I couldn't hear but was pretty sure I
understood: "Take care of her."

Only once we were all inside the waiting cab did he turn
and go back to the party.

The Chicken Box was a squat building that looked like it could
just as easily hold horses and cows as people. Like the buildings
to the left and the right, it had gray shingles along the side,
white flower boxes filled with snow, and a pitch-black roof, but
that's where its adherence to the Island dress code ended. The
shutters were crooked, the cobblestones ended just before the
drive, and light glared out from the windows as garish as neon

signs on the Vegas strip. We heard the music pulsing out the open door long before the cab pulled to a stop in front.

Julia jumped out of the car, leaving me to scramble after her with her coat and purse and Sebastian to pay the fare.

The bouncer at the door was wearing a puffy coat that made him look like a marshmallow stuck on two toothpicks. His ruddy face was barely visible under his ear-flapped hat and raised collar. He held up his hand even before we got to the door.

"Twenty-one and up tonight."

"Oh, we're twenty-one," Julia said, grabbing her coat from me and fishing through the pockets. "See." She handed him her ID, and I thought I saw a flash of green beneath.

I glanced at Sebastian more out of embarrassment than for confirmation that Julia was trying to bribe the bouncer, but he had his hands in his coat pockets and was looking down at the frozen ground.

"Buchanan, huh?" the bouncer asked, and if he was smiling it came across as a grimace. He handed Julia back her ID, the money still tucked underneath.

"Yup," said Julia, shoving her ID in her purse. She held the bill in her hand for a moment before slipping it in there as well. She shrugged at Sebastian and me, as if to say, "I tried."

"Put out your hands."

All three of us obeyed. The bouncer reached into his pocket, pulled out an ink pad, and stamped our hands with a green star.

Julia made as if to pass through the door, but the bouncer smacked a hand across the frame right before she got through.

"I catch you drinking, I kick you out. I catch you looking at a drink, I'll kick you out. If I catch you even thinking about drinking, I'll kick you out. Got it?"

We all nodded; then Julia ducked under his arm and disappeared inside.

"Good. Have a lovely evening," said the bouncer, moving his arm from the door. "Oh," he said as he shoved his hands into his coat pockets. "Tell your dad Jim Bellows says thanks again."

Sebastian and I must have looked confused, because he added, "He'll know what I mean."

"Will do," Sebastian said, and I followed him through the door.

We dumped our coats on a small side table near where Julia had stopped to watch the packed dance floor.

"Now, this is a party." She grabbed a cocktail napkin from the table behind us, dunked it in an unfinished drink on our table, and began scrubbing furiously at the green star on the back of my hand. Once she had spread it to a messy splotch, she moved on to Sebastian, and then her own hand.

"*Voila! Allons boire, maintenant.*"

I knew Julia well enough to guess the gist of what she had said. "Ummm, first, it looks like we all have mold growing on our hands. And second, remember 'if I catch you even thinking about drinking, I'll kick you out'?" I said.

"Charlie!" Julia grasped my face between her hands, which were sticky from dunking the napkin in the drink. "First, this place is so crowded, the bouncer is lucky if he can see his hand in front of his face. And second, well . . . *vivre un peu.*" She kissed my forehead with a loud smack and bounced to the bar, where she handed a wrinkled bill to a wrinkled man with an enormous beard but no hair on his head. She raised three fingers and he nodded.

Sebastian and I stood watching the band, the crowd, the plastic Mardi Gras beads being flung through the air. Though we stood apart looking at anything but each other, I didn't forget for a second that he was close enough to touch.

Then Julia came back with three glasses filled with ice and pink liquid. I grabbed one of them from her, grateful to have something to do with my hands. We drank. Then Sebastian went and got three more. We drank those, and then the night started to blur. A mishmash of sights and sounds that pulsed at the core and softened at the edges.

Suddenly, Julia and I were on the dance floor, and Sebastian disappeared into the wall of bodies near the bar and I was disappointed, but then I forgot why. The band was part punk, part rock, and a little bit of country. They played covers of all the songs that normally made me change the radio station when I was driving with my dad, but that night I loved them all. Guys in torn jeans and T-shirts and girls in sneakers and clingy dresses pressed around us, yelling along to the songs just as loudly as Julia and me. The heat of so many bodies packed together made the air above the dance floor steam, and I wondered how I had ever been cold.

The music was in my limbs, lifting my arms above my head like I was praising something higher than myself, making my feet turn while I spun Julia, then she me. She was a ballerina, a rock star, a cabaret dancer, laughing with her head thrown back. I was her partner, stepping in to twirl and dip her so the world could admire her more.

We had one more drink. Then someone bought us another. Then I lost count.

When a girl with brown skin as smooth as polished marble in a black tank top and pants so tight they looked painted onto her whippet-thin body stepped in to dance with Julia, I let her. I melted into the crowd that lined the periphery of the dance floor, admiring the beautiful bodies pulsing to the sounds of music that demanded to be danced to.

When I reached the far side of the bar, I leaned against it, exhaling gratefully. I eased one foot out of one heel, then the other, sinking down and crunching my toes on the rough wood floor.

"We're about the same size now." Sebastian appeared near my right side.

"Oh. Hey." I swayed slightly, dizzy from the drinks or spinning around so much or a combination of the two. I grabbed a cocktail napkin from the bar and swiped it across my forehead. I could feel makeup dripping down my face like paint flung against a wall. He leaned against the bar, too.

"Where have you been?"

He had taken off his jacket and his tie was undone and draped around his neck. He ran his hands through his hair, making the curls stand out from his head even more. I had to resist the urge to smooth them down.

"Talking to some college friends," he said, swaying when he gestured toward the nearest corner. He grabbed a stool to balance himself, but it wasn't enough to keep him from knocking an empty glass back into the bar. "Oops."

"Careful." I reached as if to grab him, my fingers grazing his shoulder just before he righted himself.

"These hurricanes. These are damn good." He took a gulp from the glass in his hand, emptying it. "Want another one?" He didn't wait for my answer before leaning across the bar, gesturing for the bearded bartender to make his way toward our end.

"Where's Julia?" He twisted his head as much as he could while lying half on the bar and searched the dance floor. At that moment, with his wrinkled forehead and the concern in his eyes, he looked exactly like Boom watching us leave the White Elephant.

"Dancing," I shouted. The band had started playing a loud number with a lot of drums. Whatever was in those drinks was making my fingers tingle, making me bold. I rested near him, letting our elbows touch. "Can I ask you something?"

He must have seen Julia, because he slid off the top of the bar and went back to gesturing for the bartender. He nudged my shoulder with his own. "Sure. We're old friends now, right?"

My brain felt filled with clouds. I couldn't figure out if he was teasing.

He pushed against me again. "Hey, I found Pip. Take a look at her. You have to, because as her brother, I'm not sure how much more is good for me to see."

I scooted to try to look at the dance floor from his angle. It was no longer just our elbows touching, but our entire sides. I could feel the heat of his body from my hip to my shoulder. The starched fabric of his shirt stuck to my arm, and his belt pressed into my hipbone.

The girl from before was dancing inches from Julia, who would step closer and then spin away, as if daring the girl to try and catch her.

"She's amazing." I paused, then said, "How come Boom doesn't care that we're here?"

Sebastian handed the bartender a twenty and turned around to pass me a glass, putting an inch of space between us. The pinkish liquid had sloshed over the sides and my glass was already sticky and dripping. I grasped it with both hands, but didn't drink.

"Sorry, what'd you ask?" He bent in close enough for his

breath to tickle my ear, and I had to close my eyes to remember my question.

"Uh, why doesn't Boom flip out that we're out here, instead of back at the White Elephant?" My words felt like marbles rolling across my tongue.

Sebastian took a sip of his drink, and when he leaned his back against the bar to look out at the room, I used it as an excuse to do the same so our arms could keep touching.

"I know it's messed up. I know it's not like normal families or anything—"

"What's normal, anyway?" I shouted, even though the band chose that moment to switch to a slow song where the piano twinkled instead of pounded and the guitar muffled instead of wailed, making my question hang in the air like a half-empty balloon.

"It's complicated." He sighed. "Boom can't say no to Julia. He's just so happy when she's happy that he can't say no." He shook his head. "She went through a pretty rough patch . . . after the accident. Can't really blame him. We just want her to be happy." He took a sip of his drink. "Besides, Charlie Ryder's here. What could possibly go wrong?"

For the first time since we had kissed in October, we held each other's gaze without looking away. "To messed up and complicated." I clicked my glass against his.

"To 'what's normal, anyway?'" He took a drink from his glass, set it down on the bar, and glanced at his watch. "It's almost midnight. Wanna get some air?"

I nodded, placing my full glass next to his and slipping painfully back into my shoes. I followed him toward the table where
we had dumped our stuff.

"Can I tell you a secret, Charlie?" As we both shrugged on
our coats, he balanced on the balls of his feet like he was getting
ready to sprint.

I nodded again.

He leaned in close enough for me to smell his skin: sugar,
sweat, and rum. "This might be the best night of my whole
life."

He grabbed my hand and we worked our way through the
crowd to the open door, where the light spilled onto the street
like paint from a tipped can.

Outside on the sidewalk, I could feel the sweat that had been
collecting between my shoulder blades trickle to the small of
my back. I felt shivery, flushed, and bold. So even though there
were people pressing around us—drunks stumbling toward the
next bar, groups of girls giggling and holding one another up,
tottering on their high heels on the cobblestone street—I pulled
Sebastian's hand to make him stop.

From across the street the sounds of an entire bar starting
the countdown drifted: *ten, nine, eight, seven.* Then I could hear
through the open door of the Chicken Box everyone just one
beat behind: *six, five, four, three.*

Every inch of my hand felt his when he tightened his grip.

Two. One.

Happy New Year!

Someone knocked him toward me from behind, and that was all it took. His lips. My lips. Kissing him wasn't something I could control.

I couldn't get close enough to him. He pulled me tighter and tighter to his chest until I didn't know where he ended and I began, and still it wasn't close enough. When someone bumped me from the side, we didn't separate.

Any part of me that wasn't touching him was instantly bitten by the January night. I ignored the cold. We kept kissing.

I ignored the catcalls and whistles as New Year's partiers flowed around us like they were water and we were two stones in a river.

It took a drunken girl grabbing my arm to steady herself for us to separate.

This was not supposed to happen again. I couldn't stop it from happening again. I wanted so much for it to happen again.

I took a step back, and he did the same. We didn't speak. A silver plastic necklace dropped between us, landing on his shoes. We both looked up and saw her at the same time, leaning with her arms crossed against the doorway of the Chicken Box, the party lights and music behind her and the bouncer staring where she was staring: at us. Her expression was unreadable. She didn't move until the stunning girl from the dance floor slipped her arms around her waist and dragged her back inside, leaving a pile of necklaces where Julia's feet had been.

Sebastian reached down and grabbed the beads off his shoes and slipped them around my neck.

Then he kissed me again.

NINETEEN

DID I EVER GO TO sleep? Or did I just keep floating in that waking dream that began when Sebastian and I kissed the night before?

I couldn't stop replaying everything, even though my head was foggy and my body exhausted. I couldn't stop smiling.

Three raps on my door in the morning, however, were all it took for the smile on my face to turn into a twisting in my stomach. The clock on the bureau said 7:00 a.m. It could only be Julia.

I scrambled out of the small twin bed, knocking into the side table hard enough to send a leather-bound book to the floor.

"Coming." I replaced the book and then shuffled to the door, trying to keep one hand pressed against the spot on my knee that I could already feel was going to bruise. I eased open the door, but it still creaked loud enough to make me wince.

Julia's hair was piled on top of her head. Stray wisps floated out of her messy bun and drifted as softly as whispers against her pale face. She had a blanket over her shoulders like a cape and a pair of felt slippers on that looked large enough to belong to Boom. She didn't say anything, just gestured for me to follow her, not turning around to see if I did. She knew I would.

I pulled on a pair of wool socks over the cotton ones I already had on. A draft crept up from the first floor, so I grabbed a blanket off my bed as well. The stairs groaned in a way that felt painfully loud, making me pause each time I put my foot down. Julia was already out on the porch, curled up on an Adirondack with her blanket wrapped around her like a patchwork cocoon by the time I made my way out the door.

I folded into the chair next to her and tucked my blanket around myself, feeling the cold prick my face. I waited.

When Julia didn't speak, I waited some more, trying to look out where she was looking, trying to see the frost-covered lawn, boarded-up boathouse, and white-capped winter ocean through her eyes. If she was angry, the wonder of the frozen view would be lost on her.

"I owe Sebastian a lot," she said finally, her smoky voice cutting through the stillness like a wire through clay. "He was the one who found me . . . after the accident, you know?"

I raised my chin out of my blanket. "No, I didn't."

"Well, he did. He knew where I'd be, even when I didn't know where I was."

"Julia—"

"I'm not mad," Julia said. "Not even a little. I knew it was only a matter of time before they got to you, too." She sighed and kept her eyes fixed straight ahead at some point on the January horizon. "I just hoped it wouldn't be so soon."

"Julia," I said, feeling every muscle it took to form her name. "I tried not to. I tried so hard. It was a mistake. We were being stupid and drunk." My voice wavered. "It didn't mean anything. Just kissing."

Julia rested the side of her head on her knees and finally looked at me. "If that was just kissing, then Mother Teresa was just a really nice old lady." Her cheeks and nose were pink from the wind.

"I'm your friend first," I said as I struggled to sit up straight in the deep chair. "Before anything else, I'm your friend."

She sighed. "I suppose it's my own fault. I brought you to Arcadia and introduced you to them. They can be so damn charming. Even Bradley has his moments. As for Sebastian, I'll talk to him later. *On pardonne tant que l'on aime.*"

I couldn't tell if she was seriously mad at Sebastian or just joking, so I said nothing.

She started humming.

"Julia?"

"Yeah?"

"That time on the roof." I cleared my throat. "You know . . . last summer?"

"Uh-huh?" Julia had tucked her head into her blanket like a

turtle drawing into its shell, but I kept going.

"Well, it was nice, but I'm not . . . well, you know that I'm . . ." My words tripped over themselves like passengers rushing to get out of a crowded bus. "I'm ninety-nine percent sure I like boys. Not that kissing you wasn't very—"

"Pardonne-moi?" Julia's laugh was muffled by her blanket until she drew her face out and her giggle cracked against the cold air. She raised a pale hand to her mouth. "Oh! Charlie. No, no, no, no, no. Not that you're not a terrific snogger, but a lady knows what she knows and you were . . . you *are* so obviously not in my boat."

She scooted over on her Adirondack until there was room for one more. I untangled myself just enough to shuffle over and squeeze in beside her. Once I had arranged the blanket so my body was again completely covered, she rested her head on my shoulder and I shifted down so I could rest mine on top of hers.

"The thing is that you were supposed to be mine. Just mine. I found you and now I feel like they're taking you away."

"That's silly. No one's taking me away. I'm still your friend. We're still us. Here. Together. *Contra mundum.*" The burst of love I felt for her spread through me like blue paint turning red to purple. She was my Julia. I was her Charlie. I wouldn't let anything change that.

"Just promise no secrets. I can't stand secrets. Even if you think I don't want to know something, you have to tell me. Deal?"

"Deal."

"Okay," she said, leaning against me with her whole tiny body so that our blanket cocoons were the only things that separated us. "I feel it's only fair to warn you that when Sebastian was seven he insisted everyone call him Jack because some kids were teasing him about his name. Then when he was ten he went for over a week without changing his underwear because he thought it would help the Red Sox win the World Series."

"Julia, I'm okay with *some* secrets," I said, trying and failing to smack her arm through our layers of blankets.

I settled back down beside her, once again resting my head on top of hers. "If it means anything, I think I really, really like him . . . name insecurities, dirty underwear, and all."

"Of course you do. How could you not?" She shifted her blanket so it covered more of her neck. "He's *my* brother. Some of my sparkling personality and wit was bound to rub off on him eventually."

The sun was just breaking over the harbor in the distance, making the frost on the brown grass glisten like someone had painted each individual blade. The wind that swooped over the lawn and hit our cheeks was full of ocean, ice, and a new year and all its possibilities.

Tucked in beside my best friend, with the boy and family I adored still asleep upstairs, I was sublimely, irrationally, and perfectly happy.

NOTE #2

Charlie,

Good luck with your final semester! I can't help you with your Latin translations, but if you need ideas for a senior prank I'm your guy.

Sebastian

P.S. I'll come visit after study hall on Thursday. Ask Pip if she needs anything from the outside world.

P.P.S. If Pip says nice things about me, you can share the chocolates with her. I think they're the ones you like.

P.P.P.S It's been less than forty-eight hours since I saw you. I miss you already.

The chocolates were the same kind that had survived my first trip to Arcadia.

The flowers Sebastian sent smelled like summer, and I kept them on my desk long after they started to droop and should have been thrown away.

The note I slept with under my pillow—until I worried about smudging the ink and put it in my memory box instead.

A PERFECT PRANK

"We need to start planning."

"Isn't it a little early in the year? We're barely into January."

"Charlie, it's never too early to plot. Let's start with a list of all the past senior pranks. Three years ago, they filled Dr. Mulcaster's office with Dixie cups of fruit punch. Unoriginal. Are you writing this down? The year after that they parked all the vans on the quad. Boring. And last year they put Vaseline on all the bio lab beakers. That's just mean. *Quel gâchis!*"

"What about when they put all those animals in the dining hall? It took the custodians a whole day to get the chickens out of the kitchen."

"That one was *éclatant!*"

"So what are *we* going to do?"

"I'm not sure yet. But it'll be unforgettable."

TWENTY

THE TIME BETWEEN WINTER BREAK and spring vacation was a gray blanket that spread over campus.

Everyone seemed slower. Formal dinner felt longer, classes more tedious. And winter sports were outright unbearable, which is why Julia and I skipped rec basketball as often as we could get away with it. Plus we were both terrible.

By February, it was easy to forget having ever felt warm or that the snow that pressed against the sides of the buildings and muffled the ground was ever anything other than dirty and depressing.

We were a campus of sleepwalkers for nearly three months each year—which is why there was a Headmistress's Holiday to wake us from our stupor.

Because she had done so well running the board for the fall musical, Julia was put in charge of operating the sound system three days a week for morning assembly. Most of the time, my advisor, Mr. Bates, let me keep her company in the control booth rather than making me sit with the rest of his advisee group in the theater. I didn't complain about classes or sports, and my dad and Melissa never called him about my grades. I asked little of Mr. Bates, so he demanded little of me.

While coaches got up to announce game scores and teachers stood behind the podium to talk about dress code and schedule changes, Julia and I sat in our little bubble high above the rest of St. Anne's.

Sometimes we did homework, but most of the time we read magazine quizzes to each other or pored over old yearbooks that had been abandoned and piled in the back corner.

By mid-January, my daydreaming had become a joke beyond Julia and me, and by February even the faculty were teasing me.

One morning, my Latin teacher, Dr. Merton, threw a pencil at my desk to get my attention.

"*Amor vincit omnia*, Charlotte. Love may conquer all, but it will not conquer your worksheet."

I had mumbled an apology, picked up my pen, and started to work.

Still, when I got to one particular translation I hadn't been able to help smiling. "*Beatitudo nos efficit omnes stultos.*" Happiness makes us all fools.

Fools and so much more.

"There you go again," Julia said, swinging back and forth in her chair, her feet resting on the soundboard.

"Sorry. I was thinking about Latin class."

Julia rolled her eyes and went back to studying the yearbook in her lap while I looked at the stage and tried to pay attention.

"Look."

"Huh?" I had been semi-watching and listening to Coach Archer talk about the latest JV volleyball game, but most of my thoughts had drifted back to Sebastian and the fact that he was visiting that night.

"Attention!" Julia dropped her feet and pointed at a picture in the yearbook.

"Yeah. Volleyball."

Julia shook her head. "Charlie, you're hopeless." She pushed her feet against the light display, ignoring that she lit up several buttons, in order to roll her chair closer to me. Her finger never left the page. "Look."

Julia's finger was on a black-and-white picture of the kitchen staff standing on the dining hall porch. I recognized Mrs. Peterson, the head cook, and a few others, but the rest were strangers to me. Mrs. Peterson's hair was different: longer, swept into a ponytail instead of cropped close to her ears.

"How old is this yearbook? Everyone looks younger."

"It's from Gus's freshman year, but that's not important," Julia whispered, even though we were at least thirty feet above anyone who could possibly hear us.

I glanced at the podium on the stage. My environmental

studies teacher was talking now. The top of his hairless head shone in the stage lights. I knew I probably should listen, but I turned back to Julia instead. "So what's so important about a shot of the kitchen staff?"

"Look at the truck in the background."

It was huge and white with cartoon animals on the back and sides.

"The cow looks kind of like a dinosaur."

"You are so out of it lately. Sebastian is rotting your brain." Julia jabbed her finger at the page. "Look, Cross Family Farm. Gus's boyfriend's last name was Cross. David Cross. They must have met when he came to make a delivery at St. Anne's. I knew his parents had a farm in Hyannis. It's not that far from where we catch the ferry—but I never put together how they met."

"Oh," I exclaimed. Not because I was surprised at Julia's find, but because it had taken me that long to realize that the truck was the same one that had been parked in front of Sebastian and me that day on the ferry. I took the yearbook from her without realizing I had reached for it. Same bright red. Same dented bumper and peeling lettering. It was definitely the same truck.

"Why—"

"Why is Mulcaster getting up?" Julia interrupted me. She stood so suddenly her chair rolled all the way to the back wall, hitting it with a thump.

I didn't look up from the book. "Hmm."

"*Merde!* She's doing it!" Julia leaned against the control panel. "She's reaching for the hat."

That got my attention. "You think?" I stood beside her, my chair drifting back until it bumped hers.

"Look." Julia pointed. "She's got one hand under the podium and she's been babbling about class attendance—"

"There it is!" I clapped as Dr. Mulcaster retrieved a huge hat, like the kind women wear to garden parties and horse races, from under the podium and stuck it on her head. She only wore that hat twice a year: once in the fall and then again in the winter. That awful, ugly hat, with its huge fake flowers and droopy brim, meant a day of canceled classes and no formal dinner. It meant no sports for the afternoon, no club period, and no study hall. It meant that the entire school, all five hundred of us, could do whatever we wanted on campus.

Julia and I were quiet long enough to hear her say, "Happy Headmistress's Holiday!"

"Hallelujah!" Julia shimmied, her arms raised above her head. "I don't have to take that English test. No stupid rec basketball. *Fantastique!*" She stopped dancing and put her hands on her hips. "We've got the whole rest of the day to do nothing. Anything."

Below us, the auditorium was in pandemonium as girls and teachers cheered. Any announcements Dr. Mulcaster tried to make were lost in the noise of people pushing to get out the doors.

There were only a few stragglers left in the stands when I got my great idea. "Julia, this is perfect. We can go to the farm."

"What?"

"David's farm. We can go talk to his mom and dad. You said you wanted to know more about Gus. We can ask them about her. If she spent a lot of time there, they probably knew her really well. And it can't be more than an hour—"

"Neither one of us has a car. We can't."

"We can borrow one. I'll drive. Marsha won't care. We'll be back before check-in."

"No."

"Wait. What? Really?"

"Charlie, I don't want to go."

"But—"

"Please don't make me explain."

"Okay."

"Okay, what?"

"Okay, I won't make you explain. I was just trying—"

"I know. *Merci.* I know."

You would think Dr. Mulcaster had said she was taking the whole school on a Caribbean cruise with all the shouting and music that pulsed out of the rooms in Campion Hall.

Julia shut the door right after I followed her into our room, muffling the chaos outside. She flopped down on her bed, not bothering to take off her shoes.

"So," I said, picking up Aloysius, who had fallen out of her bag when she dropped it in the middle of the floor. "What do you want to do on our last Headmistress's Holiday?"

Julia mumbled something incoherent.

"Great answer." I shook Aloysius to dust him off and then put him on her desk chair. Why had I brought up the farm anyway? I sat on the edge of my bed wishing I could knead out the knot in my stomach with my fist.

Julia turned over to her side. "I said that I don't really feel like doing much. Besides, *il fait froid!*"

This time I had a better, great idea.

I sat up. "You love the cold. Find your boots. We're going to the dining hall."

"I'm not—"

"Not for food—though we definitely need to grab stuff. For trays."

Realization came across Julia's face like the sun through a window blind being raised in the morning. "Really?"

Julia didn't actually have boots, so I wore my heaviest sneakers and gave her mine. We had to stuff socks in the toes, and then I had to borrow a ski coat for her from a junior on the second floor. We walked—or waddled really; we were both wearing so many layers—to the dining hall, stuffed our pockets with cookies, and then, when we thought no faculty or staff were looking, slid trays under our coats.

The sledding hill wasn't technically on campus, and we were technically not supposed to be there. Tray sledding had been forbidden my freshman year when a girl ended up in the hospital with a broken arm. I hadn't been since. But it was my last Headmistress's Holiday and Julia needed to smile and I needed to make things right again and let out the happiness that had bubbled in the core of me since New Year's.

We weren't the only ones with the great idea.

A group was already at the top of the hill, all seniors. Amy, Jacqueline, Rosalie, Piper, and Eun Sun, and three girls I recognized from English class and the fall musical all stood together in a huddle like a group of penguins gathered around an egg.

Their tight circle wasn't surprising. It was cold. They were probably protecting their faces from the wind. What made me pause was that they were talking like they all hung out regularly instead of existing at opposite sides of the dining hall and quad.

In my shock, I dropped my tray and had to scramble down the hill after it.

"Smooth, Charlotte," Piper shouted. I heard someone giggle as I started back up the hill, my eyes down so I wouldn't have to deal with one of Piper's drop-dead looks.

Julia, oblivious to the tension of our situation, or maybe defiant to it, ignored Piper as she walked by her, plunking her tray down to the left of the group and then plopping on top of it.

"Who wants to race?" she shouted, pushing her hat back off her forehead.

The group stopped talking.

"I'll race," said a girl in a green scarf. She placed her tray next to Julia's. "What does the winner get?"

"She's Queen of the Hill, of course," Julia replied as she adjusted Aloysius so his nubby antlers weren't caught in her pocket zipper. "Ready?"

The girl nodded so vigorously that the pom-pom on her hat swung across her face.

"*Un. Deux. Trois.* Holy—" Julia's laugh bounced off the snow. She hit a bump at the bottom of the hill, landing in a spectacular belly flop that made her look like she was making a facedown snow angel.

"That's only a five," Jacqueline yelled. "Terrible dismount."

I glanced at her, almost dropping my tray again. She looked at me, readjusted her earmuffs, and might have even smiled.

Maybe a truce had been granted—at least for the day.

Julia took a bow, but she stood up with too much momentum and fell backward into a snowdrift. The group on the hill laughed, even Rosalie. Everyone laughed except for Piper. She stood off to the side, leaning against a tree, her expression gray but not entirely unhappy.

A girl from English class went down the hill. Jacqueline only gave her a four.

Amy went, sliding within feet of the trees at the bottom. She jumped off her tray and kept running. Jacqueline gave her a nine.

Rosalie and Eun Sun raced each other down the hill. Both sevens.

I went against the girl in the green scarf and skidded over a patch of ice that sent me sliding toward the small creek.

"That's a five, Charlotte," Jacqueline said.

I was so happy she used my name that I didn't even care that my sneakers were soaking.

The time I raced Rosalie, I dragged my feet in the snow, letting her reach the bottom first. When she jumped off her sled, her arms raised in victory, she nodded at me as if she knew what I had done. I didn't say anything. Recognizing each other was enough for one day.

We kept sledding until the cookies in our pockets were crumbs and the fading sky hinted at night.

It had been a good, crazy, great idea.

Since winter break, Sebastian had driven out from Cambridge at least once or twice a week to visit with me during the hour of freedom between the end of study hall and check-in. Boys weren't allowed in the dorms, not even in winter, so sometimes we went to the art center, sometimes to the student lounge. But most of the time we stood outside because it was the only place we could be alone.

When he came to visit that night, both Julia and I were still high with adrenaline from sledding. I wanted to skip out to the oak tree where I knew he'd be waiting, but I stopped myself and tried instead not to walk too fast.

"Watch that you don't get frozen stuck to each other!" Julia yelled out our window before slamming it shut and letting the curtain fall.

"So, your day obviously wasn't exhausting enough," Sebastian said, reaching for me and rubbing the sides of my arms. His breath came out in little clouds. "Julia looks like she's dancing around your room. Look at her shadow." He pointed toward our window.

I didn't bother glancing. I wanted to look at him. No matter how many times he ended our phone calls with "See you tonight," no matter how many little gifts he sent—a set of paints, an art magazine, flowers, and more flowers—or how many times he signed an email "Can't wait to see you," I didn't fully trust he would really be there. I didn't trust it until I could touch him, and once I touched him, I couldn't take my hands off him.

"Charlie?" Sebastian said.

"Sorry. I think Julia got an extra handful of crack cookies when I wasn't looking."

"I don't think crack makes you hyper."

"No, they're these real cookies. They only make them on Headmistress's Holidays and they're sooooo good, they're addictive. So we call them crack cookies." I was talking twice as fast as I normally would. It had been that good a day, and the sky was clear and the stars were like pinpricks of light against all that black, and even though my face was cold and my toes were still frozen from that afternoon, the rest of me was warm.

"Ah." Sebastian wrapped his arms around me so tightly my own were pinned to my sides.

For a moment we just stood like that, rocking back and forth on the crunchy snow. Our breath melding together in puffs of white. I wondered if we looked as happy in that instant as Gus and David looked in the photo on Gus's shelves at Arcadia. I hoped so.

"Sebastian," I said, remembering the trip Julia and I had not taken that day, "did you know Gus's boyfriend had a farm nearby?"

He dropped his arms and started to pack a snowball with his bare hands. "Sure. I guess I knew it was kind of close." He threw the snowball against the side of the oak tree so hard snow sprayed us both in the face. "Sorry."

"Why . . . never mind," I said, wiping my cheek off. "It's not important." I wasn't going to ruin a perfect day.

"You're a very odd girl. Who asks very random and odd questions," Sebastian said as he packed another snowball with his red fingers. This one he threw at a car parked in the dorm driveway, missing it by a couple of feet. "There goes my base-ball career."

"And . . ." I said.

"And?"

"And that's why . . ."

"That's why what?"

"And that's why you like me." I tugged off my mittens and took his wet, cold hands in my own.

"Oh no, I like you because when you're a big-deal artist I can tell people I used to make out with you. Maybe get on a reality—"

I kissed him to shut him up. And I kissed him because I'd wanted to kiss him since the last time we'd stopped.

To: cryder@stannes.edu

From: jbuchanan@buchananfoundation.org

Date: February 25

Subject: RISD, JULIA, Etc.

I spoke to my contact at RISD. They've got all your materials, including the reference letter I promised you.

Waiting is the hardest part. Don't worry, kiddo, you're a shoo-in.

Could you get Julia to finish up her Wellesley application? I told Teresa I'd ask. Knowing you're on it will make life calmer in the office and on the home front.

I want you two to get out some more. Stop eating all that microwave junk. Sophie's sending a gift card for that café near campus. It'll go to your mailbox. Julia might lose it.

If you need anything, Charlie Girl, call my cell or leave a message with anyone at the foundation. They all know who you are.

Boom

WHAT DO YOU WANT?

"What do you want for your birthday?"

"Oh no, don't try to distract me. We're finishing your application tonight and then proofing your essay. All this is going in tomorrow."

"When'd you become such a bore? Besides, I'm not even sure I want to go to college right away. I might take a year or two off."

"Really?"

"So, what do you want for your birthday?"

"Are you asking as Julia or are you asking as Pip, Sebastian's sister?"

"I am asking as a representative of the family."

"That makes you sound like you work for the mob."

"I kind of do."

"Maybe we can do something quiet next time we go out to Arcadia. Sophie can make—"

"Quiet? *Absolument pas.* You're turning eighteen."

"Yeah, but my birthday falls during March break."

"So we'll celebrate here that Friday."

"Campus is closed that Friday."

"*Exactement.*"

TWENTY-ONE

THE LIBRARY WAS THE REASON a lot of girls
came to St. Anne's, or at least it was the reason their parents
made them. It was a Gothic castle, an imposing structure that
belonged in a European city. Inside was a mess of hidden corners, a sky-touching rotunda, and a vast basement that confused
me every time I tried to find my way from one end to the other.

It was also one of the few buildings on campus that Julia and
I hadn't found our way into at night. The first Friday of spring
break, three days before my actual birthday, it was almost disappointing how easy it was for us to sneak in.

Julia had propped open a window in the reading room that
morning. We tossed our backpacks through, the bottles in them
clanking, then the sleeping bags, and lastly we climbed in ourselves. That was it.

There was no need to whisper. All the other students had
left that afternoon, and only a handful of teachers stuck around

campus. But there was something about the orderly rows of books, the burned smell of old pages, and the yellow haze of the security lights that demanded quiet.

"*Viens par ici.*" Julia gestured for me to follow her.

When we reached the rotunda, she took a right turn into the Art History stacks, and as soon as I stepped into the wood-paneled room I saw the three figures, one standing, two sitting, in a circle of light around a camping lantern.

Julia rushed ahead of me, threw down her sleeping bag, and sat on top of it.

"Happy birthday, Charlie!"

"Shhhhh. Do you want to get caught?" I recognized Jacqueline's voice before I could completely make out her face. It wasn't until I reached the end of the study tables that I realized who the others were: Amy and Rosalie.

"Oh, Julia," I whispered, adjusting my sleeping bag against my side to buy myself some time. "Why, why, why did you invite them?" The night was going to be a disaster.

"Campus is deserted. Quit being a worrywart," said Julia to Jacqueline. She rolled out her sleeping bag and lay down on it, splayed across the ground like a starfish.

Jacqueline crossed her arms and leaned against the old radiator behind her. The other girls were silent as Julia sat up and began to pull out the bottles that had been clanking in her backpack.

I shuffled forward and dropped my things near a row of encyclopedias.

"Hey," I said, waving at the two cross-legged figures on the ground and the one standing by the window.

Jacqueline shrugged. "Happy birthday."

We all listened to Julia set out cups, open bottles, and pour. From the stinging smell, I knew she wasn't making fruit punch.

"Happy birthday, Charlotte," Amy said, standing up to give me a quick hug, and that was all it took. Jacqueline hugged me, and then, after hesitating, Rosalie did, too.

When she moved to let go, I made her stay a beat more, hoping she would understand that it meant I was sorry.

"Well," Rosalie said. "This is awkward."

"Thanks for coming. It means—"

"Your boyfriend called me . . . and Amy and Jacqueline, too. I guess Julia told him about tray sledding, and he thought . . . who knows what he thought." She frowned. "How he got Jacqueline to come—"

"Considering she hates me, too," I said, crossing my arms. "I have no idea—"

"I don't hate you," Rosalie interrupted me. "Remember, you're the one that dumped me."

"I didn't *dump* you." I leaned against the rows of art encyclopedias behind me more for comfort than support. "I'm just . . . look." I kicked my sleeping bag just to have something to do with my feet and ran my hands across the spines from "C" to "T" just to have something to do with my hands.

"I didn't *mean* to dump you. I did a bad job of trying to

make people happy." I looked at Julia shaking one of the bottles so hard her whole body moved. "And balancing being a good friend." I pushed the "M" volume back and forth on the shelf, not looking at Rosalie. "A really, really awful, terrible job."

Rosalie slid out a book and passed it back and forth between her hands. "'Terrible' doesn't begin to—"

"I don't know what more to say. I'm sorry."

"K." Rosalie shifted the book a few more times, then used it to gesture toward the others. "Let's just have some fun, eh? First night of our last spring break."

Now Julia was perched on the edge of a study table, a paper cup in her hand. Jacqueline and Amy were on the floor with their own cups beside them. They weren't smiling, but they weren't frowning, either.

"Okay," I said. She had at least listened to me. That was something.

When we joined the other girls, it was still weird. But it was a little better than before.

By the time Sebastian arrived with his roommate Vinay, a guy who talked and acted like a California surfer but was actually from outside Chicago, we had all finished a cup of Julia's "library moonshine." When they walked in from the rotunda, Amy was demonstrating how long she could hold a back bend, while Rosalie and Jacqueline had a headstand contest. Julia was standing on the radiator and reading from a book of puns she'd found on one of the chairs.

"A hole has been found in the bathroom wall. The police are looking into it."

"I'm reading a book about anti-gravity. It's impossible to put down."

I was laughing so hard that when I saw Sebastian, I had to pull myself up using the side of a table. "Hey. *Pour moi?*" I kissed him and slid a large bakery box out of his hands.

"Yeah. Cupcakes. I picked them out," said Vinay. "Happy birthday, Charlie. Eighteen. So now you can buy porn and cigarettes."

"I can vote now, too," I replied, giving him a one-armed hug around the large box. "Don't forget the civic duty part. It's nice to finally meet the famous Vinay in person. You pick up Sebastian's phone more than he does."

"Only because his side of the room is neater than mine," Sebastian said, kissing me again, letting his hand rest on my hip. "I'm not surprised he forgot the voting part."

"I thought of them, 'cause those are my gifts, man," Vinay said, zipping open his messenger bag and handing me a cigar and a plastic-wrapped magazine.

"Thanks," I said, turning the magazine so the cover was against my chest. "I'll give the cigar to Boom. And the magazine . . . I hide under my mattress?"

"Oh, it's feminist-approved porn. My older sister's a women's studies major. She picked it out. You should display it with pride." Vinay pointed to the girls, who were now sitting on their sleeping bags and watching us. "Aren't you going to introduce me to the rest of the party?"

I was leaning comfortably against Sebastian when I thought of it. He was warm and I was warm, full of sugar and library moonshine. I didn't want to move ever, but my idea was too fantastic not to share.

"Julia." I thought I had whispered, but everybody turned to look at me. "Didn't Gus write poetry for Dr. Blanche for her senior project?"

"*Oui.*"

"Well. They. Keep. All. The. Projects. Here." I pointed to the floor so she would understand.

"They have them in back near the war books," Amy said from the other side of our circle, where she was sitting very close to a very happy-looking Vinay.

Julia grabbed my elbow.

"I'm a library aid," Amy said. "I know where they are."

Vinay looked at her like she had just revealed she was a superhero.

Amy struggled to stand up, swaying enough for Vinay to raise a hand for her to grab.

"Thank you," she said before she started walking.

Julia and I fumbled to our feet and followed her.

*　*　*

"Wait. Wait. Wait." Julia was laughing so hard that her words came out in gasps. "*Écoute.* Listen.

> "There once was a man from Nantucket, whose . . .
> Ha, ha, Dr. Blanche. I would never.
> But as limericks go,
> That one steals the show.
> And now you'll know it forever."

"I want to read one," Jacqueline said, snatching the thin book from Julia's hands. She flipped until about halfway through. "Really?"

"What?" Rosalie leaned over her.

Jacqueline elbowed her away. "This one's called 'His Feet.'

> "His feet are always dirty.
> Always caked with soil,
> Always covered with grass.
> His hands.
> His hands are always callused,
> Always bent as if holding a tool.
> His skin.
> His skin always smells of all my favorite things:
> Salt. Earth. And time.
> When he's with me, it's always spring."

"Who writes a poem about feet?" Jacqueline looked up, her forehead wrinkled, her glasses slipping down her nose.

"My turn," Amy said, pulling the book gently from Jacqueline's hands. "Oh, this one sounds pretty." She cleared her throat. "Okay, 'Be Not Proud.'

> "Death be not proud, so the poems say.
> The poems I read on a summer afternoon,
> Just me, my boat, and the wide-open soon.
> And I can't help but wonder, what is death this day?
> I am invincible on the water. The sun guides my way.
> At one with the wind, sun, and waves.
> To feel so alive—this is all I crave.
> Death be not proud, not on such a day."

I felt Sebastian's arms stiffen around me and I knew that, like me, he was searching Julia's face for a reaction. She had her eyes closed and her face tucked toward her shoulder. What she was feeling was as fuzzy as my thoughts.

"Dude, that's deep. I got the next one," Vinay said. He flipped through Gus's book until he found another semi-dirty limerick. Then I read a haiku and Jacqueline took another turn. Everyone read but Sebastian. With each poem his arms around me tightened, and I could feel his pulse through the veins in his wrists.

I wanted to stop for his sake. But then Julia started smiling, and then she laughed. So I smiled and laughed, too. The whole time I held Sebastian's hand as if my touch could protect him from the outside from whatever was hurting from within.

We read until the library moonshine was gone and our heads were too heavy to hold up anymore.

I couldn't have been asleep for more than an hour when I felt someone shaking me. "Hmmmm."

"Charlie, come with me."

I opened my eyes to see Sebastian's face inches from my own. I smiled and then closed them again. I was so sleepy.

He shook my shoulder once more, this time with a little more force. I grumbled into my sleeping bag, but sat up.

Sebastian gestured for me to follow him. He grabbed his sleeping bag, so I grabbed mine, too. We walked across the rotunda to the room on the other side. My feet felt like I had concrete boots on, and my mouth like I had fallen asleep with a sock in it. I was going to feel terrible in the morning, but I was too tired to care.

Sebastian dropped his sleeping bag between the first stacks of books and sat cross-legged on it, running his hand through his hair in the way he always did when he was thinking. I tried to snap out my sleeping bag like a waiter spreading a tablecloth, but I ended up hitting the bookshelves as much as the floor. I shrugged and plopped down, my crossed legs mirroring Sebastian's.

He pulled the edge of my sleeping bag toward him, making me fall on his lap. "Still tired, birthday girl."

I suddenly was not, so I raised my head and kissed him. My head was a different kind of cloudy when his lips were against mine. His knee pressed into my hip, but it was a good kind of hurt, one that made me sure I was awake. I twisted myself in his lap so I could unbutton his shirt. I slid it off him, one arm, then the other, all the while thinking how good he smelled and how warm his skin felt.

He shifted so I was leaning against a shelf of books and started to pull my shirt over my head.

"Sebastian, wait."

"You okay?" He dropped my sleeves.

"Call me old-fashioned, but I'm not losing my virginity with the *Autobiography of Benjamin Franklin* looking down on us."

He pulled my shirt back down so my stomach was covered and then shifted a little away from me. "Charlie, I didn't think we were going . . . or that you were a . . . or that you weren't either . . . I—"

"Sebastian, unless you count Aston Bose kissing me behind my dad's garage the summer after freshman year, you're my first boyfriend."

"Well, now I really hope I didn't mess up your birthday gift." He reached into the bottom of his sleeping bag and pulled out a small jewelry box. "Open it."

I did. Nestled on a tray of navy velvet was a set of earrings, diamonds set in a cluster of gold seashells. Looking at them, I felt like I was choking.

"Sebastian, I can't keep these," I said once my voice returned.

"You don't like them?" He grabbed my hands and pulled me so our foreheads touched. "I wanted it to be a big deal. You're turning eighteen, and you're basically responsible for Julia making it through her senior year and you're her best friend. It's the least I could do."

"I couldn't even get her to finish her college essay on time." I tasted tears in the corners of my lips. I hadn't realized I was crying. I didn't know why I was crying. "They're beautiful, Sebastian. Thank you, so, so much, but I can't keep them." I forced myself to laugh as I wiped at my face. "They cost more than my dad's truck."

Sebastian sat up so quickly that he hit his head against the row of biographies behind him. "Ow." He rubbed the back of his head. "So I can't get you a gift because your dad drives a junky truck?"

My back stiffened. I dropped the box and moved away from him. The shelf of books behind me was the only thing that stopped me from going farther. "Do you know how stuck-up you sound?"

"Jesus, Charlie. That came out wrong." He kept a hand pressed against the back of his head. "I was . . . was hoping for a better reaction. I spent a long time picking them out."

I felt dizzy, like the room was a merry-go-round with me in its center.

Sebastian raised a hand as if he were going to touch my face.

"Please. Please don't touch me right now," I whispered, turning to curl my side into the books, so I didn't have to look at him. "It's more than your stupid truck comment. It's the stuff you said about Julia being my responsibility—"

"Charlie, I was joking."

"It's not a joke. It's a lot, Sebastian, to be responsible for another person." I glanced at him out of the corner of my eye.

"You're right. Okay." His face was etched with hurt, but I had to keep going.

"You, Boom. Maybe Julia doesn't need protection. Maybe she doesn't need saving. Maybe she just needs a friend. That's all I can be to her is a friend . . . I'm just as confused as everyone else sometimes."

"Okay."

"If you were looking for someone perfect, then maybe . . ." I pressed a hand against a book spine, grateful for the scratchiness of cracked leather under my fingers. "Maybe, I'm not good enough for you."

Sebastian picked up the earring box and pressed it between his palms, his head bowed. For minutes the only sounds were the occasional squawks from the birds that claimed the quad as their own during the night.

Finally, he spoke, his eyes still on the earring box. "Charlie, most of the time I think you're *too* good for me."

"I want to believe that," I said, my temples pounding. "But right now . . ." I stood, grasping the bookshelf when my head started spinning. "I don't." I reached down with one hand and pulled half my sleeping bag under an arm; the other half I let drag on the floor as I walked away.

"Charlie," I heard Sebastian call, but I didn't pause in my stumble across the rotunda.

When I unrolled my sleeping bag next to Julia, she said nothing. When I settled into the flannel, with its stubborn scent of campfire smoke and plastic tent, she didn't even open her eyes. But when I finally lay still, staring at the library ceiling, my heart racing so furiously I felt like it might pound out of my chest, she scooted until her sleeping bag overlapped mine. She worked her arms out and threw them around me, holding me until I fought my way to sleep.

TWENTY-TWO

"JULIA TOLD ME YOU'D BE here." Rosalie dropped into the pew. "Seriously, who does a walk of shame away from her own birthday party at six in the morning . . . to a chapel?" She looked around as if noticing for the first time where we were.

"It's my hiding place," I said, leaning forward on my arms, which were folded across the pew in front of me. I turned my head so I could look at Rosalie. "Did the other girls take off?"

"Yeah, but Amy had to be pried off Vinay. Poor guy didn't know what to do with himself." She snorted and crossed her arms. She was still wearing the T-shirt she had slept in, with a zip-up St. Anne's hoodie over it. "Sebastian was gone even before you were. Wanna tell me what happened last night?"

I shook my head, then turned my face so it was buried in my arms. My head felt like a giant was trying to crush my skull between his two hands. The wood smelled like furniture polish. It was an oddly comforting smell. "We got in a fight."

"About?" Rosalie scooted down until her bent knees each rested against a hymnbook in the rack on the back of the pew. She crossed her arms again, letting me know she was prepared to wait me out even if I didn't want to answer.

"He was snobby . . . and asks too much . . . and sometimes . . . he's not telling me something . . . he cages up and I know he's not being a hundred percent honest."

"Charlotte, nobody is. We are solitary creatures that come together in packs so we can survive as a species. We'll do anything to preserve the social status quo, including omit, deny, and lie. Complete honesty would be detrimental to the survival of the race."

I twisted my head and raised an eyebrow at her.

"What? I want to major in anthropology. It's a theory I'm working on."

"What happened to psychologist Bernard?"

Rosalie examined the ends of her hair. "I'm over my crush on Mr. Campion. Our imaginary children turned out to be brats."

It hurt my head to smile. I set my forehead back on my folded arms, grateful for their coolness. "I don't even know what I'm doing with him. He's probably going to be president and I'm probably going to get denied from the one school I really want to go to and have no idea what to do with my life." I breathed heavily out my nose. "Look what happened with my parents.

My mom thought she could handle being married to a guy who loved working on cars. That sure turned out well."

"Who do you think you're fooling with the tough-guy act? Look. Do you like him?" Rosalie said, dropping her knees from the back of the pew and sitting up as abruptly as she had sat down.

"Yeah," I mumbled into my arms.

"Do you love him?"

I paused as if I had to think, but I knew the answer even before she asked the question. "Maybe."

"Then stop being such a wimp and just jump in. What the hell do you have to lose, eh?"

"Umm, my sanity, my dignity. My concentration and ability to say no were gone a long time ago," I said, sitting up and clasping my hands in my lap. "Whatever we've got, Sebastian and I, it's not even cracked and I'm worried about breaking it."

"What's that phrase? 'If it's not shattered, don't glue it.'" Rosalie nudged my shoulder with her own, keeping her eyes on the shadow-crossed altar.

"If it's not broken, don't fix it?"

"You know what I'm trying to say."

"Yeah," I said, staring up at that endless ceiling. A ceiling built to contain prayers and heartaches, dreams and wishes. "I do."

After the echoes of our words faded, the walls and the stained glass windows themselves seemed to press down with silence. It

wasn't a bad silence. It was the kind of quiet that happens natu-
rally on long road trips when the sound of the wind through a
sunroof is conversation enough.

I was the one to break the stillness. "When'd you get to be
so smart?"

"Must've happened when you stopped bringing my IQ down
with those dumb movies you like to watch."

"Those aren't movies. They're *films*." This time I bumped
her shoulder, shoving her hard enough that she had to catch
herself on the other side of the pew.

"When did *you* turn into such a brute? I think you left a
mark." Rosalie pretended to examine her arm for a bruise.

"Does this mean you don't hate me anymore?" I said.

Rosalie chewed on her lip before answering. "I didn't hate
you. I was just really, really pissed at you for a while."

I made as if I was going to bump her again, and she braced
her arms against the pew in front of us.

"Ugh," I said, groaning as I dropped my head back. "I feel
like death and I have a four-hour bus ride."

"Need a lift to the station?"

"You sure?"

"Yeah, it's out of my way anyway," Rosalie said, looking at
her watch. "Come on. Julia's car is coming in five, so we'll go
say good-bye, then hit the road."

As Rosalie started to stand up, I grabbed her hand and pulled
her down into a hug.

"Thank you."

"You don't have to thank me, Charlotte," she said softly against my neck, all traces of sarcasm gone. "Getting your heart broken isn't the worst thing in the world. But not taking that risk? That's just pathetic."

Rosalie let go first. "You obviously haven't brushed your teeth today, 'cause you have dragon breath, so why don't you do that before we're stuck in a car together. Oh, and you're buying me a coffee, a huge, giant coffee with more sugar and cream than necessary, eh?"

"Done and done," I said.

We stuck to the side of the buildings as we darted across the quad back to the library and the south gate where Julia's driver would meet her. I knew we were supposed to be keeping quiet in case there was any faculty left on campus, but every time Rosalie peeked around the side of a wall with her fingers held up like a fake gun I laughed. She might not have been a real spy, but for a few minutes her pretending to be one helped me forget about him.

For a few minutes, I got to be happy to be running around a place I never wanted to leave on a spring morning I didn't want to end.

PHONE CALL #1

He called me later that morning, and he kept calling until I finally picked up that afternoon when I was home in New Hampshire.

"I'm sorry." His voice was a saw cutting through knotted wood.

I said nothing.

"Charlie, Charlotte, look, I didn't mean what I said. About Julia and you being responsible. And I know I sounded like a rich jerk about the earrings and the truck. I'm sorry."

I didn't reply.

"Look. I speak first and think much, much, much later. It's a character flaw. I'm working on it."

I didn't feel like laughing.

"Okay. It's too soon for jokes . . . I know it doesn't excuse what I said, but I really did just want to get you something amazing. You like to collect stuff and you're always taking shells from Arcadia, so the earrings, they reminded me of you." He paused. "And I meant what I said about you being so good for Julia. She hasn't been this happy since . . . since before the accident."

My insides loosened a little, and I put down the throw pillow I had been hugging since I answered his call.

"I'm sorry. Charlie, you said that you were confused. Some-times I am, too."

"I'm sorry, too. I shouldn't have gotten so defensive." I for-got that the phone Bradley gave me was much nicer than my old one and I didn't have to shout into it.

"No, you were—"

"No, I was—"

"Tree pose?"

"Excuse me?"

"Buchanan truce. Tree pose."

"Right. Tree pose." I could picture him pacing in front of the Buchanans' Boston house, kicking his feet against the uneven bricks that lined the sidewalks of Beacon Hill. "It's okay. I understand."

"I know you do. That's why this works. You get it."

"I get it."

"Let me come up and visit you. Let me come up for your actual, real birthday. I want to see where you live."

I looked around me, noticing not for the first time how the TV room couch sagged in the middle and Melissa's collector's plates did nothing to hide the water stain on the far wall. The room smelled a little like the boys' sneakers and forgotten lunch bags, and I had left the door open to the den, which meant I would be finding action figures and small footprints all over my unmade futon. I picked a pillow off the floor and threw it on the couch and nudged a dog-eared comic book under my dad's recliner with my toe.

"I'll bring Julia," he said, as if he could sense my thoughts. "She's driving us all nuts already. It's like she goes through Charlie withdrawal."

I perched on the edge of the coffee table in front of one of the windows and ran a hand over the scratched glass surface. I heard Melissa and my dad drive up before I saw the truck pull in.

"Charlie? You still there?"

My dad whistled as he slammed the driver's-side door shut and grabbed a box from the bed of the truck. Melissa came around the other side swinging a large white paper bag with bottles and the Styrofoam head she practiced styling hair on poking out the top. He said something to her that made her laugh and knock his cap off his head. He was grinning as he put down the box and dusted the cap off on his pants before swatting at her with it.

They were ridiculous, but they were *my* ridiculous.

"Maybe."

"Okay. I can work with maybe."

TWENTY-THREE

"**CHARLOTTE EVELYN RYDER, STOP PACING** or I'll tie your feet together." Melissa used the same tone she took with Sam and AJ when they refused to brush their teeth. "If you have to be a nervous Nellie, go outside and do it in the driveway where you won't wear a hole in my floor." Her platinum blond hair was twisted into a loose, complicated braid that fell like a shiny rope down the middle of her back. At her part, her dark roots were already creeping in.

She reminded me of an elf as she moved around the kitchen, opening and shutting the oven door, poking one of her manicured fingers into the casserole, reaching for the salt on a shelf way too high for her.

The restlessness was unlike her. She was the steady calm that reined in the craziness. Whenever one of the boys got a scrape or broke something or played too close to the road, she was always the first responder. The time my dad nearly cut a finger off with a table saw, she was the only one who could handle all the blood on the long ride to the hospital.

But on the day of my birthday party, she was nervous, too.

Impulsively, I hugged her, resting my cheek on her back just long enough to mumble, "Thank you. I really, really appreciate it. This is already the best birthday ever."

"Oh, honey," she said, putting down the knife she had just picked up and turning around to hug me back. "Of course. Now get out of here before you drive me batty or make me cry and ruin my mascara."

For once, I didn't argue with her. I grabbed a carrot stick from the cutting board and tapped her on the head with it before crossing the hall and leaning in the doorway to the TV room. I shoved the carrot in my mouth, crunching loudly.

Sam and AJ were both on their stomachs on the braided carpet, poised like penguins preparing to slide down a hill. They had their hands under their chins and were gazing with open mouths at the lion stalking a zebra on the TV screen. I finished chewing and I waited until the lion was airborne before I jumped into the room, landing between them.

"Roooooaaaaar!"

"Ahhhhh!" Sam screamed while AJ curled into a ball like an armadillo in defense mode. Once each saw that the other had been scared, they both jumped up and began hanging on me wherever they could.

"Not funny," said AJ as he jerked on my right arm. "You

made us miss the best part."

"Yeah, the best part," Sam echoed while he tried to ball my left hand into a fist and make my arm swing so I punched myself.

"I thought it was hilarious." I twisted my arms free and gave each of them a noogie.

"Mom!" they screamed in unison, darting out of my reach.

"Boys, don't mess up that room before Charlotte's friends get here," Melissa shouted from the kitchen.

Rubbing his head, Sam asked, "When's your boyfriend going to get here?"

"Yeah," said AJ. "Where's your boooooyfriend? Mom let us make the cake and she said I could light one of the candles. I'm hungry."

"My *friends* are late." I held my arms up like I was preparing for a boxing match.

"Noooo, Mom said you had a boy—" AJ was interrupted by the sound of tires in the driveway.

I took a deep breath and moved toward the mudroom, but just as I reached the door, Sam and AJ attacked. Sam attached himself to my left leg, plopping down on my left foot, while AJ did the same on my right. Each wrapped his arms around my calves like they were masts on a lifeboat and they were clinging for life.

"Guys," I hissed. "Very funny. Let go. I have to go get my friends." Prying at their little fingers got me nowhere. I tried shaking my legs a little, but the boys were too heavy for me to do anything but keep shuffling forward like a prisoner in shackles.

"I'm stronger than a giant octopus," said AJ.

"I'm a gigantic koala," Sam added, tightening his grip. I could feel his fingernails through my jeans.

"If you guys don't let go, I'm going to fix the TV so Animal Planet never—" The doorbell ringing interrupted me. I tried swaying my legs from side to side to knock them off. It didn't work. "I won't forget this," I hissed. When I opened the door, Julia, Sebastian, and Vinay were standing in the middle of the porch, the part where water collected each time it rained. All three were staring at my feet.

"Hi, guys."

"Nice footwear." Sebastian pointed at my legs, and I could feel the boys muffling their giggles against my shins.

"These things? I only wear them around the house." I tried knocking AJ and Sam together, but I couldn't get my knees close enough. I gave up. "Vinay, I didn't know you were coming."

"Yeah." He shuffled his sneakers on the uneven porch. "I'm a buffer or something in case you were still pissed at my dick-head friend here." He jerked his thumb in Sebastian's direction.

"Dickhead?" said AJ, taking his face away from my leg.

"Oh, whoa, sorry, little dude. Don't, like, repeat that to your mom or dad." Vinay's cheeks turned red under his tan skin.

"They're parrots. They repeat everything," I said.

"They're parrots. They repeat everything," Sam said.

"Well, I know for a fact that parrots are very ticklish." Julia bent down and went right for where AJ's T-shirt had rolled up, exposing his stomach. He started laughing so hard he was snorting as he lost his grip on my leg and fell on his back on the porch. Julia then tickled Sam until he, too, was rolling on the floor, begging her to stop.

When she finally did, the boys looked up at her from their splayed positions, absolute adoration on their faces.

"Your coat has holes in it," Sam said, pointing up at Julia's jacket.

"Sam, that's—"

Julia interrupted me. "That's because the witch who gave it to me put magic in the holey parts."

AJ turned over on his stomach, pushing the front of his body up so he looked up at Julia. "I like your coat. Will you marry me?"

Julia laughed her champagne laugh, and for the first time since Sebastian had asked me if they could visit I felt the knot in my stomach relax. "You guys want to come in? Dinner will be ready soon."

The boys latched on to Julia, one on each arm, pulling her into the TV room. Vinay followed. Sebastian waited until the others were inside, and as he came through the doorway, he kissed me, sending warmth from my lips to the tips of my toes.

"Hi," he whispered, his lips still by my ear.

I shivered. "Hi."

He squeezed my hand and followed me inside.

AJ insisted on sitting next to Julia. Sebastian was next to me. Vinay ended up next to my dad, who barely said three words the entire dinner. All I caught of the one-sided conversation was a series of "likes" and "whoas" and "awesomes." I was too busy trying to keep Sam's hands off Sebastian's plate and AJ's hands off Julia so she could eat to tell Vinay to talk about baseball or power tools if he wanted a response.

The casserole wasn't Melissa's worst, and that was something to be grateful for. Everyone politely chewed, politely complimented her cooking, and politely drank a lot of water. No one had seconds.

The party was officially over after Sam and AJ had licked the frosting off of all eighteen candles and the elastics on the cardboard hats they insisted we all wear started to break.

As soon as Melissa began clearing the plates and covering what was left of the lopsided cake, AJ and Sam started tugging on Julia to go play in the sandpit in the backyard.

"Guys. Guys! My friends and I are going to go for a drive. Maybe go to the old ski lodge. You'll see them when we get back." I tried to unpeel their fingers from Julia's arms.

"But . . ." Sam's face fell, but his grip didn't ease.

"You know who's fantastic in a sandpit?" Julia bent down so she was Sam's height.

"Who?"

"Sebastian."

Sam looked up at Sebastian, then at Julia, his mouth twisted as if he was still waiting for the punch line.

"No, really," said Julia. "We used to build these huge sand castles on our beach and Sebastian was always chief architect." Julia peered over her shoulder at Sebastian, who was standing close enough for me to feel his sleeve against the inside of my wrist.

Sebastian shifted, his fingers brushing mine. "Well yeah, I think Charlie and I are—"

"Okay." Sam interrupted him, nodding solemnly. He let go of Julia and grabbed Sebastian's hand. "You can be the triceratops."

"You can play, too." AJ patted Vinay's arm. "I like you."

"*Eh bien.*" Julia clapped her hands. "I guess Charlie and I are off for some girl time. Let's go." She didn't wait for a response. Just disappeared out the front door.

"I'm sorry," I mouthed at Sebastian as Sam tugged him toward the back.

"You can be a triceratops, which means you have three horns, but I get to be the T. rex, which means I can eat you," I heard Sam explaining, just before Julia and I climbed in the truck.

I parked as close to the Wycliffe Mountain ski lodge as possible. The truck was the only car in the lot, which was more dirt and

piles of rocks and broken branches than asphalt. The owners
had gone bankrupt when I was in middle school, and the place
had been left to nature and partiers ever since.

When we slammed our doors shut, the sound echoed off
the mountains. It took Julia and me ten minutes to hike up to
the top of the first trail, following a path of faded beer cans and
deep snowmobile ruts, and another few minutes to figure out
how to scramble into one of the rusty ski lift buckets without
landing in a patch of lingering snow. Spring always came late
in the north.

Once we were rocking back and forth, Julia leaned against
the far side of the bucket and put her legs across my thighs.
"C'est le bonheur." She closed her eyes and tilted back her head.
"It smells like floor cleaner up here."

I pretended to shove her legs off my lap. "Those are pine
trees!"

She opened her eyes and lowered her head. "I didn't say I
didn't like it. *J'adore nettoyer le plancher.*" She dug a heel into the
side of my leg for emphasis. "This is nice. Just me. Just you. I
never get you to myself anymore."

"It's always me and you, Julia. *Contra mundum.* I promised
you that doesn't change." I slid my hands over the safety bar
we had ducked under to get in the bucket until they were as
cold as the metal. "You showed me your hiding place. This is
mine."

"Contra mundum," she repeated, dropping her legs and sitting

up so our sides were touching, our legs dangling into space over the edge of the seat. "So your place is a chapel, too."

I paced my legs so they kicked out in time with hers. I never thought of it that way, but Julia was right. This was my chapel. The mountains, which were capped with snow even in August, were my altar. The place where the top of the evergreens met the sky was as stunning as stained glass. The ski lift was my pew. It was where I came after I got into St. Anne's and had to decide whether or not I could ever leave.

The ski lodge was where I thought about the past and day-dreamed about the future, but it took Julia saying so for me to realize it was holy.

Julia tapped my foot with her own. "So, your folks are *très, très* nice."

"Yeah. I think I'll keep them." I pressed my cold hands to my cheeks.

"I was just wondering how much you told them about us?"

"Who?"

"Your parents."

"No, I meant who did I tell them about?" I said.

"Us. Us. How much have you told them about the *Great Buchanans*." Julia waved her arms in the exaggerated motion of a conductor starting a concert.

I stopped swinging my legs. "Well they know Sebastian is my boyfriend. And that you're my best friend and that your family is wicked generous." I nudged her with my shoulder.

"Actually, Melissa feels bad that Sophie gives us so many care packages. She's threatened to send homemade cookies."

Julia didn't smile.

"What's wrong?"

She pressed her hands between her legs, looking down like a person in prayer. "It's just the parties. Mummy and Boom doing whatever obsessive thing they're doing with the foundation—it's not real. It's just what we do to try to forget. It was nice today to be your best friend Julia and not Julia Buchanan."

I glanced down at the ground, noticing how the melting snow had formed a barrier around a small pool of water beneath our seat. If it had been a little deeper, perhaps I could have seen my face in the reflection. I turned back to her and nodded. "Yeah, it was nice."

Julia looked up from her lap. "Let's go away."

"Where? I promised Melissa I'd babysit for the rest of the break."

"No." She laughed. "I don't mean now, now. After graduation, let's travel. Only the two of us. We can go wherever for however long we want. Just being Julia and Charlie, *les grandes aventurières.*"

I shifted into the corner of the lift, so I could look at her straight on. "Are you being serious? What about Wellesley? What about RISD? If I even get in."

"You'll get in. Of course you'll get in. They'd be *imbéciles* not to see how amazing you are," she said, smacking the safety bar for emphasis. "We can both defer. Mummy and Boom will definitely say yes if they know you're going. They'll handle the money and everything if you're worried—"

"It's not about money, Julia. What about my family . . . and Sebastian? I know it hasn't been that long . . . and I have no idea what will happen, but . . ." I trailed off. I didn't know how to finish.

Julia patted my hand. "You're cute when you ramble. My charming brother can visit us wherever we may be over his breaks. I even promise to leave you two alone for scheduled makeout sessions."

"You're crazy," I said, but already I was imagining.

Julia continued as if she didn't hear me. "Mummy and Boom have friends in London, and we can stay with Nanny's cousin in Paris. I'd let you spend an entire week in the Louvre."

"I'd need a month . . . or so I've read," I said.

"Charlie, I'm serious." She took both of my hands and clapped them together between her own. "Say you'll at least think about it. I want to run away and I want my best friend with me."

I would have promised her the moon, if it had been mine to give.

I nodded. "Yes."

"Yes, you'll go, or yes you'll think about it?"

"Yes, I'll think about it."

She flung an arm around me, making the bucket dip

dangerously forward.

When we finally stopped swinging, I said, "We should get back soon. Sebastian and Vinay have probably had their fill of sandpit dinosaurs." I pinched her right above her elbow just like Sam and AJ had taught me.

"Ow! That hurt." She tried to pinch me back, but I scooted to the other side of the seat and held up my arms in defense.

"Just imagine how long the plane ride to Asia is going to be if I keep pinching you to keep you awake."

"Asia?"

"Or maybe Argentina. We'll see."

"Five more minutes." She patted beside her.

I slid back over until we were once again shoulder to shoulder.

Five silent minutes turned into ten, and ten into fifteen. When Julia whispered, "Beautiful," I didn't know if she was talking about the night's first stars or the future we were beginning to plan.

WORDS OF WISDOM

He left the tissue-lined bag next to Sam's plastic T. rex on the kitchen counter. I dumped it out on the TV room floor and lined the caps up one by one. There were over fifty.

> *Animals that lay eggs don't have belly buttons.*
> *The tongue is the fastest healing part of the body.*
> *Hot water is heavier than cold.*
> *A day on planet Venus lasts longer than a year.*
> *Shakespeare was the first to use the words "unreal" and "lonely."*

The card was just a piece of folded stationery with his initials at the top.

> *Here's your REAL birthday gift.*
> *I had to drink a lot of lemonade to get them.*
> *I'm still sorry.*
> *Love,*
> *Sebastian*

I kept all of them in my memory box. Even the caps with facts I already knew.

Dear Ms. Ryder,

The faculty in the visual arts program has reviewed your application and supporting credentials.

Congratulations! This letter is to inform you of your acceptance into the Rhode Island School of Design (RISD). Your stellar portfolio and glowing personal recommendation letter from Senator Buchanan give us no doubt that you'll be a successful addition to our community.

Your enrollment at RISD is contingent upon your successful completion of your secondary education. To confirm your intention to enroll, you must submit your nonrefundable matriculation fee by May 1st.

Since you will certainly have many questions, we have assembled pertinent information in this folder for your careful review.

Congratulations again! We look forward to seeing you in Providence this fall.

Sincerely,
Michelle Samgrass
Dean of Admissions
Rhode Island School of Design

TWENTY-FOUR

SEBASTIAN TOLD ME HE WOULD take me anywhere and do whatever I wanted to celebrate RISD. He'd take me to Australia if that was where I wanted to go.

I told him I wanted an afternoon at Arcadia, just the two of us. I told him what I wanted to do, and I heard the sound of the phone dropping, him swearing and scrambling to pick it up.

He asked me if I was sure.

I said I was.

Julia and I had signed out for the weekend. She, Boom, Cordelia, Sophie, and Mrs. Buchanan had all driven out to the nature reserve. Bradley was in Tokyo on a business trip. As I requested, Sebastian and I had Arcadia to ourselves for an entire April afternoon.

"Okay, I've got water, granola bars, a ten-pack of condoms, not that we have to use them all, it's just sometimes they can tear when you take them out of the foil thingies, and—"

"Do you always approach sex like you're packing for a camping trip?" I was sitting cross-legged on his bed, watching him pace back and forth in front of his windows.

"Yeah. I mean no." He paused in front of the window that looked out over Arcadia's beach. "I'm sorry. I'm nervous."

"Don't be." I ran my hands over his quilt, tilted my head and met his eyes. "I'm not."

"You sure?" He crossed over to his dresser and picked up the box of granola bars, passing it back and forth between his hands.

"I'm sure. Are you sure?" I said.

"Oh, I'm sure. I'm sure, sure, sure." He shook the box for emphasis.

I laughed. "Okay, but I'm opening the condom. You have clumsy fingers."

He put down the box and then leaned against the dresser, studying me.

I was still running my hands over his bed. My fingers itched to sketch him just as he was in that moment. How his bare feet rooted him to the wooden floor. How his hips came out at such an angle that one side of his pants was higher than the other. His hands in his pockets. His brown eyes watching me watch him.

How do you capture love in paper and pencil? Is it even possible to come close with metal and stone?

Sebastian padded across the floor and knelt down in front

of me, prying my fingers from the quilt and weaving them between his own.

"I love that you appreciate bottle cap wisdom. I love that you're sarcastic and funny and so talented and that you take people just as they are . . . even if they're a little uncoordinated." He looked up at me and smiled, his hands still wrapped in mine. "You're not afraid of anything, Charlie. It's kind of crazy, how you're not afraid."

He was wrong. I was afraid of so many things. I was afraid of being terrible at this. I was afraid of whatever we had ever ending. But him believing I was fearless let me pretend I was.

I stood up and pulled him to his feet. His lips were on mine and then his hands were on my stomach. My hands on his hips. Then there was fumbling, and laughing, and a stack of books being knocked over when he went to take off his pants. Clothes were flung and we didn't care where they landed. I got stuck in my tank top and he had to help me peel it over my head. When I was in just my underwear and he had taken off his shirt, I wrapped my legs around him, smiling into his kisses as we fell back on the bed.

His hands. My hands. Both restless and exploring. I couldn't get enough of his skin. He couldn't stop kissing my neck, my throat, my stomach, my bare legs.

"Okay," I whispered into his ear. I felt short of breath and slightly dizzy.

He took my face between his hands, his chest rising and

falling in the same rhythm as my own. "I don't want to hurt you."

I shook my head. "You're not going to hurt me."

But I lied, because it did hurt. It hurt so much I had to bite my lip to keep from crying out. But then it hurt less the longer we stayed pressed together.

I felt part of a world that was so large and so strange I could never understand it, and that was okay. I was happy to give myself up to it.

Much later, after the early evening shadows had crept up the walls and the cooling spring breeze had started to drift through the windows to where we lay with our legs and arms still intertwined on the bed, we got up to put on our clothes.

When I bent down to pick up my tank top, I noticed that on the bedside table, next to the condom wrapper, was an upturned bottle cap.

The urge to fall in love is, like sex and hunger, a primitive, biological drive.

He must have been saving that one.

TWENTY-FIVE

WHEN AMY DROPPED A STACK of computer printouts in front of my easel one Wednesday afternoon, I knew she had forgiven me completely.

"I was bored at work, and Julia got such a kick out of her sister's poems I thought she'd be interested in these, too. These are all the *Gazette* articles that mention her sister." She patted the pile gently, like it was a small dog.

"Wow. Amy, thank you."

She twirled her hair around her finger. "So are you and Julia eating with us at lunch again tomorrow?"

I put down my oil crayon and wiped my hands on my jeans. "That's the plan. Is that okay?"

"Yeah," Amy said as she picked up the papers and shuffled them. "It's nice. Julia isn't like I thought she would be. She's not snotty at all."

I took the stack from her. "Julia isn't like *anyone* thinks she would be."

Amy looked confused.

I was confused myself. "I don't even know what I mean by that. Thank you." I held up the printouts. "For this."

"I've got to get to theater. Enjoy." Amy walked out the door, but then swung back in, holding on to the doorframe so only the top half of her body was visible. "There's some pretty interesting stuff there." She swung back into the hall before I could respond.

Most of the articles were about the sailing team. A few were about events Gus helped plan or trips she took with the debate club. They were little more than recitations of wins and losses and fuzzy black-and-white photos with quick captions. I wasn't sure Julia would have the patience to work through half of them.

The last article in the stack, however, was about the best prank ever pulled at St. Anne's.

How Amy figured out that the "anonymous" source in the interview was Gus, I don't know, but to me it was obvious. The source asked to be identified by the initials A.A.O.N.B.

I circled the best parts with my oil crayon.

Who came up with the idea of creating a petting zoo?

A.A.O.N.B.: I had some help from a friend. He knows

a lot about animals, so he was a good guy to have around when we actually brought them on campus. I learned the hard way that chickens will run away first chance they get. [Laughs] He was the one who thought of bringing grain and hay so girls could feed the animals like in a real petting zoo.

And where did you get the animals?

A.A.O.N.B.: We borrowed them from a local farm. I can't tell you which one. That's top secret.

What's the fallout been?

A.A.O.N.B.: All the animals made it back safe and sound, and the kitchen staff thought it was hilarious. The trustees, however, don't have as great a sense of humor.

Has anyone gotten in trouble?

A.A.O.N.B.: [Laughs] Not yet!

Julia would flip. Gus had pulled the dining hall petting zoo.

TWENTY-SIX

"MISS RYDER, TO WHAT DO I owe this pleasure? Did we have a meeting I forgot about?"

Dr. Blanche was sitting at the round table in the Keble Hall tower. The windows behind him overlooked the quad and the table in front of him was mess of papers, a Styrofoam coffee cup, pens, and a giant bag of sour candies.

He must have noticed me looking because he held up the bag. "Want some?"

"No, that's okay. Do you have a second?"

"I'm feeling generous today. Take twenty," he said, leaning back from the table and resting his hands on his round stomach. Dr. Blanche looked like Santa Claus—if Santa was balding and favored corduroys, sweater vests, and round tortoiseshell glasses.

"It's not about me," I said as I stepped into the room.

"Is it about a hypothetical friend who I'm not supposed to know is really you?" He gestured toward the chair closest to his and I sat down, pulling my backpack into my lap, grateful for the comfort of its weight on my legs.

"No." I paused. "I wanted to ask you about Gus Buchanan. Augustine. It says here you were her advisor." I riffled through my backpack, pulling out the wrinkled folder and opening it and pushing it in front of him.

Dr. Blanche leaned forward like someone had pushed him from behind, his elbows on the table. He was silent.

"Dr. Blanche?"

"What would you like to know, Miss Ryder?" he said. His voice was as heavy as sadness, and his eyes were fixed on his clasped hands.

"I just . . . I want to know why it says Harvard, question mark in her folder. Right here." I flipped to the final page and pointed.

Dr. Blanche dropped his eyes to my finger. He tugged his hands through what little hair he had left. "Why are you curious about Augustine?"

"I'm curious for a friend," I said, letting my backpack drop to the ground.

"Ah, there's the hypothetical friend." Dr. Blanche rapped his knuckles against the table. "Miss Ryder, how long have I been your teacher?"

"Two years."

"That long? *Tempus fugit*, as the Romans said." He clasped his hands in front of him again. "Well, I believe I have enough of a grasp on your character to trust that when I say this stays between you, me, and your *friend*, that will be the case."

I nodded.

Dr. Blanche took a drink from the coffee cup. I could see his throat working to swallow. "It says Harvard question mark in her file because Miss Buchanan, Augustine, almost flunked out of St. Anne's—"

"But she was so smart," I said.

Dr. Blanche looked at me over the top of his glasses.

"Sorry. You were saying . . ."

"Her senior spring she didn't turn in assignments, and when she went to class she was late or her head was in the clouds. Augustine was popular, and so in love with that boyfriend of hers." He moved the bag of sour candies from one side of the table to the other, leaving a trail of sugar. "But she thought the rules didn't apply to her. When she realized that Harvard could take back its offer, she pleaded with us all to raise her grades. She offered to do extra-credit projects, volunteer tutor—anything. All her teachers took her up on it. They let her get by on that Buchanan charm just one more time." He sighed. "Except for me."

"Oh." I thought of the girl in the picture in the hall downstairs, the girl in the picture beside Julia's bed, the girl in the picture in the room that was never opened. It was hard to imagine that girl, Gus, failing at anything.

"Miss Ryder, before you leave St. Anne's, I'll let you in on a faculty secret." He leaned toward me, setting the sleeves of his tweed blazer right in the trail of sugar. "We know everything that goes on here."

"What do you—"

"I had been her advisor for four years and her teacher for two. I pretended not to notice when she was late for check-in, and I pretended not to see a tall shadow moving around the edges of the quad after lights out. I let her stay chatting with me long after she should have been in first period or study hall."

"Why?"

Dr. Blanche slouched back in his chair. "They tell you you should never have favorites—"

"But she was your favorite."

His silence was his confirmation. The grandfather clock by the stairs down the short hallway ticked as loud as a heartbeat.

I waited.

"I believed in her. That's why I had to hold her accountable," he said. Dr. Blanche took off his glasses and pushed between his eyebrows as if he had a headache. "She was so furious with me that she didn't even say good-bye after graduation."

"I'm sorry," I said, not knowing exactly why, just knowing that I was.

"She died before Harvard made a decision about whether or not they would rescind her offer of admission." He put his glasses back on and started shuffling the scattered papers in front of him into a stack. "And that, Miss Ryder, is why it says

Harvard, question mark, in her file."

"Okay." I didn't know what else to say. I was out of questions and out of words. "Thank you . . . thank you a lot." I scooped my backpack from the floor and hefted it on one shoulder. "I'll let you get back to what you were doing then." I started toward the door.

"Miss Ryder."

I turned around, one hand already on the doorframe. "Yes?"

"I'll pretend to forget to ask you how you got a hold of that file, if you'll pretend to forget the ramblings of a tired old man."

"You're not old, Dr. Blanche," I said.

"Ah, today I am very old indeed." He smiled, but it was a sad smile, and maybe a little old, too.

WEAR PANTS

"You know what it means, right?"

"What what means?"

"That Gus masterminded the dining hall petting zoo?"

Sigh. "What does it mean?"

"I have to one-up her."

"Really, Julia?"

"Really."

"You don't even have to come. Julia's not bringing anyone, so—"

"Oh no, I definitely want to. I can be that creepy old college guy lurching in the corners of the gym, watching all the girls dance."

"Prom is in the dining hall, not the gym."

"Great. Now, do I have to wear pants?"

"You're going to make me regret asking you, aren't you?"

"You don't already?"

"You're insane."

"And you love me for it."

I did.

TWENTY-SEVEN

THE SATURDAY OF PROM JULIA went to that place where I knew I couldn't reach her. She spent the morning on her phone or staring at it waiting for it to ring. When it did she'd whisper and then duck out of our room to go talk in the hall. She spent the afternoon on her bed looking out the window, her expression as impenetrable and troubled as the ocean before a storm.

I gave her space. I left our room to go to the studio, the library, to take a break from her radiating unease. When I came back hours later, she was in the same position: tucked into the corner of her unmade bed, Aloysius in her lap, the photo of Gus on the sailboat in her hands. The room was dark. She hadn't moved to turn on the lights. When I dropped my backpack on the floor, she jumped like the sound had reached out its hands and shaken her.

I had to remind her three times to get ready. I turned on

music. I put out her dress. I danced around the room with
Aloysius in a stumbling waltz. Slowly she melted. Slowly she
began to smile. Slowly she came back.

By the time Sebastian knocked on our window, she was
jumping on her bed and I was still only half-dressed. But she
was happy. I was happy.

Prom theme was "Impressionists' Spring," so I wore a vin-
tage yellow and orange dress that Mrs. Buchanan swore she
hadn't worn in years. Julia wore a purple and blue strapless that
looked like she had dragged it from the back of Mrs. Buchanan's
closet and snagged the tulle on every hanger along the way.
Sebastian, I was happy to see when Julia and I met him on our
dorm steps, wore pants.

The dining hall was lit brightly enough to be seen from
an airplane, never mind from across the quad. Julia actually
skipped when we walked through the doors. The round tables
had been removed and the wooden beams wrapped with little
Christmas lights in green, yellow, pink, blue, and orange. A DJ
set up in the far corner was playing a jazzy old song, and no one
was dancing yet.

I felt Sebastian's arms slide around me. He pushed my hips so
I swayed with him along to the music.

"Gross. *Beurk!*" Julia said, looking at us. "*Je me tire.* Because
if you guys start making out—"

She started walking away before I could hear the rest.

"Julia, wait," I said, pulling away from Sebastian. But she

had already worked her way through a group of girls huddled around a cardboard re-creation of Monet's Japanese bridge.

I groaned.

"What?" Sebastian said, drawing me back toward him.

"I spent all afternoon trying to snap her out of a weird mood. I just want her to have fun tonight."

Sebastian settled his chin on my shoulder. He nuzzled my neck when he spoke, and his chest was warm against my back. "You need to have fun, too, Charlie."

He was right. I knew he was right. So I let myself lean into him just a little bit more, and when he once again swayed to the music, I moved with him.

I tried not to look for her as the night went on, but it was as useless as trying to get a song out of my head. Sebastian and I took fake champagne from the trays of passing waiters and waitresses. We danced, and I steered him to another part of the dance floor any time Piper and her date came too close. We found Jacqueline, Rosalie, and Amy, who had invited a confused-looking Vinay to be her date. But only when we snuck away to the patio and wrapped ourselves up in each other did I stop searching the room for Julia.

That was where we were when her voice came over the loudspeakers.

"Ladies . . . and the handful of brave gentlemen, *allons-y!*"

Sebastian dropped his arms from around my waist and pulled me back inside. "Is Julia on the prom com—"

He stopped speaking when an impossibly thin, tall Asian waitress near the dance floor shoved her tray of drinks into the arms of a very surprised Dr. Merton, who had the bad luck to be standing near the DJ stage. The waitress slowly raised one arm above her head and jutted her opposite hip out at an unnatural angle.

"What the—" The music cut me off.

"Wellllll, you know you make me want to shout!"

With the first burst of sound the waitress leaped, landing on the balls of her feet and swinging her hips side to side. Within seconds, a waiter with a square jaw and a long nose standing nearby had thrust his tray full of empty glasses at a blond girl I recognized from my history class and joined the first dancer movement for movement.

"Kick my heels up and shout!"

Another waiter-and-waitress couple met them in the center of the floor, each arm wave and hip thrust perfectly in sync. The crowd began forming a circle around them.

"Don't forget to say you will."

A waiter with broad shoulders burst into the space the two

couples had created and ripped off his vest and shirt, sending a few buttons flying into the audience and revealing a bright pink unitard that looked like it had been painted on his pale skin. His pants came off next with one swoop, the Velcro in the sides screeching. Just as the four dancers fell to the ground in a combination of rolls and splits, he joined them. They moved across the floor, expanding their circle. Two more waiters fell into the center of the group.

"Don't forget to say, yeah, yeah, yeah, yeah, yeah."

They rose together as if they were all puppets being pulled on the same string. One of the men lifted the pale guy with broad shoulders off the ground and swung him on each side like he was weightless.

The music changed abruptly to a pop song that I had heard pounding from beneath practically every room in my hall that spring. Four more waitresses and waiters joined those already dancing, shedding their vests and pants until they were all a swirling mass of neon.

I didn't realize I was smiling so hard until my face started to hurt.

Sebastian leaned into me, not taking his eyes off the dancers. "You have to wonder where she got such coordinated waiters."

I threw my head back and laughed. "It's Julia. I can only imagine." A female dancer clad in a fluorescent yellow leotard that left little to the imagination erupted into the air in a full split and landed in the arms of a male dancer in a blue unitard that also left no secrets. "That was—"

The music switched to an upbeat oldies tune I knew from long rides in my dad's truck.

"Do you love me?"

Sebastian whispered in my right ear and rubbed my arms, sending goose bumps down to my fingertips.

"I can't hear you," I shouted, my nose bumping his cheek when I turned my head.

"Now that I can dance."

"I love you—"

I stopped swaying my hips and twisted so I was facing him. The dancing circle had expanded and now students and even some of the teachers on the fringes were mimicking the movements of the dancers in the center.

"Watch me now, oh."

"I love—"

"I heard you," I said, much louder than I needed to. The dancers jumped, the music pounded, and the people surrounding us had started to dance.

"I love you!" I flung my arms around his neck. He stumbled backward, but caught me.

It was true. I loved him so much I had to either laugh or cry, my heart was that full.

"And I can do the twist.
Tell me baby, mmm, do you like it like this?"

The waiter and waitress dancers were grinding together in ways that made even Coach Hassle, the youngest faculty member by years, look away from the dance floor.

"Yeah?" Sebastian shouted.

"Yup!" I laughed and kissed him, not caring who saw.

"Tell me. Tell me. Tell me. Do you love me?"

He unclasped my arms from around his neck and pushed me arm's-distance away, his hands on my hips, his eyes studying my face. What he saw there must have convinced him, because he pulled me into a tight hug and we rocked back and forth amid the sea of people pulsing, swaying, and turning around us.

Just as the music turned to another pop song and the dancers dropped to the ground, leaving everyone else standing, I spotted Julia over Sebastian's shoulder. She was leaning inside the arch of the back entrance. Her dress stuck out around her like a badly cut tutu and she had lost the flower I had put in her braid.

She was a princess surveying her domain, a master chore-ographer enjoying her masterpiece, and an illusionist taking in the magic she had created. She was a legend, a genius. She was my Julia.

I let go of Sebastian and raised a hand above my head in a mock toast.

She stepped away from the wall and made a deep curtsy.

I bowed.

Sebastian kissed me and then stepped to the side, so when Julia ran from the wall and threw her arms around me we had room to spin until we were so dizzy we had to cling to each other to keep from falling down.

"Let's go next year. I'll put off RISD. You'll put off Welles-ley. Let's run away," I shouted, just before turning her out from me.

When she turned back in so our hips bumped she threw back her head and laughed. "*Tu ne le regretteras pas.* We're going to conquer the world, Charlie."

We danced the rest of the night, Julia and me. *Contra mundum.*

GET A DRESS

"Julia, it's fine. My mom sent me money for my birthday and Melissa paid me a little for watching the boys over spring break."

"No. I want to pay for the dress. I was the one who dragged you off campus to shop. Besides, it's my brother's party you're getting it for. We should buy the dress, Mummy said."

"I doubt Bradley cares who pays for the dress. He won't even—"

"Actually, since *he* was the one who sold a start-up, I'll make him pay Mummy back."

"You guys already do too much, and I'm not really comfortable—"

"Just pick out a damn dress, Charlie!"

The woman at the cash register looked up from the stack of receipts she had been sorting. A woman near the entrance of the boutique turned so suddenly she dropped a pair of pants from the top of the pile in her arms.

I stepped behind a jewelry display, pulling Julia with me. "Why are you shouting at me?"

"I'm not shouting." Julia pressed her fists against her eyes. "Just pick out a dress. Please. I want to go back to campus now."

"Okay . . . okay." I flipped through the sales rack. "This one's pretty."

She grabbed the hanger from me. "Let's go."

★ ★ ★

Julia sat in the passenger seat of the St. Anne's van for the ride back to campus. When the driver dropped us off in front of our dorm, she whispered, "I'm sorry."

"It's okay."

"I'm just stressed."

"About what?"

But she didn't hear me—or maybe she didn't know how to answer.

BALANCE

They had told me she was fragile. First Rosalie. Then Boom. Then Sebastian. Even Julia herself warned me in her way.

But I didn't understand what they meant until she broke down in front of me, crumpling like a piece of tissue paper drifting into a bonfire, disintegrating to ash even as she floated upward.

Before that night, I didn't grasp that the shadows that sometimes crossed her face weren't momentary clouds passing in front of the sun. Her deep silences were more than daydreams. And her habit of standing with her arms wrapped around her ribs was her way of holding herself together.

I didn't get that there must be balance.

She couldn't hold so much life, light, and joy without also containing their opposites.

TWENTY-EIGHT

ON THE DAY OF BRADLEY'S party, the Buchanan cousins were at Arcadia by ten, stumbling over one another like puppies in a cardboard box as they shrieked from the house all the way down to the beach where Sophie kept watch.

Cordelia wanted no part in their games. She wanted to stay with me on the porch and learn how to fold linen napkins into peacocks.

"They're pretty. Too pretty to have out here in the wind. We'll put them inside by the cocktail tray for the party," I said, looking at our lopsided display. The napkins were more blobs than birds.

Cordelia stuck her hands on her hips. "I know that's just a nice way of saying you don't want them out here. You're just trying to make me feel better by using an oof-fin-nism."

"Euphemism." I pulled what was supposed to be the neck of one of the birds a little straighter.

Mrs. Buchanan walked over from the corner, where she had been arranging vases of lilies, and pulled Cordelia to her, kissing the top of her head. "How'd you get to be so smart?" she asked. "Huh? You should be grateful you didn't get my brains."

"I know a lot more than people give me credit for." Cordelia squirmed from under her mother's arm. "I'm going to go make sure Simon and Jasper aren't messing with my shells." Cordelia leaped down the steps, landing just near enough to one of the posts at the bottom that Mrs. Buchanan and I both jumped as if we could grab her.

Once Cordelia was lost in the circle of children, Mrs. Buchanan shook her head and put her hands on her hips, standing just as Cordelia had. She reached into her pocket and pulled out a crumpled pack of cigarettes that looked like it had been there for years. "It was just yesterday that she believed me when I told her that she couldn't go in the water when I'm not here because of sea monsters, and the tooth fairy wouldn't come if she didn't brush her teeth." She glanced from side to side, confirming we were alone before shaking out a cigarette, lighting it, and taking a long drag, her eyes closed in bliss.

She exhaled and looked at me. "You won't tell, will you? The kids think I gave them up years ago . . . and I have. It's just every once in a while my nerves . . ." She trailed off.

"I won't tell."

She hugged her left arm under her rib cage and held the other at a sharp angle from her right hip. She looked like a store mannequin, posed and vulnerable as hollow plastic. "Promise me you'll never take these up." She exhaled smoke out her nostrils in two straight lines. "My mother always told me that smoking was a sign of weak character." She took the cigarette from her lips and studied it. "I suppose she was right."

I shook my head. "I've never smoked," I said as I leaned against the railing next to her.

"Good. Don't do as I do . . . as they say." She didn't look at me when she spoke, but continued staring at the cigarette balanced between her fingertips. "Charlotte, I need your help." She paused and brought the cigarette to her lips, inhaling. "We ask a lot of you—"

"Not really—"

"It's just, we trust you. We depend on you, Charlotte." She exhaled smoke out the side of her mouth and tapped her fingernails against the railing.

"I don't want to put you on the spot. But Julia needs to behave tonight. No drinking. No pranks. Nothing but her perfect charming self. Bradley selling his company is such a big deal, and there are going to be too many important people with sticks up their asses here tonight. Pardon my French. Tomorrow, I'll let her streak through town naked if she wants to, but tonight I need her to . . . oh, I don't know." She flicked some ash over the side of the porch into the bushes.

Her eyes shifted from the horizon to me. When they did, it was the first time I noticed the lines at their corners. She had brushstrokes of gray in the hair at her temples, but they blended so well into the blond that I hadn't seen until then.

I looked down at my hands on the railing. "I can't spy on Julia."

"Charlotte, I don't want you to *spy* on her. I just need you to help her be her best self."

I watched one of the cousins—Simon? Jasper? I could never tell them apart—run down the dock and lie down flat on his stomach to dip his bucket full of stones and shells into the ocean. When Sophie yelled for him to come back to the beach, he did, leaving his collection of treasures at the end of the dock, already forgotten.

"I'll do what I can," I said.

"Well, I guess that's the best any of us can hope for. To do what we can," she said, stubbing her cigarette out on an upturned shell resting on the seat of a rocking chair and dropping it behind the bushes. Then she walked into the house, as graceful as a white sheet on a laundry line twisting in the breeze.

"Jules—"

"You never call me that."

"I do when you're up to something. Your mom doesn't want anything bad to happen tonight."

"So she made my best friend in the whole world my babysitter?"

"It's not like that. Look, why do you even need the money?"

"It's a surprise. For Bradley." She kept clenching and unclenching her hands. Tugging at her sundress.

"Can't you just make him a great card?"

"Pathetic, Charlie. *Très, très pathétique.*"

"Julia—"

"I need this. Please. I can't ask anyone else. Sebastian can't find his wallet again. Sophie would tell. Cordelia's a baby. You're it. You're my best friend."

I trudged up the stairs to get what money I had, hoping for the best, dreading the worst.

By the time I had gotten dressed, done my hair, and found my tube of lip gloss, the party had spilled from the porch to the lawn. Hundreds of white candles cast hazy light on the tops of tall tables, and rich smells drifted from the trays of passing waiters and the kitchen, mixing with the ever-present scents of seaweed and salt.

Twilight was taking its time that night. The sky was a watercolor: light blue, darkening to navy, then black dotted with the first suggestion of stars.

Sebastian stood in the middle of a group of men with silver hair and protruding stomachs. Boom, Sophie, and Mrs. Buchanan were smiling and nodding at a middle-aged Asian man and a petite woman in a green dress near the entrance of the glowing white tent, and Cordelia was showing a girl half her size how to put a marshmallow on a stick near the fire pit. Julia was nowhere to be seen.

It was only after I grabbed a flute of champagne that I saw Bradley standing by himself on the side of the porch where Cordelia and I had been folding napkins. He had a glass of ice and dark liquor in his hand.

"Young lady, are you old enough to be drinking that?"

His sternness sound so authentic that I put the flute down on a nearby table.

"Really, Charlie. You thought I was serious?"

I picked it back up, shrugging. "I've got to say, Bradley, your old-man act is pretty good. What age are you now? Thirty? Forty-five?"

"Touché." He mimed touching a sword to his nose and bowing. "Nice dress." He glanced at the silk dress Julia had bought me the weekend before.

"Thanks. It's new—"

"Pink." He spoke like he hadn't heard me. "I wouldn't have pegged Charlie Ryder from New Hampshire as a pink girl."

"Well, normally—"

"So, Sport," he said, making his voice tremble like an old man's. "I'm glad I got you alone for a moment. Cause I'm gonna tell ya a little secret before the evening gets away from us. And because it's my goddamn party and I just sold a company, that makes me much, much wiser than you, so you have to listen." He braced himself against the railing in a poor imitation of someone leaning on a cane.

"You're a good kid, and you know what?" He gestured for me to bend down to his level. "You've been good for the lot of us." He straightened and drained his glass, setting it down on a nearby table with enough force to make the ice cubes jump onto the porch.

"Bradley, are you ever ser—"

"Hey, Charlie." He rested a hand on my shoulder, gripping it tightly enough so I could feel each of his fingers. "I am serious. You've been good for all of us." He gestured behind him toward the crowd gathered on the lawn.

"Now." He smoothed down the front of his blazer and made a motion like he was straightening a bow tie. "Tell me how handsome I look."

"You're very handsome."

"The best-looking one here? Better-looking than Sebastian?"

"Well . . ." I tapped a finger against my chin.

"I'll take that as a yes. Okay." He hopped over the rail, landing just to the left of a rosebush. "I'm off to get so drunk I forget my name and pass out in a lawn chair with just my boxers on."

"Sounds like it wouldn't be the first time," I shouted after him, but if he heard me he didn't turn around.

After he left, I stood pressed against the railing, watching the guests weave around one another like tropical fish in a tank. Watching dusk turn to dark. Watching the bubbles rise in my flute and the smoke from the fire pit hover over the whole scene like the remnants of a dream.

I would have been happy to watch all night, but Cordelia dashed up the porch, a swirl of blue linen and chocolate-coated fingers, and insisted she had to teach me the best way to make a s'more.

Julia found me just as I was pulling a marshmallow that looked as chewy and crisp as charcoal from a stick.

"*Merde!*" she exclaimed. "Are you trying to give the kid cancer?"

I shook my head at a little boy in seersucker pants as he handed me two graham crackers. "She's just kidding." Nonetheless, after I scraped the marshmallow onto the crackers, added some chocolate, and handed it to him, he ran off toward a tall black man with the same wide eyes and shoved the s'more into his hands instead of eating it himself.

I turned back to Julia. "Where have you been?"

"Shhhhhhhhh," Julia said, swaying on her heels. "It's a surprise." She stuck a finger in front of her lips, missing the center.

I sighed and plucked the remnants of the cancer marshmallow off my stick with my fingers and stuck it in my mouth. It tasted like burned toast. "On a scale of one to ten, how drunk are you?"

"Oh." Julia broke a piece of chocolate off from one of the bars melting on the wooden bench near the pit. "How little you know me after all this time. I've been keeping a steady buzz since the first clowns piled out of the first car." She shoved the chocolate in her mouth, licking her fingers.

"Maybe you should ease up."

"Oh, dear, sweet Charlie."

"And the money. What's the gift?"

"What kind of magician would I be if I gave away the surprise before the big finale?" She patted my arm, leaving a smear of chocolate near my elbow, and walked away, disappearing into the tent on the other side of the lawn.

The fireworks were amazing—until they weren't.

When the first one went off, I didn't even turn around. Sebastian had his arm around me as he chatted with one of Bradley's investors. From time to time he would squeeze my side, as if to say, "I know. This is boring me to death, too." I would squeeze him back to let him know I was okay. I was content with entertaining myself by trying to squint just enough so that the swirls of women's dresses and the candlelight blended together into an abstract painting.

I heard a low rumble, even felt it course through my body, but I didn't turn around. I thought it was the ferry making its final run for the night, sounding its horn as it pulled out of the wharf. Or I thought it was an old car passing on the road, or any number of reasonable things.

But by the second firework, she had figured out how to

launch them properly. The second one soared off the dock, splitting the sky into shards of red and orange with a crack before dripping down like the branches of a willow tree. I saw all of this in the reflection of the investor's glasses. Already his neck was craned back, his small mouth slightly opened.

All it takes is one explosion and people expect a show.

"Pip," Sebastian said.

I nodded and turned around, looking skyward with the rest of the party. "Your mom is going to kill me."

A third firework exploded off the dock: green and blue sparkles, glitter thrown in the air. A woman near the bar clapped, and the kids by the fire pit woke out of their sugar-induced stupors to clap as well.

We heard a fourth bang, but no light.

A fifth firework: a purple starburst.

A sixth: yellow splashes of paint thrown against a black canvas.

A seventh, eighth, ninth. The bright colors made the upturned faces and the huge tent glow green, red, and blue.

"I didn't give her that much money," I said to Sebastian. "How'd she get them all?"

He pulled me back so I was leaning against his chest. "It's Julia. She can be very charming when she wants to be."

By the fifteenth firework, we could smell the smoke. It was the rotten-egg stink of sulfur, but it was also the smell of a bonfire: damp, old wood protesting before catching flame.

"What's that smell? Is somethin' on fire?" slurred a woman with short red hair standing just to my left.

"Shit." Sebastian let go of me and started jogging toward the shore. "Julia!"

He was halfway to the boathouse by the time my brain caught up with my feet and I ran after him. The fireworks had stopped and the guests had begun to pace like nervous cats. I reached him just as the flames began to crawl over the top of the roof, reflecting off the water like they were beneath the waves instead of in the night sky. If it hadn't been terrifying, it would've been beautiful.

"Julia!" Sebastian shouted.

"Would she have gone in to try and put it out?" I said.

Through the curtain of smoke, I saw that the flames weren't just red and orange. Like the fireworks that had given them life, they were blue, white, gray, and purple.

The heat swept toward us in waves, riding the wind that whipped the flames even higher. Out of this haze, Julia stumbled toward us, her arms clutched against her chest like she was cradling a doll.

"Julia, Jesus!" I ran toward her. "Are you okay?"

"I think I burned it." She looked into the night over the ocean, where the light from the fire didn't reach. Her eyes were unfocused, and her lips hung open slightly as if she was a fish gasping for air.

I put an arm on her lower back and steered her toward the

house. One glance was all it took to see that her arm was red and blistering. As I sat her on the front porch steps, Bradley rushed down from inside the house, holding a fire extinguisher. When he met Sebastian, they both sprinted toward the burning boathouse, where some partygoers had gathered and were using their cocktail glasses to throw seawater at the flames.

I held her gently and rocked her against me, making the same soothing sounds I made whenever I picked Sam or AJ up after a fall.

Despite Sebastian's and Bradley's efforts, despite the martini glasses of water and the shouting, the fire spread, creeping from the boathouse to the dock, and then, finally, to the little red sailboat. The same sailboat I had seen in the picture in Julia's room over a year before. The same sailboat that was in the photos in the room where no one was allowed to go. Gus's sailboat was engulfed in minutes. There was nothing to do to save it. I pushed Julia's head down on my shoulder, hoping that she wouldn't see.

By the time the fire truck roared onto the lawn, I was as dazed as she was. Within an hour, the fire was out and only a smoking black skeleton remained of the boathouse.

The party broke up after that. Guests drifted to their cars like refugees tramping across the desert, whispering among their small groups.

Sebastian trudged toward us. His once crisp shirt stuck to him in patches, and he had lost his tie. Julia had begun to shiver, but she had stopped whimpering.

"She needs to go to the hospital," I said.

His face had streaks of soot on it and glowed with sweat. He nodded and helped Julia to her feet.

I was still sitting on the porch steps, clutching my head in my hands, getting ready to follow them, when Mrs. Buchanan found me.

"Did you help her buy those things?"

I nodded without looking up.

"Charlotte. Why would you do this to us? After I asked you . . . I trusted—"

"I didn't mean . . . I wasn't trying to hurt anyone." My head ached. My eyes stung from the smoke, and Mrs. Buchanan's words made my heart hurt.

"Teresa, calm down," Boom said as he jogged down the porch steps. He hugged her to him. "It was an accident. What matters now is that we get her to the hospital."

Mrs. Buchanan turned into his chest and mumbled something that I couldn't hear.

"I know. I know," Boom said in return. He looked at me over her shoulder. "Charlie, you and Sophie will stay with Cordelia?"

I nodded as I rubbed my hands up and down my arms, as if getting rid of my goose bumps would somehow stop my chest from feeling like it had caved in on itself.

They walked over to where Sebastian was easing Julia into

the passenger seat of an SUV with rust on the bumper and dented doors. It was the car we used to drive on the beaches and the dirt roads of the nature preserve—outings that suddenly felt like they happened lifetimes ago. Bradley was already at the wheel. Sebastian held the door for Mrs. Buchanan before sliding in after her.

I was left standing alone on the lawn, looking up at that magnificent house. Not even on the day that Sebastian first brought me to Arcadia did I feel so acutely how much that world—where a home could be lit up like a beacon, like a chandelier—didn't belong to me.

Much later that night, as I lay sleepless in what I had come to think of as "my room," I heard the sounds of a car turning into the drive, the front door opening, and then Sebastian's voice drifting up from the base of the stairs.

"Doctor said . . . just watch her . . . blame . . . fine."

I heard the steps creak as someone helped Julia up to her room. I heard Boom clear his throat, Sophie saying something in French, and Mrs. Buchanan softly crying.

And when I finally heard only the normal night sounds— the waves on the shore, the flap of the flag against the pole, the occasional wail of a foghorn as sad and lonely as a solitary bird—I saw a shadow outside my door.

The shadow hesitated, shifting left, then right, then left again, but eventually disappeared.

Not long after dawn, I did, too.

I went into Julia's room, first just standing in the doorway and trying not to cry at the sight of her thin arms wrapped in layers of gauze so thick it looked like she had wool mittens on. I set the note I had written her on her bedside table and then snuck downstairs and out through the kitchen door to Sophie's cottage. She was up. Her red-laced eyes made me wonder if she had slept at all.

Sophie grabbed her car keys with a nod, knowing what I needed without me even asking.

We were silent during the drive to the ferry, but when I opened my door to get out of the car, she grabbed my arm.

"Just give them time, *chérie*. Sometimes they forget that the world is not against them."

"Will you tell Mrs. Buchanan I'm sorry?"

"Oh, darling girl, *je suis désolée . . . je suis désolée pour ton cœur brisé.*" She kissed the palm of my upturned hand and let me go.

I sat on the upper deck for the two-hour ride to Hyannis, letting my phone ring and ring until I shut it off completely.

"I'm sorry," I whispered. But the only people I wanted to hear me were already miles of ocean away.

I'M SORRY

Julia,

I wish I was strong enough to stay, but I'm not. I don't know how to face your family after I messed up so badly. I messed up, and you got hurt, and I don't expect them to forgive me for that.

Love,

Charlie

PHONE CALL #2

"Charlie, I've been trying to reach you for hours. Where the hell are you?"

"Hyannis. Waiting for Rosalie to pick me up."

"Why did you leave like that?"

"Will you tell your mom I'm sorry? I'm so sorry. I couldn't see her this morning, Sebastian. I couldn't."

"Oh, Charlie." I knew he was running his hand through his hair, pacing, drumming his fingers. "Whatever she said, she didn't mean it. She was upset and Julia having to go to that hospital again just brought back a lot of bad feelings. My mum loves you. You know that."

"I didn't know she would get hurt."

"Of course you didn't. You're the best friend she's ever had. Anything Mum said last night, it wasn't about you. Okay?"

"Okay."

"She might not be back on campus for a few days."

"Okay."

"I love you."

"I love you, too."

Sophie arrived to pack up her things two days later. Julia never came back to St. Anne's at all.

THE END

Non est ad astra mollis e terris via
(There is no easy way from the earth to the stars)
—Seneca the Younger

TWENTY-NINE

JULIA'S ABSENCE SUCKED ALL THE meaning from graduation.

It was as if nature had predicted my mood and decided to coordinate. The sky was heavy with the threat of rain—the clouds like gray water balloons that had been filled to the point of near-bursting. The air was as sticky and suffocating as a pond of melted licorice.

I sat through the depressingly predictable speeches, trying not to scratch at the polyester robe that clung to my skin and twisted through my legs no matter how many times I rearranged it. The valedictorian, an earnest Yale-bound girl, gave a speech that was full of sayings from all the right poets, philosophers, and pop stars. The alumna guest offered sage advice on how to succeed in life without really trying, and Dr. Mulcaster's talk about not wasting our potential felt like it was directed right at me.

I sat still until my name was called. I threw my soggy cap, the cardboard square thing at the top bent at the edges, with the rest of my class. It was a small victory that I had only turned and searched the folding-chair-perched crowd two dozen times during the ceremony.

I hated my weakness. I hated my hope. I hated that I still thought just maybe, maybe I would see him casually leaning against the giant oak at the back of the quad, her near the fringes of the crowd, or Mrs. Buchanan and Boom standing with Cordelia, Sophie, and Bradley somewhere, anywhere.

When it was all over, I didn't search for my dad, Melissa, and the boys—they knew to meet me at my dorm—or anyone to say good-bye to. Amy, Jacqueline, and I had made our good-byes the night before, sitting on the half-packed boxes in my room, talking long past lights out. Rather, they talked and I listened. I didn't have the energy to giggle and wonder about college. But I was glad to watch them. Glad to not be alone with only my regrets for company.

Rosalie would find me later, after she packed up her car. She had agreed to give me a ride. I'd been a bad friend to her, and she was being a good one to me. I didn't know why, but I was grateful.

I sat beside the side door of what used to be my dorm on top of one of my cardboard boxes and waited. The rain that had held up the sky all afternoon finally started to come down in pinpricks of drizzle.

I was so caught up in staring into nothing that I heard the click of Piper's heels before I saw her coming toward me. She had taken off her black robe and seemed not to care that the blue dress she wore was getting ruined by the rain. She gestured for me to move over, and once I had, she leaned against my box next to me.

"You'll recover, you know? From the Julia hangover, that is." She spoke without looking at me. She was close enough that I could see the mascara smudges hidden beneath the foundation around her eyes. She either hadn't had time to wash her makeup off from the night before or just didn't care. I guessed the latter.

My hands tightened around the edge of the box. I was having a hard time pretending to be interested in looking at the Dumpsters behind the science center.

"Is that a known medical condition?" I said. "A Julia hangover? I'll have to look it up later. In the meantime, my dad's going to be here any moment. He'll be driving a truck, so you might want to leave just in case someone you know walks by."

Piper ignored my sarcasm and reached across me, her arm briefly touching my shoulder, to grab my Magic 8 Ball from a box I hadn't quite been able to close. She straightened up and shut her eyes tightly. She had the pained expression of someone hit by a sudden migraine. When she opened them she just looked tired. "I know I haven't been a peach to you."

I shrugged. "You spent half of last year and most of this giving me the death stare."

"Listen, I'm trying."

I didn't say anything. I pulled at the loose strings dangling from the hem of my dress. It was old anyway.

"I just wanted to say I'm sorry. I'm sorry for being such a bitch." She tugged at the top of her dress, before whispering, "I'm sorry that I ever met Julia Buchanan."

I drew my knees up to my chest, even though I was probably flashing every grandparent on campus, and hugged them. I couldn't pull my body tightly enough together to keep myself from feeling like I was falling apart. "You don't mean that," I said into my legs.

"No, I suppose I don't . . . but maybe I'd be a nicer person now if I hadn't." Piper shifted on the cardboard box next to me. The drizzle had eased, but the air still hung with the weight of water, and heat, and all the good-byes and uncertainties that clouded any campus on any graduation day.

St. Anne's was my home. Before Arcadia, it was the place where I felt most at peace, and in that moment, I already missed it.

My dorm room, with shadows from the trees outside the windows running up my walls like streaks of dark paint. The quad saturated with so much color it became like a box of crayons each fall. The library, cool and soaring in the early-setting winter sun. The studio full of sawdust and half-finished projects and empty paper coffee cups. I was still there, but I already felt like I should prepare myself for the pain of leaving. The beauty of those memories that weren't even memories yet made me generous.

"It's okay. I wish it could have been different—that no one had gotten hurt."

Piper studied the Magic 8 Ball as if it might actually contain the secret to her future.

I straightened up and pretended to be fascinated by a family across the quad. A girl from my environmental science class was trying to shove an armchair into the back of an SUV while her dad pulled from the inside.

Piper slumped at the waist. Her blond hair was starting to frizz and her blue eyes were tight at the corners like she was pinching them to keep from crying. "I was only a bitch because I was protecting Julia. Most people don't get her and she used to be my best friend so . . ."

I gave her my best you've-got-to-be-kidding-me stare.

"Whatever," Piper said as she wiped at the corner of her left eye with her free hand. "I might have been jealous and trying to scare you away from her, too."

"Didn't work."

"Yeah, I know. It was stupid." She looked up from the Magic 8 Ball. "Before you were Julia's person, I was her person." She shivered and I saw goose bumps rise on her arms. "But last spring, like a week after you came to her room that time, I figured a Buchanan secret out, and after that she couldn't stand to be around me." She looked at the quad as though she was noticing where we were for the first time since sitting down. "God, I'm so glad to get out of this place."

I was still watching the father and daughter in the SUV. I could see the girl's mouth move as if she were counting, and then she gave a gigantic push as the outline of her dad inside the vehicle gave a huge pull. The chair slid into the car.

What do you know?

"I think I'm going to miss it," I said. "What did you find out? About Julia? About the Buchanans?"

"Ha, you really think I'd tell you that?" Piper said, shaking her head. "If I had to find out the hard way, you do, too."

"I doubt I'll get the chance."

"Now that we've had our moment," she said as she slid off the box. She turned back abruptly, remembering the Magic 8 Ball in her hands.

She gave it a little shake. "Will it all turn out okay?"

She turned the ball over, and her forehead was wrinkled as she read. "'Better not tell you now.' Well, that's beyond not helpful." She slipped the ball back into the open box and walked away, her heels once again clicking on the wet middle path through the quad.

TEXTS #3

C: Graduation was miserable w/out U

C: Call me?

C: Do u want me to come out to ACK?

C: Is ur mom still mad? Family time still?

C: K. U know where I am when you're ready. Feel better, Julia

C: I'm sorry. I miss u

S: Graduation?

C: Awful

S: Ugh! Wish I'd been there. Things still messy here

S: Mum & Boom r wrecks. Sophie keeping it all together

C: Julia?

S: Arms feeling better but really quiet

S: Think J's sad about graduation. Maybe missing Gus. Def missing u

S: J might go to grandma's for bit. All up in air. Really not talking much

C: Tell J CM for me

S: CM?

C: J will know what it means

S: I love u

C: I love u 2

THIRTY

THE CROSS FARM WAS FARTHER out on Cape Cod than I thought it would be.

Rosalie and I left St. Anne's right after we had packed up our parents' cars and sent them driving north. We went east, toward Hyannis. Once we left downtown with its coffee shops and antique stores, the asphalt road turned into narrow dirt where the gravel pinged against the side of Rosalie's car as frequently as insects smashed against the windshield.

"Disgusting!" Rosalie said after a particularly fat bug hit her side. "These things have a death wish or something." She had to pump the windshield washer button twice, and even then the wipers spread the bug guts around more than they got rid of them. "Remind me again why we're doing this."

"Because I need to figure something out." I lifted my head from where I had been resting it against the window. "Julia didn't want to come out here, and Sebastian . . . he's . . . never mind. I need to know why."

"Charlotte, I realize he's your boyfriend and Julia's . . . like your soul mate or something—"

"Are you being mean?"

"Come on, it's kind of true, eh? But you gotta let go. Her sister died. That sucks. She set her house on fire. That sucks. Sebastian hasn't asked you to come out there. That—"

"It was only the boathouse," I said. "Just the boathouse caught fire." I slumped back against the passenger door.

We didn't speak again until I saw the bright wooden sign announcing the Cross Family Farm with a smaller one below declaring, "Strawberries are in season!"

"This is it. Turn here."

Cotton ball clouds drifted against a freshly washed June sky. A huge maroon barn that looked like something out of a milk commercial stood at the end of the drive. Beyond it, a yellow and brown field was dotted with cows, sheep, and possibly llamas; it was hard to tell what they were.

The weathered white farmhouse on our left was comfortably shabby and uneven, as though it had been put together with glue in some places and now the stickiness was losing hold. Flower boxes guarded a freshly painted blue farm stand like a protective barrier.

Rosalie pulled to a stop, raising a cloud of dirt that made my eyes water when I slid out of the car. Otherwise, the air was sweet and salty, full of cut hay and the nearby ocean.

"Be careful where you step," Rosalie yelled, slamming her door and stepping gingerly around the car. "I bet there are cow patties everywhere."

"Actually, they are called manure, and the cows stay in field always."

Rosalie and I both turned at the heavily accented words. The most beautiful girl I had seen outside of a magazine approached us from the direction of the plant fields on the right of the barn.

She couldn't have been much older than us. Her practically white blond hair was in a tight bun on the top of her head, and that, coupled with her height and posture, gave her the appearance of a ballerina picking her way around farm tools and wheelbarrows. When she was just feet from us, I saw that the dramatic angles of her face were tempered by her full lips, which guarded slightly crooked white teeth. She wore her beauty with the ease that comes from a lifetime of being stared at.

"Holy . . ." Rosalie whispered.

I nodded, still staring.

"Can I be of help to you? We are not open on Mondays, but strawberries are in the barn if you like." The girl wiped her hands on her jean shorts, then shaded her eyes to look at us.

"Yeah, actually." I swallowed loudly. "We're here to talk to the Crosses. Mr. and Mrs. Cross, that is. Are they around?"

"No, they are away today." She emphasized her words like each one was the end of her sentence.

"When will they be back?" I felt Rosalie shift to stand beside me.

"Not until very late. They pick their daughter up from college today and it is long drive." She sighed, still shading her eyes. "But if you have questions about farm, I am Helen. I have worked here many summers. If you want, I can answer. But I have to keep working. Come with me." She started walking toward the plant fields.

Rosalie and I glanced at each other. She shrugged, and then we both followed.

Helen plopped down in the middle of a row of strawberry plants, picked up a trowel, and started loosening the soil around the roots. "What is it you want to know?"

"Where are you from?" Rosalie said.

"I am from Romania. I come over every summer to work for Cross family. They are great people. Very nice family. But this is not why you are here, no?"

"Actually . . ." I cleared my throat. "We wanted to ask about David, about the Crosses' son."

Helen stopped digging.

"Were you here? When the accident happened?"

Helen nodded, but didn't look up. In the quiet that followed I heard the jumping of gravel as a dump truck passed by on the road, and I noticed that some hidden insects were maintaining a steady buzzing like an orchestra warming up before a performance.

"We want to find out more about what happened that day." Rosalie uncrossed her arms, stepping forward. "We were friends with David when he was little."

I shot her a poisoned look.

"What?" she mouthed.

"You knew David?" Helen's face was so full of hope, or maybe it was happiness or maybe it was awe, or maybe it was all three, that I couldn't help myself. I nodded. Even squinting into the sun she was stunning.

"Everyone loved David," she said. "He was so nice. Never made fun at my bad English. Took me to a movie my first summer. It was first time I see American movie. It was kind of movie he liked, lots of cars . . . big explosions." She smiled, though her eyes were glistening. "The worst movie I see in my life . . . but I was happy because he took me."

"He sounds . . . yeah, he was wicked sweet," I said. Helen looked back at the ground and so didn't see me punch Rosalie, hard, in her right shoulder.

Rosalie clutched her arm. "Bitch!"

Helen didn't understand her or didn't care. "The accident summer . . . that was very, very bad summer. For Cara and Jon, the Crosses, and me. Like it happened yesterday. All the time." She picked up her trowel and started loosening the soil again— this time furiously, as if she was digging against stone.

"What about after the accident?" I knelt on the ground beside Helen, letting my knees fold into the freshly turned dirt.

I wanted to touch her shoulder, to help her weed, to do any-thing to comfort her, but I sensed that she wasn't the kind of girl who liked help from anybody—especially strangers. "Did the Crosses keep in touch with—"

"David was a good driver. Never speeds. Drove the tractor since the pedals were at reach of his feet, he told me. Drove me to the airport at the end of every summer. He was very, very good driver." Her voice caught. "Something must have been wrong with car. He was a very good driver."

"Hey, well speaking of driving," Rosalie said as she pointed at the huge truck parked by the side of the barn. "The Crosses must be doing well. That truck looks brand new, eh?" Her attempt at cheerfulness felt as natural as a snowstorm in July.

Helen snorted. "There is no money in farming. Augustine's family has been *very* generous." Her sarcasm was not lost in translation.

"They gave them a truck?" I said.

Helen stood up just enough to shuffle to the next set of plants, forcing Rosalie and me to follow her. She started digging again. "Truck is nothing. After car crash, we have new spreader, baler, and Becca, David's sister, go to the Dartmouth University. Very smart girl. Smarter even than David. First, there was no money. Dartmouth University is very expensive, you know? So she decide maybe go to the community university and work for year. But after David dies, suddenly there is money and the Dartmouth University lets her in spring semester. Just her.

Nobody else," Helen said, tearing a handful of brown leaves off a plant. "As they say, you do the mathematics."

She ripped at the plants in such a way that her motions seemed in sync with the buzz of the insect orchestra.

"He loved Augustine very much. He would bring her here all the time and take her out on the tractor or in the truck . . . they laugh very much," Helen said. Though her voice was without bitterness or jealousy, it was what she didn't say that struck me: She had loved him, too. She had loved him, but couldn't compete with the dazzling, rich girl who had won David instead.

"I'm sorry," I whispered. I didn't know whether I was sympathizing with her broken heart or apologizing for a family who had had theirs broken, too.

"It is not your fault." She hiccupped into the dirt, then turned her beautiful face up toward Rosalie and me. Even with her red-rimmed eyes she was the reason artists painted portraits. "People are not to be treated like toys to break. You know this?"

I nodded.

"I think Buchanan family do not."

Rosalie and I left Helen in the strawberry field. We barely spoke on the drive into Hyannis until she hugged me good-bye at the bus station. I stared out the window the entire long ride home.

If I could have unlearned what I had learned, I would have. I would have chosen ignorance over doubt. But I could no more go back to believing that everything the Buchanans had led me to think was true than I could swim across the Atlantic.

David had been an excellent driver, Helen said. But the Buchanans' gifts and Sebastian's and Julia's strange behavior told me that perhaps Gus had not.

My only distraction from my suspicion was the stone I had worked out of the soil for my memory box. I passed the time by running my fingers over its pointed edges, clutching it in my palm so hard it hurt.

AT LEAST

In over a year of searching, Julia and I had discovered nothing and everything. Gus hadn't been a saint. She hadn't been without flaws.

She was a sailing star, a girl in love, a prankster, and a person who made an enormous mistake. And like with any legend, the real version of her could never live up to the memory.

But at least she was no longer a stranger.

THIRTY-ONE

I SPENT MOST OF THE first day I was home in my makeshift bedroom, looking out the windows or at the boxes that I had no intention of unpacking.

I spent most of the second day staring at my phone, willing it to ring with Julia's or Sebastian's number.

By the third day, I couldn't stand to be in the house anymore. So I wasn't. I walked the ski trails at Wycliffe Mountain until my legs ached from all the snowless black diamonds and my feet were blistered.

By the fourth day, I was so tired of my own company that I went and begged for my old job at the resort. I gave no end date and signed up for every double shift the restaurant would give me. Any moment where I was not working I spent in the garage. Hammering. Pounding. Welding. Anything that kept me from thinking.

But I did not touch the half-done sculpture in the corner.

* * *

"Table four asked for you." Zack snapped his gum loudly, as if daring the manager on duty to come remind him yet again of the rule against chewing gum while working. But then again, Zack had neglected to take out his nose ring and button his black vest, so the gum was probably at the bottom of his violation list. He was lucky the resort was swamped that July. Management was too concerned with the delivery of shrimp cocktails and martinis to go through the ritual of firing and rehiring him.

"Why?" I was focused on refilling salt and pepper shakers for table eight.

"Dunno." He snapped his gum again. "But she looks like a wine-spritzer-and-salad kinda lady, so if you give me table ten we'll call it even."

"Fine. Cool." I'd never been wicked friendly with my coworkers, but that summer I was particularly low on the sociability scale. Though everyone was nice enough to my face—Emily, the bartender, even invited me to a few house parties and bonfires—I got the sense that they all were smiling behind cupped hands, glad to see me brought down a peg or two. I'd gone off to a fancy boarding school, and where had it gotten me? No college. No plans for the future. Broken in so many places I didn't know where to begin repairs.

I slapped the shakers on table eight and glanced at the harried young parents who probably couldn't wait to drop their french-fry-throwing kids off with the summer camp staff. I took my pad of paper out of my apron as I wove my way to the two-person window table. Table four looked over the golf course and the White Mountains, and I was surprised the hostess hadn't made a party of one sit at the bar, but maybe the wine spritzer woman's persuasiveness would translate to a generous tip for me. I forced my mouth into my best fake smile.

But when the blond woman turned away from the window, the smile melted from my face like sugar dissolving in hot water.

"Your dad told me where to find you."

"Mrs. Buchanan," I choked. "What . . . what are you doing here?"

"Teresa."

"Why are you here?"

She shifted away from the window slowly, as if the movement hurt her. "She disappeared yesterday. Joe and I, Boom and I, we don't want to send police or strangers. She'd just keep running." Her voice quivered. "Charlotte, I am immensely sorry for how things ended at Bradley's party. I was scared. I wasn't thinking . . . but I need you to talk to Julia and bring her back." She clasped her hands against the edge of the table. "Sebastian . . . Sebastian said you would know where she'd go . . . that she'd listen to you. He said that out of all of us, you should be the one to bring her home."

His name was enough to make my throat feel like it was closing. I hadn't seen him since the party or talked to him in days. It felt like my words were scratching me as I spoke. "Why would he think that? Julia . . . she won't answer any of my calls or texts."

Mrs. Buchanan looked down at her hands, her long fingers twisting her wedding band almost like she was trying to pull it off. "Joe's left for Vermont this morning to start a new project, but before he went, we agreed with Sebastian." She leaned across the table as if she were about to touch me, but then dropped her arm, seeing something in my expression that made her reconsider. "Charlotte, please. Go talk to her. Bargain her anything. Just get her home."

"What if she won't come?"

"Convince her."

"Mrs. Buchanan—"

"Please. Please just try. If you're her friend . . . if your time with my family meant anything to you, you'll bring her home. I can't—" She closed her eyes as she spoke next. "I can't do it all again. I'm not that strong."

"I know that you give the Cross family money," I said without realizing what I meant until the words were out of my mouth. I was sick of secrets, sick of all I knew, and even more of what I didn't.

Remembering the packed tables behind me, I whispered, "I know that Gus was driving the car, not David . . . so you, you and Boom, pay for things. I went to the farm. I saw."

She stared out the window for a long minute, looking at the snow-topped mountains. "Charlotte, you need to talk to Julia

about that. Tell her." She swallowed hard. "Tell her it doesn't
matter anymore." I could see her reflection in the glass. She
was a marble statue left too long outside; time and weather had
taken their toll. She was worn. Defeated. Unreachably sad.

The click of knives and forks against thin china, and delicate wineglasses pinged against half-filled water glasses, and
meaningless conversations floated into the silence between us.
Busboys yelled at the waiters and waitresses, who yelled at the
bartenders, who yelled back and forth to each other and the
hostess, who spoke louder than all of them to couples, and families, and wedding parties escaping for spa weekends. The din
filled my head. I couldn't think. I could only feel.

"Okay."

"Thank you." Mrs. Buchanan wiped at her eyes with the
back of her right hand, opened her small leather purse, and took
out a white envelope. "To pay for the gas and incidentals. Anything you need, you know you can call. More money. A rental
car. Anything. I've left the check blank."

She rose in one fluid motion, slipping the envelope into my
hand and then picking her way through the tables the same way
I'd seen her weave through her own crowded parties.

I ran after her, ignoring the cries of "Miss" from my
neglected tables. I caught up with her right after she passed the
hostess stand. "Wait! How is everyone?"

She paused in the center of the restaurant entrance, oblivious that customers had to duck around her to get in and out.

She glanced over her shoulder for only the briefest of moments, knowing what I really meant. "He misses you." The noise surged as she left, but I thought I heard her say, "We all miss you."

Or maybe I only heard what I wanted so desperately to be true.

"What a rich bitch," Zack muttered behind me. "She totally f'd up the table and didn't even order anything."

I gripped the hostess podium with two hands. "Zack, take over my tables for me, okay?"

"Huh?"

I didn't stop to explain. I tore the envelope into shreds, scattering the remnants on a tray of dishes a busboy had abandoned nearby. I untied my apron as I walked through the staff door. I would get demoted to kitchen prep or fired. I didn't care.

I knew where Julia Buchanan would be.

THIRTY-TWO

"**WHAT ARE YOU DOING HERE?**"

The smudges beneath her glassy eyes were like purple bruises. She was sitting cross-legged in our little stone alcove, and her skin was so pale that under the light of the stained glass windows it looked almost translucent.

"Mum and Boom sent you, didn't they?"

"I'm here because I want to be." I lowered down to the floor a few feet away—not ready to fold myself in beside her just yet. The chapel stone was a welcome cool against my sticky legs. The air conditioning in the truck had blown before I crossed the state line into Massachusetts, and the open windows had only let in more humid July.

"Your hair's growing out," she said, reaching forward to spin some strands between her fingers. "That's too bad. I loved your hair."

I scooted a couple of inches closer so she didn't have to reach so far, a couple inches, but no more. I was afraid that any closer and she would disappear into a wisp of smoke or a pile of dust.

"Where'd you stay last night?"

She dropped her hand and picked up Aloysius. I had not noticed him at her feet. "Here. There. Everywhere. Nowhere. What does it matter?"

"Julia," I said. "Can we go somewhere? Get an iced coffee? We haven't talked since the party—"

"*Now* you want to talk? You. Left. Me." Julia twisted Aloysius in her hands and her face crumpled inward. She braced her legs against the floor, as if she was getting ready to spring over me and run for the chapel door.

"Hey," I said, louder than I'd meant to. "You left me, too. Do you know what it was like to go through the final weeks without you? I had to pack up your stuff with Sophie. I had to wait through graduation, hoping they would call your name but not surprised when they didn't." I listened to my words echo through the cavernous nave before I continued.

"Since the party I've barely spoken to any of you. Sebastian hasn't called me in days. . . ." I took a deep breath and clenched my hands so hard that my nails dug into my palms. "And then all of a sudden your mom comes all the way to New Hampshire."

"*Tu as raison,*" Julia whispered into Aloysius's matted fur. "I abandoned you, too."

"It's okay, you needed—"

"I thought it would all be easier . . . I did so many things to try and make it easier. I thought it would hurt less by now, but it doesn't. *Ça fait encore plus mal.*"

"Tell me what you mean." I crossed my legs and turned so I was looking at her, so I was her mirror.

"Coming to St. Anne's, sneaking around campus at night, the prank, the surprise for Bradley . . . they were all the kinds of things Gus did when she was alive."

"Julia, I know Gus was your sister . . . and amazing, and you should love her, but she wasn't perfect. I—"

"I'm not upset that she wasn't perfect, Charlie," Julia said. "I just . . . just wish that she had gotten the chance to be great. She never got the chance." She slapped a palm against the floor. "She would have been so much better than me. It's not fair."

"Julia, that's not true. You can't think that way. It's not like because she died you got to live. It doesn't work like that."

She sniffled and rested Aloysius across one of her bony knees. She petted his patchy fur. "When I was little and we were all in the car at night, I would tilt my head and look out through the window to find the moon. Even if I was stuck in the middle, I would lean across Bradley or Sebastian or Gus to make sure I could follow it. I wouldn't take my eyes off it, not even if I was sleepy and it was late. I was afraid that if I stopped looking the moon wouldn't follow us home. It's like even as a kid I knew I couldn't do much for them, but if I could give them the moon then maybe—" She dropped Aloysius and pressed her fists to her eyes.

"Oh, Julia—"

"I need to know . . . if you loved me . . . for me," Julia said, gulping for air between words. "Not because I needed saving or for my family, but for me. Just plain broken, *foiré*, crazy me."

I didn't care if she tried to run. I grabbed her arms and pulled her until our foreheads were touching, our bodies so close I could feel her breath mixing with my own. "You're not crazy, Julia," I said. "You're just more alive than all the boring people out there." I started smoothing her hair, knowing I would never be able to work my fingers through the tangles. "Julia, I need to tell you something. Rosalie and I went to talk to David's family. We saw the farm."

I felt her stiffen, but I kept going. "I know Gus was driving, not David. And it's okay. You, Sebastian, your mom, Bradley, Sophie, Boom, you've all been trying to protect her. I get it. And I'm not going to—"

She tried to dip under my arms to move away from me, but I gripped her shoulders, not letting her slide backward any more than the length of my arms. "Julia, it's okay. I understand they did it to protect Gus."

"Oh, Charlie, I thought you would have figured it out," she said, shaking her head. "Or that maybe Sebastian would crack and tell you. He's never been that good at keeping secrets."

"What do you mean?" I dropped my arms and leaned back as much as I could in the small space so I could see her expression.

Her eyes were as murky as jars full of unstirred paint. She could hide anything behind those eyes.

"I thought he would have told you how they all played their parts. *Mon Dieu*. Even Cordelia figured out so much on her own."

"Julia." Her name had grown barbed edges and hurt my throat. "I don't understand." The floor felt so cold under my fingertips, I had to resist the urge to rest my hot face against the stone.

When she looked at me then, I felt her hurt like the heat coming off a bonfire. A pain so consuming and terrible, it was like falling into black.

And then I knew.

"You . . . you were driving. It wasn't David . . . or Gus. It was you," I said.

She leaned back and closed her eyes. Her voice was as even and emotionless as a waiter reciting a menu. "Gus and David had been drinking. He didn't want me to drive." Julia was crying, but seemed not to notice, not even when the tears dripped off her chin and fell on the stone. "Gus . . . she told him it would be okay. I was fourteen, but Gus let me drive her car all the time. She told him she trusted me. I didn't even see the bridge until we were at the edge . . . and then it was too late."

Julia lowered her head, her hands clasped together in front of her face. "Why did she trust me?"

"Oh, Julia." I grabbed her and pulled her toward me,

tightening my arms when she tried to break loose and relaxing them once she collapsed against me, sobbing so hard she was hiccupping. I could feel her heart beating through her ribs where my hands clung to her back.

"I'm the reason it all went to shit . . . I was alive, was the logic. David and Gus were dead," Julia said in between sobs. "I had my whole life in front of me—why ruin that, too? A future with a capital F. Not that it mattered, I've gone and screwed it up anyway." She wiped her nose against her shoulder as she pushed me away.

"You were only a kid. You shouldn't even—"

"No bullshit, Charlie. Not from you." She shook her head and wiped at her eyes with her sleeves. "Go home. Go home and make things right with Sebastian and make art and go to college and be happy. I want you to be happy."

"No. I'm not leaving without you."

"You don't have much choice. *Le coeur a ses raisons que la raison ne connaît point.*"

"I don't know what that means."

She fell forward until her knees were pressed to her chest and her hands were pressed to her beautiful face.

I wrapped my arms around her again.

"I'm just so tired. *Très, très fatiguée.*"

"Shhhh." I smoothed her hair back with one hand and clutched her to me with my other. I rested my chin on her head and held her as if my touch alone could absorb her despair. I would have taken it all from her if I could have.

"A slow march into the ocean, letting saltwater creep over you inch by inch until the last wave crashes and you go under. That's what it feels like to be trapped in my head. A slow walk into water." Julia clutched at the front of my shirt and tugged until my face was right next to hers and she could whisper in my ear.

"I tried to bargain with God right after she died. Once I was awake in the hospital and I realized what had happened, I asked him to take me instead. Gus was the best of us, so I begged him." She let go of my shirt and crumpled down into herself again. "Now I just wonder if he'll take me at all."

I was out of thoughts. I was out of everything. So I did the only thing I could do. I held her, whispering, *"Contra mundum. Contra mundum,"* until she was empty as well.

When she had no more tears left, we crawled out of our hiding spot and crossed the empty campus to the truck.

In Hyannis, I let go of her hand only when our arms couldn't stretch any farther up the boarding ramp to the ferry. I stood on the dock until I couldn't pick her out from the other figures on the top deck—and even after that I lingered.

Julia told me she'd call once she got to Arcadia.

She never did.

PHONE CALL #3

"Yes? Hello, may I please speak with Mrs. Catherine in admissions?"

"Please hold."

"But I've been holding," I said, even though there was no one on the other end of the phone to hear me. Classical music played in the ear that was pressed against the kitchen phone while the sounds of whatever morning cartoons Sam and AJ were watching in the TV room played in the other.

"Miss Ryder?"

"Yes!" I jumped in the spindly wooden chair. "I mean, yes. Hi. I know it's early, but I just want to leave a message for—"

"Please hold."

"Jesus!" I clutched my free hand to my forehead because it was all I could do to keep myself from smacking it against the kitchen table.

"Charlotte." Sam padded into the kitchen and tugged at my sleeve. "Hey, Charlotte. I didn't mean to answer, but it was buzzing so bad it fell off the coffee table." I raised my head and saw him holding my cell phone in his marker-stained hands.

"What is it with people in this family not being able to keep their fingers off my phone?" I squeezed the kitchen portable between my shoulder and my ear and grabbed my cell out of Sam's hands, holding it to my chest. "Who is it?"

Sam shrugged. "He didn't say." He raised his thumb to his mouth, saw the look I gave him and lowered it.

"*He* didn't say? You're sure . . . it's a he?" I hated that my voice caught.

Sam nodded. "Yeah, he sounded growly. Like a bear."

I closed my eyes and inhaled before taking the cell away from my chest. "Hello?"

"Charlie?"

His voice wasn't like a bear's. It was deep and heavy, but hearing it felt like floating.

"Hi."

Sam shuffled up to my side and ducked under the arm holding the kitchen phone to lean against me. The looping classical music now filled the kitchen as I let the portable slip away from my ear.

"Boom's gone," he said. He sounded like a wave had come crashing down on him and left him flailing and gasping for air.

I dropped the kitchen phone. It landed with a crack on the linoleum floor. Sam slid out from under my arm and began gathering the parts that had flown around the room. I tried to speak, but my brain wouldn't work. The words were there, but finding them was like swimming toward a light in the water. I couldn't reach them.

"Boom. Has. Passed. Away." He was speaking in starts and pauses like he was reading from a prepared speech but couldn't quite make out the handwriting. "I'm sorry . . . wasn't able to call sooner . . . arrangements . . . Mum won't come down-stairs and Bradley's useless. Cordelia's trying, but . . ." His voice caught on a sob he wouldn't let himself give in to. "But, it's not fair. She's too little . . . it's not fair that she has to go through it again."

I heard the tears in the words he couldn't say. I inhaled and held it. Sam stood watching me, his mouth in an "O." But like me, he said nothing.

"Boom was trying to get back . . . to the island . . . you got Julia home . . . thanks for getting her home . . ." He trailed off, and for a moment there was only the crackle of static between us.

"Sebastian, what happened? Please." My phone was shaking against my ear and I had to curl my left hand into a fist to keep it still.

"Charlie, he wanted to get home, but all the ferries were closed. The waves were too high. The charter planes weren't even running. He . . . he paid this guy to take him in his fishing boat. But the waves were too high."

"I—"

"There was a big wave. They were almost to the point where you can see the lighthouse . . . the fisherman made it." He stopped speaking, but there was anguish in his silence.

"Oh, Sebastian. I'm—"

"The fisherman . . . he said he saw Boom right before he went under. Boom was holding on to a life jacket, but he let go . . . no, he was holding on to a life jacket and then he lost his grip. There was a wave or . . ." There was black silence again.

I shivered, and once I started I wasn't able to stop. I could imagine him pacing that library floor, walking where the wood was worn smoothest by footsteps and time. I could picture him in his rumpled clothes, the shadows under his eyes from not sleeping.

"Charlie, will you come? Sophie will call with details. I need you here. *We* need you. Please."

I stood up, but I had to lean on the table. Sam dropped the phone parts on the counter and circled his warm arms around my waist, pressing his face to my stomach. He was the only thing that kept the room from closing in on me. I nodded and then remembered I would have to speak, too. "Yes. I'll be there," I whispered.

He hung up before I did.

I looked at the phone and then placed it gently on the counter. I took a few halting steps until I couldn't move anymore. I crumpled to the kitchen floor, my back against the refrigerator and Sam on the cold linoleum by my side. I drew my knees to my chest, and that's when I started sobbing—violent, body-shaking sobs that left me gasping, light-headed, my throat raw. I tried to stop. I couldn't stop.

Sam ran out the side door to the garage. But even when my dad rushed inside and picked me up off the floor, holding me so close my tears soaked his flannel shirt, I couldn't stop crying. It felt like I never would.

THIRTY-THREE

IS THERE A LIMIT TO what a family will be asked to endure? Had they suffered enough?

Or was tragedy what made them what they were?

The funeral was subdued, somber, and unlike Boom in every way.

Cordelia read a poem. Bradley got so choked up that he couldn't finish his speech, and one of the cousins played the organ while another cousin sang. A ruddy-faced priest read a section from Corinthians, and although his bit was nice and the small island church was old and lovely, I thought Boom would have hated it.

He would rather have skipped the funeral part entirely and gone right to the party. He would rather have had people drinking dark liquor in crystal glasses on the lawn of Arcadia, smoking cigars, and talking politics. He would rather have heard loud debates than hushed conversations and a jazzy band playing instead of somber hymns. He would have wanted a party, not a good-bye.

But funerals are for the living, not the dead.

I was grateful for Rosalie beside me. Grateful that I didn't have to come alone. She'd been in a state of awe and confusion since we'd gotten off the ferry that morning. A tourist who has embarked in a country where no one speaks her language and she doesn't know the laws. Even the wooden street signs and cobblestone roads fascinated her.

Though she said little, her presence was a comfort. In the church, she patted my hand any time someone was done speaking. She held the purse I'd borrowed from Melissa and picked up my shoe when it slid off my foot and under the pew in front of us. We were among the last to leave for the reception at Arcadia. We parked at the end of the long line of cars on the road and walked close enough for our shoulders to touch while we made our way toward the gate.

"Whew. I get it now." Rosalie whistled when we reached the driveway.

The house reminded me of the children's story about a mitten that could not possibly fit even one more animal inside of it. People spilled out onto the porch, standing in close protective circles, as if they were guarding something in their centers. The first-floor windows were dense with bodies. The buzz of conversation was numbing and strange. When a laugh came from the far end of the porch, it was like a bolt of lightning had struck the center of the lawn. I had never been to an Arcadia party where laughter was the exception.

"Charlotte?" Rosalie said.

"Yeah. Sorry," I replied. I had not realized I had stopped walking.

Rosalie squeezed my arm once we reached the front porch steps. "Whenever you're ready to go, we'll go. I'm gonna go look around inside for a bit and then park at one of those chairs there." She gestured toward a set of Adirondacks at the northwest corner of the porch. "Just come grab me."

I exhaled. Nodded. She climbed up the steps and disappeared through the cluster of bodies packed by the door. Soft piano music floated out the open library window, but I couldn't make myself follow Rosalie in. Instead I wrapped my arms so tightly around myself that I could count my ribs with my fingertips. I walked around the side of the house, trying to pretend that I had never been there and I was seeing it for the first time. If I could take it all in, then maybe I could take it with me and keep it forever. Maybe I could put Arcadia in my memory box as easily as I had kept the shell Boom had given me that first summer.

I heard Henry the pug's snuffling at the same time that I felt Cordelia slam into me, wrapping her arms around my waist and burying her face in my side. "Charlie, you came. I knew you would, but I thought maybe you wouldn't or maybe you'd still be rarified of Mummy."

"Petrified." I smoothed back her dark hair. "You mean petrified."

"That's what I said. Did you like my poem? I was going to read it in French. *'Les aubes sont navrantes.'* But Sebastian said more people would understand if I read the transition instead."

I let that one slide. Henry sniffed at my ankles, circled twice, and then, deeming me a friend instead of an enemy, plopped down on my feet. He looked up at me, his little pink tongue sticking sideways out of his mouth, his bug eyes wet and glistening as if he too had been crying. If it had been a different day, I would have laughed at him.

"Charlotte," Bradley called, approaching from Sophie's cottage. Cordelia let go of me as he reached down to hug me. "I'm so glad you could come. It means a lot," he said in his charming old man voice, which today sounded forced instead of funny.

The skin of his tan face looked looser, like some structure beneath had begun to soften. He smiled at me, one arm still on my back, but the corner of his eyes did not crinkle.

"Of course." It was all I could manage.

"Mom told me you got Julia to come home." He swallowed loudly and pulled at the knot of his tie with his free hand. "Before . . . before the accident."

"Accident," I repeated, not really knowing why. Cordelia bent down and scooped Henry up in her arms, clutching him against her chest, burying her face in his shiny black fur.

"I told you that you were good for us, that you would save us all." He rested a hand on my shoulder. There was a dullness in his eyes and pain in the twist of his smile.

"I didn't, though," I said.

"But you did." Bradley bent down and kissed the top of my head. "I have to go check on the kitchen situation, but the rest of the family is on the beach if you want to go say hello, and Sophie and some girls from St. Anne's are inside. Come on, Cordelia."

They walked toward the house, but I didn't follow them. I didn't want to see anyone from school, but I couldn't make myself go to the beach. I headed toward the newly repaired dock instead, hugging myself tightly once more. There was no trace of the boathouse left. What had remained of Gus's sailboat had been removed completely. The fire was nothing but a bad memory now.

Shielding my eyes with one hand and keeping the other arm wrapped around me, I looked toward the beach. Mrs. Buchanan was holding her black heels by her side and was leaning on Julia, who stood still as a pillar. She was barefoot, too, and didn't look like she cared that the waves were filling her shoes with water and sand.

David and Thoreau were racing each other up and down the beach. Sebastian had his pants rolled up and was standing in the water. When a stick drifted near his legs, he reached down, picked it up, and then chucked it for the two dogs to chase.

I slipped off my shoes and sat down at the edge of the dock, letting my feet dangle over the edge—sitting in that same spot where we had talked that night forever ago, watching him watch the sea. When Sebastian turned and saw me, he looked confused for a moment, like you do when you see someone out of context: a teacher in the grocery store, your doctor in the library. He shouted something to Mrs. Buchanan and Julia and started jogging toward me.

Julia gave a little wave. But she made no motion to follow him. She collapsed against her mother's side, hiding her face in the taller woman's shoulder.

I had not heard from her since that day in the chapel, but I wasn't surprised. Piper had warned me that if I learned too much she would push me away and I would get my heart broken. And now I was going to break someone else's.

"You came." Sebastian stopped about halfway down the dock. Shoving his hands in his pockets, he walked the rest of the way. "I wasn't sure you would."

"Of course." I had to shield my eyes to see him.

His pants were too big and they still had creases from where they had been folded. His face looked sharper than the last time I saw him, and his dark eyes had smudges beneath them. Sleeplessness or bruises, they could be either.

"How have you been?" He sat down beside me.

"Okay," I practically whispered. "I've been okay."

"I'm sorry." He looked away from me and out toward the

water. "Look. I'm sorry about being so out of it . . . after the party. Things were just crazy around here and . . ." He drummed his fingers against the dock. "Charlie, I need to tell you something. I need to tell you the truth about . . . about what happened the night of—"

"Don't," I interrupted. "Don't do that. Don't apologize." I wiped at my eyes with the back of my hand. "Julia told me everything. I know that you lied because you love her and you, all of you, were trying to protect her. I don't want to know more than that . . . I think I'm done with secrets for a while."

He exhaled, gripping the edge of the dock like he was trying to stop himself from falling into the water. "I'm too late. I messed up and now I'm too late. I should have told you all of it that first time on the ferry." I could feel him studying my face. His hands at his sides lifted and then dropped. He couldn't keep them still, but he couldn't touch me either. "We aren't going to be able to get past this, are we?"

I shook my head.

"And you're going to break up with me now, aren't you?"

"I'm not even sure if we're together to be broken up." I couldn't look at him or I'd lose my nerve entirely.

"What if you just stayed?" Now he did touch me, his hand brushing across my cheek. "Just stay the night and we'll talk. Come say hello to Mum and Julia. Just don't go."

"And then what?" I was crying now. I had to speak between gasps. "Then a few more months before we finally recognize what was so obvious all along?" I looked up toward the house before turning back to him. "I don't belong here, Sebastian. I'm just a visitor who stayed too long."

"Charlie." He placed his hand over mine on the rough dock. "You're as much a part of this as the rest of us."

I could taste tears where they drifted into the corners of my mouth. I shook my head. "I can't. Sebastian, you know I can't. I need to walk away now or I'll never go. You're going to be great. Maybe even greater than Boom. But I need to figure out who I am when I'm not here. What's real. I thought I knew, but I think . . . I think I lost track somewhere."

Sebastian was silent for a long moment, and then he reached into his pocket. He took my hand and placed a smooth metal disk in my palm, closing my fingers around it one by one. "This," he said. "This part was real. Please trust me that much."

When he released my hand, I looked down and read, "The human heart beats 100,000 times a day."

"I do trust you that much," I said. "Bye, Sebastian."

"Take care, Charlie."

I ran up the lawn toward the porch where Rosalie was waiting, as she said she would be. Before we left I let myself look once more, but only once.

Bradley and Cordelia had joined the rest of the family. Sebastian had made his way back to the beach. The Buchanans were standing in a loose semicircle, looking out at the black water and the cloudless sky.

Mrs. Buchanan, delicate and poised even in her misery, was an elegy to herself—a tribute to the young woman she must have been before she became the wife and mother who lost so much because she had so much to lose. Bradley, his perfect posture temporarily forgotten, stood hunched with his hands in his pockets and his tie loose around his neck beside her. Cordelia, hugging Henry once again to her chest, was already a little more somber, a little older. Sebastian was skipping stones because he could not stand still.

And Julia. My Julia. I whistled sharp and clear and waited until she turned around and saw me. *"Contra mundum,"* I whispered, and I swear I saw her mouth form *"Contra mundum"* in return.

Julia and me against the world. That's how I like to remember her.

They were perfect. They were flawed. They were scarred and beautiful. They were too familiar with death and clung to life by clinging to one another. The Great Buchanans were only human, after all.

A NEW BEGINNING

Dolor hic tibi proderit olim
(One day this pain will be useful to you)
—*Ovid*

DOLOR

This is not something anyone can teach you. Heartbreak you must learn on your own.

I knew too much. So she pushed me away. It was how she stayed whole. It was how she survived. I could not hate her for that— for wanting to survive. I could not hate her for anything.

But I also know that I left them all even more than she left me. It would have been so easy to lose myself in the Buchanans, to become the Charlie they thought I was and needed me to be. They were so generous, so kind, so persistent in their belief that I could protect her from herself.

But I couldn't. I could no more rescue her than she could save me from my self-doubts and uncertainties. I had to do that on my own.

I heard that she went to college for a while, then to the west coast. After that I lost track.

And Sebastian? He did what he promised Boom. He finished Harvard. Enrolled in law school. Became a rising star.

For a time, I missed them like winter misses warmth. I could not breathe without her. I could not feel without him.

Friends helped. New friends who understood that they could never replace the family I had lost, but tried anyway. They were ever ready with cheap beer, dirty jokes, and coffee at the cafés near campus in downtown Providence. Friends who could make vegetarian lasagna to feed fourteen in under an hour. Friends with haircuts they gave themselves, tattoos from ex-boyfriends and girlfriends, and scars from past lives. They accepted my flaws because they had them, too.

Travel helped. Getting off a plane in a place where no one knew me. Walking among tombs, paintings, and strangers like a ghost was oddly comforting. I could be no one. I could be someone. I was just a girl with sad eyes, a sketchbook, and an oversized bag drifting among ordinary people.

Time helped. The pain faded from a gaping hole in the very center of me to quick moments of remembering that took the air from my body, forcing me to make excuses for the sudden watering of my eyes.

Art helped. The sculptures—the collecting of odds and ends and molding them into something striking and new. Success came gradually and then overnight. And I welcomed it, because it, too, was a distraction.

I made it to this point, but I made it on my own terms. That was her final gift to me. Helping me stand. Helping me imagine a life large enough to stand for.

CAPECODTIMES.COM

BUCHANAN FAMILY COMPOUND TO BECOME CULTURAL CENTER

The Buchanan family has transferred ownership of their family home, Arcadia, on Nantucket Island to the late Senator Joseph "Boom" Buchanan's nonprofit foundation.

The Cape Cod–style 6,000-square-foot house designed by architect Alexander Flyte will become a community center and historical museum. Renovations will begin this fall on the main home. A cottage on the southeast side of the four-acre property has been given to Ms. Sophie Girard, Mrs. Teresa Buchanan's secretary.

Mrs. Buchanan released this statement: "This house is our gift to the people of Nantucket, her visitors, and her artists. We hope it will become the cultural center of this community that has given our family so much. We have cherished every sunrise, sunset, and moment in between in this extraordinary place."

The museum's opening date has yet to be determined.

It only takes ten folds for me to turn the article into a butterfly.

THIRTY-FOUR

MY DAD, TO HIS CREDIT, does not ask why I need the keys to the new truck. He hugs me and hands them over. He doesn't ask what's under the sheet or how long I will be gone. He just lets me go. Just as I know that in a few days he will let me get on a plane and travel until my fellowship money runs out.

He is as stable as I am restless. That's why we work so well.

The trip from Hyannis to the island is longer than I remember, and the ferry strangely empty for August. Even when the massive ship is docking and folks are lining up on the metal steps to go down to their cars, I linger on the top deck.

The drive, however, is shorter.

I park on the road and struggle with the gate, which has become rusted and stubborn. When I finally heft it open and bend down to pick up my package again, my arms are tired. But I know I'll make it to the porch.

The house looks like an old woman waiting on a bus bench. Shabby. A little sad. Hunched over and tired. Plywood covers the first-floor windows and the gray paint is peeling off in some spots like bark on a birch tree. The lawn is dotted with dandelions, and the grass grows in patches in the circular drive. A porch step cracks as I walk up. I hold the package close to my chest, trying to ignore the wood and metal edges that poke me through the sheet, pricking the bare skin that my sundress doesn't cover.

I set the sculpture down by the kitchen door. Exactly where Sophie had told me she would find it later that day. She told me it would have a place of honor. She told me she would explain who it was from to the family and that the parts all had a story.

I could not finish before because I was not done collecting memories. I had not seen that it needed my bottle caps and champagne corks, stones, shells, and origami animals. I have used it all—all but one, which I am keeping for later.

I see him standing at the water's edge after I jump off the porch. Instead of the piercing sensation in my chest I used to suffer at just the thought of him, I feel only the vibration of a once-broken bone that has long ago healed.

"I didn't see your car," I call as I walk toward him.

He turns and smiles that smile that once had the power to take me apart and put me back together in the same instant. "I parked at the neighbor's," he shouts. "I thought you might not come if you knew I was here."

"I read somewhere that you were selling it." I point at the house.

"Nah. It's better than that. They're giving it away. It's going to be a museum community center thing. I think they're even going to bring someone in to teach French, and there'll be sailing lessons and stuff. It would have made Boom and Gus happy." He tilts his head. "Actually, who knows what they would have thought."

"Ils auraient aimé que cela puisse rendre les gens heureux."

Both hands are in his pockets. His hair is shorter, tamer. He has on real shoes instead of sandals and his shirt looks ironed.

His fingers, I notice as I close the space between us, are not drumming. His feet are not shuffling or tapping. He is no longer perpetually in motion. He has become accustomed to stillness. It suits him—being still.

"You speak French now."

"Oui."

"Nanny told me you were coming today."

"Je pensais que c'était la situation."

"I read the papers." He leans back on his heels, as if getting ready to look up at the sun. "I mean I read about your Boston show—in a couple of places actually. I should have been studying for my tax law exam, but your interviews were much more interesting. They love you, don't they?"

I take the edge of my dress up in my hand and rub the linen between my callused fingers. The fabric catches and pulls at my skin as I approach him. "They love me today. We'll see about tomorrow."

"Julia would have liked that you made that sculpture about her. The one you talked about in the long interview . . . about your travel fellowship. Is that what's on the porch? Sophie told me that you were bringing something for the museum."

"Don't you remember?" I say. "The beauty of art? It is what you see in it." I stop five feet away from him. "I'm glad if you find her in something I've made. How is she?"

"We don't hear from her that often, but she seems okay. She's hopping around. Cuba, India, somewhere in South America." He looks at some point in the distance, as if Julia herself might be out there to wave to us. "Besides fame and fortune . . . and graduation, right? How have you been?" He shades his eyes to look at me.

"I'm okay. Actually." I look at my feet before raising my gaze to meet his. "I'm good. I'm really, really good."

"I'm glad." He smiles. "Everyone's happy for you. Mum, Bradley, Cordelia, Sophie, Julia . . . wherever she is right now. I'm sure she's—"

"And everyone?" I interrupt him. I am tough, but there's no need to test my strength today. "How are they?"

"They're okay."

"Good. Then I'm *glad*, too." I try the word out on my tongue like a sip of something sweet. "I only came by to drop off the piece. I have to go, but good luck, Sebastian." I gesture toward the lonely but still magnificent house. "I'm sure it will be great."

I turn and begin walking in the direction of the driveway.

"Charlie," Sebastian calls after me. He jogs to where I stand and stops in front of me. "Look, I wanted to see you, so I could say I'm sorry. I'm sorry for the way things turned out. I'm sorry for lying and that you got hurt so much. I'm sorry for the whole mess."

"Don't be, because I'm *not* sorry. I would do it all again."

He grasps his hands together and then drops them, letting his arms swing by his sides. "Wouldn't it be great if I could just be me and you could just be you, meeting for the first time?"

I do not answer immediately. I rest my head to the side and put my hands on my hips and look up at him. "You know what I recently discovered? The Earth is four and a half billion years old."

He smiles. "Those bottle caps. You learn something new every day. Don't you?"

"You up for a boat ride?"

When the ferry nears the lighthouse, I take a penny from my pocket and hand it to him. I take the smooth stone from the night I met Julia and clutch it until it grows warm in my palm.

"On the count of three," I say. "One. Two." I bring the stone to my cheek for just a moment. "Three." Then I whip it with all my might toward the peninsula.

Sebastian looks at me, and his grin is contagious. "What'd you wish for?"

I laugh, a real laugh. *"Le dire, ça porte malheur."*

"Fine," he replies. "I'll tell you what I asked for: a fresh start."

I lean against the railing next to him and look at the island dissolving into the waves.

I wish for the same thing I've hoped for since the beginning. I wish for a life so brave, so unpredictable, so full of unexpected joys and unforgettable love that no box could possibly contain all my memories.

Such a life won't be perfect. It'll be something better.

It'll be my own paradise.

ACKNOWLEDGMENTS

I AM SO VERY LUCKY to have the indefatigable and gracious Stephen Barbara for an agent. The stars were certainly aligned on the day he matched me with editor extraordinaire Sarah Dotts Barley. Thank you, Sarah, for your wisdom and guidance, and for softening your corrections with smiley faces. I am filled with gratitude for the whole HarperCollins team that has made *Even in Paradise* a beautiful reality: Renée Cafiero, Christina Colangelo, Alison Donalty, Erin Fitzsimmons, Christopher Hernandez, Alison Lisnow, and Tara Weikum.

To the friends and second families who have given me spaces to write, encouragement, and unconditional love, thank you. I am indebted to Chelsey "Beane" Canavan, Hsiu-Hsien Chiang, Elysha Ertas, Carolina Fasola, Lori Gassie, Briann Greenfield, Morgan Hanna, Katie Johar, Courtney Markle, Barbara and Billy Pollex, Laura Rossbert, Ashley Stone, Divya Vasudevan, Vanita Vishnubhakat, and Mari-liis Visnapuu.

I will always think of my teachers, professors, and librarians (past and present) with bottomless appreciation. The work you do is crucial. It is life changing. It is never forgotten. Thank you. A thousand times, thank you.

My coworkers, editors, and mentors, I will never stop learning from you. I am grateful for every opportunity you've trusted me with or led me to.

Thank you to my dedicated and kind brothers-in-law, Chris Fischer (my most optimistic champion) and Jason Pergament (my favorite road trip partner). I am so, so happy that you both joined our family. We did not know we needed you two until you were here.

I am filled with admiration for my talented, amazing siblings: my older sister, Natalie; my younger sister, Saeger; and my little brother, Harris. You are my greatest friends, the sources of so much inspiration, and the keepers of my best memories. Thank you for the terrible nicknames, keeping me humble with barn chores, and believing in me so much. *Contra mundum* forever and always.

Finally, I cannot do justice to how much I owe my parents, William and Karen Philpot. You've provided me with books, education, travel, and endless support. I can live out of a duffel bag and have my adventures because where you are will always be home. You've given me the world. Will you accept a book in return?